T0125495

KANAZAWA

a novel by
David Joiner

Stone Bridge Press · Berkeley, California

Published by
Stone Bridge Press
P. O. Box 8208, Berkeley, CA 94707
TEL 510-524-8732 · sbp@stonebridge.com · www.stonebridge.com

Book design and layout by Peter Goodman.

Front-cover illustration by Kawase Hasui: *Shimohonda-machi in Kanazawa* (*Kanazawa Shimohonda-machi*) from the series Souvenirs of Travel II (*Tabi miyage dai nishū*); in public domain. Map background from Shutterstock.com. Snowflake-crystal designs from *Sekkazusetsu*, published in 1832 (National Diet Library Digital Collection).

The translation "All living things . . ." is from *The Manyoshu: One Thousand Poems Selected and Translated from the Japanese* (Tokyo: Iwanami Shoten, 1940).

Text © 2022 David Joiner.

Printed in the United States of America.

First printing, 2022.

p-ISBN 978-1-61172-071-6
e-ISBN 978-1-61172-953-5

for Harue

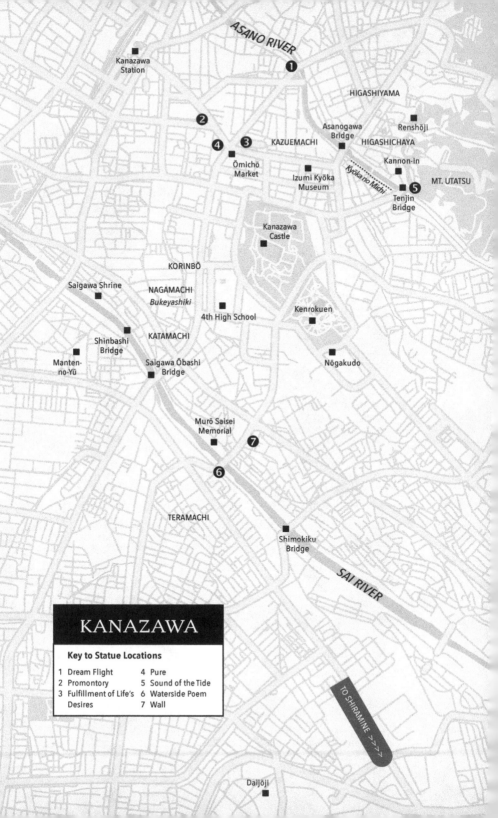

ASANO RIVER

Kanazawa
Station

1

HIGASHIYAMA

Renshōji

Asanogawa
Bridge

2

4 **3** KAZUEMACHI

HIGASHICHAYA

Kannon-in

Ōmichō
Market

Izumi Kyōka
Museum

Kyōka no Michi

5

MT. UTATSU

Tenjin
Bridge

Kanazawa
Castle

KORINBŌ

Saigawa Shrine

NAGAMACHI
Bukeyashiki

Kenrokuen

4th High School

Shinbashi
Bridge

KATAMACHI

Manten-
no-Yū

Saigawa Ōbashi
Bridge

Nōgakudo

Murō Saisei
Memorial

7

6

TERAMACHI

Shimokiku
Bridge

SAI RIVER

TO SHIRAMINE >>>

KANAZAWA

Key to Statue Locations

1 Dream Flight   4 Pure
2 Promontory   5 Sound of the Tide
3 Fulfillment of Life's 6 Waterside Poem
  Desires   7 Wall

Daijōji

KANAZAWA

"Time flows in the same way for all human beings; every human being flows through time in a different way."

KAWABATA YASUNARI, *BEAUTY AND SADNESS*

1

OVER THE COURSE OF Kanazawa's long winter, February was the whitest month.

As Emmitt stood before the living room window, a heavy snowfall muted the wail of a passing ambulance and the illumination of its red emergency light. Although the ambulance's interior was brightly lit, he couldn't see anyone in the vehicle, not even the driver at the near window.

A moment later the ambulance dissolved in the snow. What remained was the reflection of his wife Mirai and her mother cooking dinner behind him, and he resumed his surreptitious observation of them.

Over the sounds of cooking, and the TV his father-in-law was watching, a brief conversation arose.

"You're quiet tonight, Mirai. Is everything all right?"

"Am I? Maybe I'm a little tired."

"Haven't you been sleeping?"

"I'm fine, Okāsan."

Half an hour ago, when Emmitt was changing out of his university teaching clothes upstairs, Mirai had confessed to having second thoughts about the lease they were to sign in two days. They had agreed to renovate and rent for fifty years the one-hundred-and-twenty-year-old *machiya* his friend in real estate, Kimura, had introduced them to in December. The owners had surprised Emmitt and Mirai by agreeing to the fifty-thousand yen monthly rent Kimura suggested. They wanted to find someone to take the traditional townhouse off their hands so they could create a fund for their grandchildren, who eventually would inherit the property. For Emmitt and Mirai, the contract ensured low rent for most of their lifetimes, and the nonrefundable deposit, though equal to two years' rent, was negligible compared to their total investment. That they would assume the financial burden of renovating it gratified the owners, too.

"What happened?" he said, watching her reach behind her head to retie her short ponytail. "I thought we were ready to do this."

"I'm worried about the money. And what happens if one day we want to move?" They had discussed this before, and Mirai had seemed content with committing long-term to Kanazawa. What was more, she had always agreed with him that living in an old *machiya* was a more exciting prospect than living in a modern house, which offered little charm in its design and materials. "But we like Kanazawa. Where would we move, anyway?"

Not long ago they had considered spending a few years in America. The plan was for both of them to return to school, but after a spate of mass shootings in the state they wanted to move to, and then an unexpected presidency they wished to keep far away from, their enthusiasm for this plan dissipated. Since then, from their far-off perspective, the whole country seemed to have caught on fire. America was no longer a viable alternative.

"I have no idea where," Mirai said. Then, as if the idea just occurred to her: "Tokyo, possibly. Especially if Asuka settles down there."

Emmitt looked at her, speechless for a moment. "Your sister's being there isn't a reason for us to move there, too."

She shook her head, as if to say there was no point arguing over it. "My biggest worry is money. You're planning to walk away from your job, and the renovations loan we were offered is less than what we'll need."

Then her mother had called her into the kitchen. Mirai had hurried downstairs, leaving Emmitt half-dressed and baffled by what had transpired.

He continued to watch Mirai in the window's reflection, wondering how serious her concerns were about signing the lease. After disagreements like this, living with her parents and younger sister increased his agitation and restlessness. Although he got along well with his in-laws, and the arrangement helped him and Mirai save money, he didn't want to live like this forever. He was convinced that without their own house they couldn't feel as confident about the future, and he feared that if they relinquished this dream they shared, one thread that helped connect them might unravel.

Over two months of negotiations, he thought in annoyance, *and now she changes her mind?*

"Your *machiya* will be cold on winter nights," his father-in-law said, gesturing to the printed photographs of the *machiya* in Emmitt's hand. "I expect you'll want to stay here then." He set down the remote he'd been holding to refill a small cup with hot sake—unwilling, apparently, to admit his own house was freezing.

"When the *machiya's* ours, we'll make sure to insulate it well."

"Let's just hope we can afford a renovations company," Mirai said. "Eiheiji should hire one. Those temple rooms look uninhabitable in winter."

She was referring to a temple in Fukui Prefecture where Emmitt had suggested they stay after signing the lease. Eiheiji offered Buddhist meditation classes and lectures on Buddhist life. He was happy that the basic accommodations didn't deter Mirai from wanting to go.

His mother-in-law turned to Mirai, who was wrapping a short towel around the neck of a sake carafe she had heated to replace the one her father now drank from. "I didn't know you were interested in Buddhist retreats."

"I'm not," she said, laughing. "I'd prefer to visit in the spring or summer. But it's always nice to see someplace different."

"I may be too busy in the summer," Emmitt reminded her. They had talked about him fixing what he could of the *machiya*, then hiring specialists to finish what he wasn't able to do. He hoped to work on it starting in April. This was an argument for quitting his job, one his in-laws didn't yet support: The money they would save by having Emmitt, rather than a renovations company, work on the house for one year would equal what he'd earn teaching at the university. And surely there were ways to stretch the renovations loan they'd been offered to make the house livable.

"The house isn't ours yet," Mirai said, carrying the towel-wrapped carafe into the dining room. "Don't get ahead of yourself."

His mother-in-law called everyone to dinner.

As Emmitt sipped his miso soup his mother-in-law said to him, "Do you remember the Izumi Kyōka stories my literary club asked you to help translate in November?"

"Of course," he said, feeling guilty still for having turned the request down, though his work schedule had left him no choice. "Why do you ask?"

"I gave a copy of them to a native English speaker last week."

The stories were part of a collection of Kyōka translations the city had helped fund. She and Emmitt had avoided talking about them over the last three months.

"Who did you find to translate them?" he asked.

"An American housewife in Tokyo; she's a friend of a member in our group. But she doesn't have a formal background in literature, and we had to work with her closely on each story. It was more troublesome than we'd anticipated."

Of the various novelists Kanazawa had produced, Kyōka was its most famous, but for some reason he lacked the readership many of his peers enjoyed. Emmitt's mother-in-law once told him that Mishima Yukio, Tanizaki Jun'ichirō, Akutagawa Ryūnosuke, and Kawabata Yasunari, among other important Japanese writers, credited Kyōka with being "the most Japanese" writer from before World War II. Mishima even claimed that Kyōka's writing represented the apotheosis of the Japanese language. From what Emmitt understood, the only surprise in the city's push to translate more of his works into English was that it had taken this long. He found it hard to believe that he hadn't yet read any of them—but then, his university teaching left him with neither the time nor energy to read for pleasure. It was one of his biggest frustrations. Until a few years ago, he had read other Japanese authors of Kyōka's time and found their work fascinating—the lives depicted in them antiquated yet familiar, connecting him to a simpler, less Westernized time. They brought him deeper into a culture that in certain respects remained a mystery to him.

For his birthday last month his mother-in-law had bought him all the Kyōka books she could find in English and a few, too, in Japanese, and even a critical biography of the author's life. Her effort and generosity had astonished him. And although he knew she'd done so, at least in part, with ulterior motives, he felt ashamed for not having read them yet.

"I never thought a translation could be completed so quickly," he said.

"She'd been working on his stories for two years. That's one reason we thought she'd be ideal. But this afternoon the English reader told me the translations weren't as engaging as other translated Kyōka stories she'd read. She suggested that the ones we chose might not have been as good, but she doesn't read Japanese, so how can she judge the original stories? When I asked if the English read smoothly at least, her hesitation confirmed my fears."

She served her husband salad from a bowl and added, "It would have been nice if you'd contributed. My group still doesn't understand why my own son-in-law wouldn't help."

"But would his Japanese have been up to the task?" Mirai said, smiling archly. "Weren't you in the living room last night when our first date came up in conversation?"

"It's the only language we've ever used with him," her mother answered. "I trust Emmitt's Japanese completely. Besides, that was a long time ago. Since then he's worked hard to become fluent."

Smiling, Emmitt said to her parents, "It's amazing how a single blunder marks you for life."

Tugging her sweater sleeve, Mirai leaned into him playfully and exposed the pale underside of her arm. "Even though it was eight years ago, it still makes me laugh."

She was referring to their first date at a café near the language school where she'd studied with a colleague of Emmitt's, when she had complained that her skin wasn't as white as Asuka's. Trying to assure her that her skin was beautiful as it was, he'd confused the word *gyūnyū* with *gyūtan*, and his statement that her skin color resembled "cow tongue" rather than "milk" made her (and two women at a table nearby) burst out laughing. Mirai retold the story often.

"I'm not sure what I could have contributed," Emmitt said, nearly explaining again that he possessed neither training nor experience as a translator. His mother-in-law had told him before, however, that his literature degree and fluency in Japanese was sufficient; he would come to translating as a beginner, but one had to start somewhere. Emmitt thought that if he'd been involved, she would have had the same criticisms of him she had just expressed about the American woman in Tokyo.

"Anyway," his mother-in-law said, mercifully changing the subject, "I was going to suggest visiting Renshōji temple this weekend, but with this bad weather and your work schedule, I'm afraid we'll have to try another time."

"Why Renshōji?" Emmitt asked.

"It's the setting for *Rukōshinsō*, the last story Kyōka wrote. But maybe it's better to go in the spring or summer when its grounds are lush and full of life—even though the story takes place on a warm winter day."

Emmitt knew the story by its English translation, "The Heart-vine." If not for the pile of essays he had to grade by tomorrow, he would have been willing to go. Several months had passed since he'd been able to make such an excursion, and he felt desperate to find a way past the chronic overwork that was affecting his health and spirits.

"Isn't Kyōka buried there?" Mirai asked.

"He's buried in Tokyo," her mother said. "I guess you've forgotten, but my literary club visited his grave shortly after you and Emmitt got married."

Mirai protested lightly: "There are monuments to him all over Kanazawa. If the city wanted to claim him, why is he buried there?"

"It was his decision, not the city's. Although he sometimes wrote about Kanazawa, he didn't much like it. He wouldn't have succeeded as a writer if he'd stayed."

"I used to feel that way myself when I was younger," Mirai said.

Her mother nodded as if remembering. "Even now, anyone ambitious from Kanazawa would probably feel drawn to Tokyo.

after he drank too much, though Emmitt hadn't thought he'd reached that threshold tonight. He seemed either angry or terribly sad.

"Why do you need to spend two days at Eiheiji?" the old man said.

Emmitt saw he wasn't the only one bemused by the return to their earlier conversation. Mirai and her mother laughed at the clumsy question.

"Do you plan to become a monk one day? If not, it sounds like the dream of a young man pretending he has no responsibilities, and I can't help but say it's a waste of money. Even if you rent this *machiya* so cheaply, you'll still spend far more than if you lived here."

Emmitt poured his father-in-law a cup of sake then filled his own. Gazing at the cups, he remembered giving them to him on his birthday last year, bought on a one-day trip to Kurashiki and the Inland Sea for an ikebana exhibit Mirai had participated in. The cups were beautiful examples of *bizenyaki* pottery.

"I'm salaried until the end of March," Emmitt reminded him. "That's a month and a half of getting paid to do nothing. But I'd rather not do nothing. I'd rather look for some way to improve myself and better our lives."

"I still don't understand your plans," his mother-in-law said. "University teaching is good money, and it's respectable. Also, you have another year on your contract. Even if you can't continue there, you could parlay that into a position somewhere else. It saddens us to see you throw that away after working so hard for so long."

"I'm not throwing anything away. The *machiya* is a great opportunity, and eventually Mirai can teach ikebana there." He had told them many times he was tired of teaching English—a subject his students cared nothing about, and on behalf of a department that forced him to bear more responsibilities every term. Here he was at thirty-six, already burned out on work he once thought he wanted to do forever. "Up until now, I feel like I've been wasting my life trying to forge a path forward."

His mother-in-law said: "Well, you have to make a living somehow. Mirai can support you with her ikebana only for so long."

His father-in-law made a disagreeable noise in his throat. "If you don't move forward, do you propose to move backward?"

Emmitt held his gaze for a moment. How could he tell him it was a more interesting question to him than he might guess?

In a city as well-preserved as Kanazawa, Emmitt's imagination rejoiced in his ability to touch the past. On the Japan Sea, Kanazawa was famed for its arts and crafts, gardens, and geisha districts, cuisine, and gold leaf—its traditions dating back to the first Maeda lord in the late sixteenth century—not to mention its annual snowfall. No longer denigrated as "the back of Japan," Kanazawa had recently become one of the country's most popular tourist destinations, and Emmitt considered himself lucky to have known it before it changed.

When he first arrived in Japan, the country's foreignness had overwhelmed him, and he used to email his impressions of Kanazawa to friends in America. But most of them either ignored what he wrote or joked about it; they found it hard to understand why the city excited him. His parents had no interest in his life here, either, which was why, over time, their long-strained relationship had ground to a halt.

Mirai's phone buzzed, and she lifted it from the table to read a new message. Emmitt saw it was from Asuka. She was in Tokyo to interview for jobs and visit her boyfriend, Shin, who had graduated last year from the same master's program in art and design she was in.

"Tell her she's missing her mom's homemade cooking," Emmitt said.

Mirai laughed. "She won't mind. Last night she and Shin had dinner at Nodaiwa, in Azabu."

"The famous eel restaurant?" her mother said, her eyes wide. "I didn't know Shin was that rich."

"He's not," Mirai said. "But that doesn't keep them from eating at fancy places."

The room fell silent in the way the snow was silent. Emmitt sensed something cold falling around him, which made him wish for its cessation followed by warmth. But Kanazawa winters were long and cold, and it wasn't even the middle of February.

He glanced at the photocopied picture of the *machiya* on the table, admiring again the dark wood and latticed doors and windows in the front; the rectangular fabric divider hanging before the entrance, the character for "rice" billowing in the middle and advertising the family's former business; the rows of black tiles on the angled roofs; the decorative stone lanterns scattered about the small garden; and the two-story white *kura* storehouse visible behind the short wall to the side.

The house was large and well located and dated back a hundred and twenty years to the late Meiji period—which meant more to Emmitt than to Mirai or her parents. To him, the *machiya* represented an earlier, more romantic era, a way of inhabiting a Japan that had nearly vanished. He and Mirai had been assured that no house of similar provenance would enter the market in downtown Kanazawa for another decade, and he didn't want to lose this opportunity.

If their marriage lacked anything after five years, it was stability, and a commitment to place, they'd agreed, would strengthen it. Her parents often reminded him, as if afraid he might take Mirai far away one day, that Kanazawa had no earthquakes, tsunamis, volcanoes, or nuclear plants on active fault lines, and thus was the safest place to live in Japan.

His in-laws had grown up in old-style *machiya*. Mirai and Asuka had, too, until their parents had enough money to tear theirs down and build a new house, which they did twenty years ago when Mirai was twelve or thirteen. The "new" house had noticeably aged. From the outside it looked like it needed a thorough cleaning and a few more layers of siding to make it appear sturdier. To Emmitt, it was merely an aluminum box with a door and windows. Too often, it seemed, that was what modernity meant in Japan.

When Mirai stepped into the kitchen to refill and reheat the sake carafe, Emmitt followed her. Lightly massaging her shoulders, he said, "You hardly ate tonight. Are you really that worried about the house?"

She forced a smile while watching the water start to boil.

"What is it?"

She shook her head and kept silent. Finally she said, "A sparrow got into our building today and flew into my classroom. I called the janitor to help catch it, and after five or ten minutes, out of frustration, he swung at it with a broom. I demanded that he stop, but the sparrow was already panicked and flying into the window. In the end it knocked itself unconscious against the glass. Only then could we take it outside. It came to after a few minutes and flew away. I filed a complaint about the janitor, but I doubt the school will do anything."

Emmitt stopped massaging her. He waited for her to circle around to what he'd asked, but her anecdote apparently had nothing to do with it. "Why are you going on about a sparrow when I asked what's bothering you?"

She removed the sake carafe and wiped it off. "Afterward I thought, 'What kind of place is that to work?'" She paused and said, "For some reason I wanted to tell you."

"You're not thinking of quitting, are you?"

bars and *izakaya*, he searched for the one where his family were celebrating.

Mirai spotted Emmitt entering behind a group of salarymen. She waved to him and pointed out his arrival to the others, who were seated at a low table.

People often said that Mirai and Asuka, despite their six-year age difference, resembled one another, but to Emmitt they were almost unrecognizable as sisters. Mirai was willowy and somewhat tall. Asuka was slightly compact, stood two or three inches shorter, and in her face took after her father more. But she was pretty, too, and her smile was quicker than Mirai's, her lips set in a way that made her always seem amused, or at least glad to be around you. Mirai's smile belied not only a greater seriousness, but also a certain guardedness he rarely saw in any of her family.

"Congratulations on your new job," Emmitt said, walking to the table.

"I'm moving to Tokyo!" Asuka grinned and clapped to herself. "I can't wait to show you and Mirai around when you visit."

"You may be hosting us a lot."

Mirai laughed and said, "Or hosting me, anyway. You've never been a big fan of Tokyo."

"I feel about Tokyo how I feel about Los Angeles," Emmitt said. "Not bad to visit, but I wouldn't want to live there."

When Mirai didn't answer, Asuka said, "You're both welcome to come whenever you want. That way, I can count on you bringing me a steady supply of Okāsan's cooking."

Emmitt jokingly asked Mirai if she'd bought them tickets to Tokyo yet.

"Of course not. But Asuka did ask me to go to Tokyo to help her find an inexpensive apartment. She wants to start looking right away." She hesitated before adding, "Otōsan's giving her a monthly allowance. Her salary won't be enough at first to cover her living costs, and she doesn't want to take a company loan." It seemed she couldn't help adding: "He's more generous than in the past."

Sitting next to Emmitt, at the head of the table, her father didn't say anything. Emmitt had never understood why he'd been stricter with Mirai.

The room was in the traditional Japanese style, with a small alcove in which a calligraphic scroll hung and local *kutani*-ware cups were aligned on a small wooden shelf. The room had tatami flooring and several tables generously spaced out, and its walls and ceiling were of dark-stained wood.

Most houses in Japan, even modern ones, had a traditional room similar to this. Mirai's parents' home had one, too. The smallest room in the house, it contained the family altar. Although Emmitt rarely had reason to enter it, he sometimes went in alone to lie on its tatami floor, redolent with the smell of incense that his mother-in-law burned there every morning. The only other times he encountered such rooms were in *izakaya* such as this, for the duration of a meal, or in traditional *ryokan* inns, which he and Mirai hardly ever stayed in.

The room's simplicity contrasted with the disarray spawned by the busyness of his life, a far cry from the orderly, even poetical existence he yearned for. Not only did living in a traditional Japanese home strike him as ideal, but it also seemed a beautiful vision worth striving for.

He resituated himself on his knees and handed Asuka the paper bag he was holding. "Daiwa was out of cakes. I got sake instead."

She raised her eyebrows at this, then handed the bottle to her father, who took it gladly.

Sitting back down Emmitt said, "How's Shin?"

"He's fine. He wanted to come back with me but couldn't

get away. He says he'll probably get promoted soon, so he's been happy lately."

"Good for him."

"I envy his spirit. I feel like I'm with a real adult around him."

Emmitt smiled, wondering what she thought of him and the people in her family she'd lived with all her life.

Talk centered on Asuka's plans for life in Tokyo. She was keen to live in Shibuya and was willing to pay half her monthly salary for a thirty-square-meter apartment. Emmitt sat on the edge of the conversation, unable to imagine paying half his wages for such small accommodations.

Mirai had once had similar big-city dreams, Emmitt knew, though for her the allure had been Kyoto. She had given those dreams up for him and he was grateful. Soon they would live in a house of their own and could start planning their own family. With a new high-speed Shinkansen line connecting Kanazawa to Tokyo, Kanazawa's economy was thriving—a rare "bubble" in Japan these days. Even so, Kanazawa remained far more affordable than Tokyo, Kyoto, and other cities of comparable size.

Mirai's excitement for Asuka showed in the questions she asked and the attention she paid her answers. If she was reminded of her father's refusal to help her when, as a student, she needed money, she didn't show it.

"You can live closer to Shibuya Station if you choose an old place with no shower or bath," Mirai said, leaning toward Asuka's phone, on which Asuka was scanning a map of the station area.

"What am I supposed to do, wash myself at the kitchen sink?"

Mirai waited for her parents to stop laughing before replying. "You can wash your hair there at the very least."

Looking stricken by the suggestion, Asuka turned back to her phone.

"When I lived on my own," Mirai said, "I went to the public baths every evening. If you did the same, you could have more space, be closer to the action, or both. And you need enough space to grow some vegetables. Tomatoes, if nothing else."

"Do you think I'm moving to Tokyo to be a farmer?"

"You totally need me to help you," Mirai said.

Emmitt thought how Mirai differed from her mother and sister. Unlike either of them, she made her own clothing and rarely used makeup. When he and Mirai dated, he'd been shocked to learn that as a college student she'd cut and sold her own hair. Since the family had never struggled financially, it had been difficult for him to understand her poverty then. Even now, Asuka and her mother were far freer about money.

The head chef delivered to the table a complimentary dish of grilled *hatahata*. He knew Mirai's family by their long-standing patronage.

"It's a migrating fish, so it seemed appropriate. When Ms. Asuka returns to Kanazawa, we hope she'll migrate back to our *izakaya*."

After thanking him, Asuka whispered to her mother that she couldn't eat *hatahata*. Overhearing her, the chef apologized and returned to his kitchen, then brought back a small dessert. Asuka's mother tried to shame her but couldn't manage to without laughing.

Mirai's father insisted that Emmitt drink with him. "Asuka leaves in two days, and you and Mirai will move out soon, too. I forget; is it said that bad luck happens in twos or threes?"

Not wanting to show that the prospect of moving excited him, Emmitt reminded him that the *machiya* was a walkable distance away. His father-in-law shook his head, clearly unconvinced.

Emmitt turned to see the old woman who owned the *izakaya* standing behind his father-in-law, where she flipped the calendar page from January to February. His father-in-law saw it, too. Since it was almost mid-February, he teased her about ignoring the passage of time.

"Winter is long here," the woman said. "The days start to feel the same."

"When you're our age, it's natural to cling to the past."

"I guess that's right."

"By the way, what year is that calendar?"

The woman looked at him oddly. "This year, of course."

"I wish it were fifty years old. It would take me back."

Emmitt recognized that the calendar's picture for February was of the local mountains in winter. "Hakusan," he said and felt his father-in-law glance at him.

"What's that?"

"In the lower right of the photo, the *kanji* says 'Hakusan.'"

Emmitt's father-in-law looked again at the calendar, as if seeking something in the snow-covered peaks. "Japan's second-most-sacred mountain, inhabited by Buddhist and Shinto deities. Even the *Man'yōshū*, compiled 1,300 years ago, celebrates it."

"At the time the monk Taichō first climbed it . . ."

Turning back to the table, Emmitt's father-in-law dipped a slice of sea bream in soy sauce and lifted it to his mouth. "You know something about it, do you?" His tone wasn't challenging so much as reflective and a little tired.

"Not as much as I'd like."

His father-in-law chewed contemplatively. "I climbed Hakusan several times as a boy," he said. "On a school field trip once, and then again with my family. Also, one time with a girl I liked before I met my wife. For some reason, I always climbed the mountain in July. I would have liked to go in autumn once."

"After ten years here," Emmitt told him, "I finally plan to climb it."

His father-in-law seemed to think an invitation lay wrapped in his words. Shaking his head he said, "It's too late for me. Though I'd like to visit it once more before I'm gone."

Emmitt refilled his father-in-law's glass, not to encourage such maudlin talk but to distract him from it.

His mother-in-law saw this. "Don't overdo it. Tomorrow we have to help Asuka."

The rebuke brought a smile to the old man's face.

He tugged Mirai's arm, interrupting her conversation with Asuka. "Are you climbing Hakusan this summer, too?"

Leaning into Emmitt she said, "Emmitt asked me to, but I won't have time. I told him I'd massage his legs every day for a week when he got back. But only if he can prove he reached the top."

"Always a catch . . ." Emmitt said.

Mirai smiled and returned to her conversation with Asuka.

Emmitt's father-in-law told Emmitt, "If you plan to climb it, maybe I should come along. You'll miss many things scaling it on your own."

Emmitt had no intention of letting his father-in-law accompany him up a mountain, especially one as tall and difficult as Hakusan. It seemed wiser to let the comment pass.

"Didn't you tell me before that where you grew up there were no mountains nearby?" his father-in-law said. "You probably have no idea what to expect climbing Hakusan."

It was true that in the state where Emmitt was from the highest point was less than five hundred meters. But he had climbed mountains before. Lesser ones than Hakusan, it was true, but he wasn't inexperienced.

His father-in-law proceeded to share a story about an old friend who had climbed Hakusan too late in the year.

"Hakusan wasn't as developed back then, and there were no strict rules about staying on official paths. He ascended alone in early October. A snowstorm whipped up unexpectedly and lasted three days. Rescuers tried to locate him, but the storm made the mountain impassable and even a helicopter sent to look for him was unwilling to risk the conditions. When the storm finally abated, they came across him buried in snow, indistinguishable from the rocks in the area, in a pose of peaceful sleep. Someone told me once that a small *ojizō-sama* statue had been placed where they discovered his body. I'd like to find it and offer a prayer."

Emmitt had heard his father-in-law mention this dead friend before, but he'd never told Emmitt the circumstances of his death. "He was a painter, wasn't he?"

"No. I was, or I thought I'd soon become one. He was a sculptor. Some people said he had the potential to be the best sculptor of his generation in Japan. He wasn't famous, but news outlets all over the country reported his death."

Emmitt listened with interest and was disappointed when his father-in-law didn't say more. "How far from the main trail is the statue?"

"I don't know. But I'm sure it's accessible." His father-in-law paused before saying, "He invited me to go with him that day and I said no. Obviously, I made the right decision, but sometimes I ask myself—would he be alive today if I'd been along? I might have talked him down before it was too late."

There was something in the wording he'd used that hinted at suicide, but Emmitt didn't press him over it.

The emotion in his face suggested a man who felt he'd lived a full life, or as long as a father and husband could reasonably hope for, and that all he had left was time to look back on. But the emotion didn't linger. He turned to refill Emmitt's glass and then his own.

Before they could talk more about Hakusan or the sculptor who died on its slopes, Emmitt's mother-in-law cried out, "Asuka, you're bleeding."

Asuka pulled away her glass where blood from her upper lip feathered out from the rim. A drop had stained a piece of octopus on a small plate before her.

"It must have been that snail shell," she said, licking the blood from her lip. It continued to trickle out, however, and her mother dug in her purse for a wet tissue.

A waitress knelt down and used her cleaning towel to wipe away a splash of blood on the table. Asuka's mother apologized to her repeatedly.

"How did you cut it on the snail shell?" Mirai said.

"I was sucking out a piece my toothpick couldn't reach. I felt a prick but didn't know I was bleeding."

The bleeding stopped with a minute's pressure, but Asuka wouldn't eat or talk afterward, worried that the cut would reopen.

Emmitt's father-in-law ordered more sake. Ignoring his wife's and Mirai's protests, he said to Emmitt, "Weren't we talking about the *Man'yōshū*? A poem from it came to mind:

> *All living things die in the end.*
> *So long as I live here,*
> *I want the cup of pleasure."*

He smiled at Emmitt. "You should study the *Man'yōshū*. It overflows with wisdom."

Emmitt looked up as his father-in-law stood and tearfully surveyed the table.

"Next fall I will turn sixty-seven," he announced. "Emmitt invited me to climb Hakusan to help celebrate my birthday. It will be the last time I attempt to conquer the mountain. If anyone opposes our plan, you may as well tell me now."

Emmitt felt disbelief and resentment emanate toward him from six female, formerly smiling eyes.

"We all oppose it," his mother-in-law said to her husband. "Emmitt probably does, too, but is too polite to tell you."

"You're drunk, Otōsan," Mirai said. "And you," she told Emmitt, "you should know better than to encourage him."

Emmitt said in English, "He misunderstood me. I'd been talking about my own plans to climb the mountain."

"You'll do no such thing," Mirai's mother said. "You can barely walk here from home without getting winded."

As Mirai's father dumped himself back on the floor, a small plastic packet shot out of his coat pocket. He picked it up and stared at it.

"Where did these *fukumame* beans come from?" he said.

Mirai laughed and said they must be three years old. Her father's regular coat was being dry-cleaned and tonight he was wearing an old one. The memory of the "fortune beans" came back to Emmitt as Mirai explained their origins to her father.

Emmitt and Mirai had gone three years ago to Utasu Shrine for Setsubun, the bean-throwing festival held every February 3rd to mark the coming spring. It involved young *geiko* women in flowing black kimono, playing and dancing to lute music, and then, with a few local celebrities, throwing packets of *fuku-mame* to the boisterous people packed together below their stage. Mirai's mother had earlier told Emmitt to look for a sardine head attached to a branch of holly hung on a tree or pole. "It's a good luck charm," she'd told him. "So are the packets of *fukumame*.

Please bring one or two back for Otōsan and me." They had stood before the large stone *torii* gate at the shrine's entrance, looking over the noisy revelers. As the bean-throwing commenced, they had deferred to the excited, energetic crowd, who screamed and lunged in every direction the *geiko* threw the beans, sometimes even pushing each other to the ground. Emmitt had brought back a single packet. It had landed on the shoulder of the woman in front of him, and he had plucked it off without her noticing. The gift had excited his father-in-law. But finding the beans in his old coat now, it was clear he'd forgotten them.

As everyone laughed, he threw the packet onto the table. The packet split and the beans skidded across the surface into Mirai. Her look of shock didn't last; a second round of laughter, quieter this time, helped erase it.

"Let's go," Emmitt's father-in-law grumbled, thrusting money at his wife to pay the bill and starting for the door. "Our celebration is over."

Emmitt steadied his father-in-law as he left the *izakaya*.

Outside, the deep cold shocked Emmitt. He stood frozen for a moment on the narrow street as businessmen wove drunkenly past, talking at the tops of their voices.

Mirai had asked their waitress to call a taxi, and by the time they were all outside one awaited them. It only had four seats, however, so Mirai and Emmitt volunteered to walk the short distance home.

A moment later another taxi rolled down the street. It halted beside them to let a passenger out, and as it did Emmitt's attention turned to the snowflakes tumbling through the beam of its headlights. Looking up, the snow seemed infinite and indistinguishable from the clouds, and he thought again of his father-in-law's story about his friend who'd died in the mountains.

They made their way toward Bukeyashiki, the small former samurai district, and turned at a corner where long, Edo-period walls were covered with straw for the winter.

Emmitt pulled his muffler down over his mouth and said, "By the way, did you review the lease today?"

"How could I after Asuka came home with her news?"

He had asked her to look at it almost every day for two weeks, and her excuse rang hollow. At her mention of her sister, he remembered that Asuka hadn't asked about the lease they were to sign tomorrow. In fact, no one seemed willing to talk about it, and if they did, it was to express their worries, not their support. Whether it was justified or not, he equated their silence with disapproval.

"Let's talk about it when we get home," Mirai said. "We still have tonight."

It hardly seemed enough time. But he supposed it didn't matter as long as they agreed to move forward with it like they'd planned.

The family's house appeared in the distance, its short driveway gleaming with light. The light wasn't coming from the house, however. Something about the scene confused Emmitt.

He increased their pace, then pulled Mirai into a clumsy run. "Something's wrong." Her hand slipped from his as they ran.

They saw the family car in the driveway. Although no one had driven it tonight, its headlights were on as if to illuminate something in the darkness, and Asuka and her mother were scurrying around on the driver's side. Emmitt's father-in-law didn't seem to be with them.

"What are you doing?" Mirai called out as they approached.

When Asuka turned around, Emmitt and Mirai reeled back. The cut in her lip had reopened, and blood now coated her chin. "Otōsan fell on the ice and hurt his leg. I don't think he's broken anything, but neither of us can help him to his feet. Come quickly, Emmitt. You're stronger than us."

Emmitt's father-in-law lay beside the car, the snow beneath him seeming to half-swallow his body. His eyes were closed, and small clouds of breath shot from his mouth, one corner of which was twitching. Snow had turned even his eyebrows white, and he looked impossibly old and frail. Emmitt knelt beside him and placed his hand on his shoulder. He spotted blood in the snow around him, and after a moment's fear he realized it had only come from Asuka's cut.

"It's nothing serious," Emmitt's father-in-law said. "Let me rest here a minute before getting up."

"This isn't a place to rest, Otōsan," Mirai said. "Emmitt's going to walk you inside the house now. Can you sit up?"

When he didn't move, Emmitt scooped him into his arms. He didn't expect him to be so light, as if his essence had evaporated in the cold air.

At the entryway, Emmitt lowered his father-in-law to a sitting position where his daughters removed his shoes. Emmitt hoisted the old man to his feet. His mother-in-law took over from there, leading her husband to their bedroom.

Emmitt was relieved his father-in-law wasn't seriously hurt. He couldn't avoid thinking about the risks inherent in climbing Hakusan and hoped that by morning he would have forgotten the idea of joining him on the mountain.

Down the hallway, Mirai, Asuka, and their mother were all talking at once, but Emmitt couldn't see them. He was looking at the long wooden floor, which shimmered in the electric light. He went to find a wet tissue with which to wipe up a droplet of blood he saw there.

3

ON THURSDAY MORNING EMMITT went to his office earlier than usual to prepare the class he'd been forced to take on. He would have preferred to discuss the lease with Mirai, but she, too, had left for work early.

At a bus stop midway home that afternoon, a tall black man with thinning hair entered at the back and took a ticket with a shaky hand.

"Thomas," Emmitt called out, waving him over and making room to sit beside him.

His former colleague had always been thin, but he looked almost stick-like now. Within the English department he was renowned for eating only boiled or grilled food, a habit indicative of a germophobia he always denied. Even more well known was his aversion to shrimp, the presence of which, at more than one faculty event, had compelled him to remove himself and return home. On his office desk was a pipe with a paper tube covering its mouthpiece, and boxes of tissues he used to avoid touching food he ate there.

Thomas sat down heavily and sighed as if exhausted.

"You're a huge mystery these days," Emmitt said. "They gave me one of your classes and I have little idea what I'm doing. I suppose you didn't get my emails asking about it?"

"Sorry, I haven't checked my university email since I left. But I can try to answer your questions now. I don't get off the bus for another few stops."

Emmitt shook his head. "I'm not as worried about it as I was. I'll be leaving after this term, too, so that eliminates some stress."

Thomas raised his eyebrows at this news. "You'll be fine, then. I've only heard good things about your teaching, in any case. And don't forget to get some rest when you finish the term. Real rest. The kind my doctor's ordered me to take."

Emmitt felt that he'd been invited to inquire about Thomas's departure. "What happened, anyway? Are things that serious with you?"

Thomas looked out the window. "I've been sick a half-dozen times over the four years I've worked here—just colds, mostly—but this time I knew things were different." He turned back to Emmitt, smiling sadly. "My doctor put me through a battery of tests. Somehow I failed them all."

Emmitt wasn't sure what to say; he was reminded of his own sickness earlier this term—chronic stomach pain his doctor attributed to stress—but he didn't mention it now. The bus stopped to let passengers on and off.

"One day before leaving for work I passed out at home. My wife found me on the floor and for ten minutes couldn't wake me. She thought I was dead, poor girl. She insisted I see a doctor, and I guess by then I just needed someone to tell me to. The doctor said I had the worst case of hypertension he'd ever seen. He said I'd never make it to the end of the term the way things were. Now I have to rest for at least half a year. I asked if he could send me to some European-style health spa like Thomas Mann wrote about in *The Magic Mountain*, but he said he'd never read it. He's from Zushi, on the Shonan coast. He suggested I recuperate there if I want a change of atmosphere."

This was the first time Thomas—or any of his colleagues—had ever opened up to him about something so personal. "If you don't mind me asking, what will you do after you recover?"

"The university promised to take me back. But if I agreed, wouldn't I be setting myself up for the same thing to happen?

In retrospect, it's ludicrous that from the beginning I prioritized my work over my health, even over my life. If I can advise
you on anything, it's that your priorities be the opposite. Why
punching the clock is so goddamn important to everyone is
beyond me. Our time is limited, after all. People have forgotten
how to live."

Emmitt agreed, wondering if he, too, was the same.

"A friend in Tokyo thinks he can get me an administrative
job at an international school there," Thomas went on. "It seems
like a good option. But for now, I'm only to rest. I'm coming back
from the pharmacy now, otherwise I'd be at home."

"I'm just sorry this happened," Emmitt said. "It sounds like
you've traded one source of stress for another."

"I don't miss the university one bit."

Emmitt laughed. "I don't expect to miss it much either."

"I didn't put the idea of quitting into your head, did I?"

"No. You've only confirmed its importance. My wife and I
plan to move into an old *machiya* soon and I want to spend a year
renovating it. We sign the lease for it tonight, actually."

"Congratulations," Thomas said, smiling finally. He looked
over his shoulder as the bus turned a corner, and then, with the
sleeve of his coat pulled over his hand, reached into the aisle to
push the button for the next stop.

"What would you have risked if you kept teaching?" Emmitt
asked as Thomas stood to leave.

Balancing himself against a pole on one side of the aisle he
said, "In a word: everything. Not just for me, but for my family, whom I love too much to leave in the lurch." The other passengers were staring at Thomas and the driver's eye was on him
in the rearview mirror. Emmitt doubted they understood anything Thomas said, but his voice as it rose had obviously alarmed
them. "It's time for me to rest," he said as the bus slowed before

his stop. "Don't forget to fit some in between one job and the next. Good luck with them both."

As he made his way to the exit, Emmitt thought he looked and moved like someone much older than he was. Emmitt waved as the bus drove off, but Thomas didn't see him. His eyes were fixed on wherever he was going.

Emmitt texted Mirai to let her know that he'd be home soon.

By the time he arrived, she hadn't replied. He texted her again to ask when she'd be home, but she didn't reply to that either. When he left for their appointment, he checked his phone again and saw beside both messages timestamps of when she'd seen them.

✳

IN THE TATAMI SITTING room of the Kurokawas' *machiya*, Emmitt sipped the tea that Mrs. Kurokawa had replenished, reassuring himself that Mirai was fine. If her car had broken down or gotten stuck in the snow, she would have called him first thing. And if she'd been in an accident, he knew he'd be the first to hear about it.

"I'm sure she'll be here soon," Mrs. Kurokawa said, brushing the tatami floor in front of her with a hand. The dark shawl around her shoulders slipped, and she pulled it back over her padded kimono, whose pine tree patterns appeared faded, even threadbare.

"Your kimono is lovely," Emmitt told her. "It complements the atmosphere."

"Thank you. Unfortunately, it's had better days."

Emmitt wondered if Mirai, after they started living here, might sometimes dress in one, too, as she often did for her ikebana exhibitions. Her kimono and several hair ornaments had been handed down to her from her grandmother, and the traditional clothing, more than the occasion, transformed her. Mr. Kurokawa also wore a kimono under the coat he still had on. Although Emmitt rarely saw people in kimono, he looked forward to having his own to wear inside the *machiya*.

Turning to her husband Mrs. Kurokawa added, "The weather is so bad, we may have to stay here tonight."

Mr. Kurokawa, his white hair disheveled, and just long enough in front that he could hide his eyes behind it, scowled. In the three times Emmitt had met him, he always had the impression that the elderly man was being forced to give up the house.

"I just tried calling her again, too," Kimura said, handing Mrs. Kurokawa several of his business cards that he'd suggested she pass on to acquaintances who might need a real estate agent. "No luck."

"Maybe she left her phone somewhere or forgot to charge it," Emmitt said, trying to disguise his concern. "This isn't like her."

Despite his worries, he couldn't help but admire the Meiji-era *machiya*. From where he sat, he could see three spacious rooms open to each other through sliding, paper-paneled doors, including the large stone-floored room to one side, whose thirty-foot ceiling, crisscrossed with dark, century-old beams the length and thickness of fully grown trees, still made him catch his breath. Most of the rooms had tatami floors, wooden ceilings patterned in squares, and hand-carved transoms with intricate avian, floral, and Buddhist designs. In the adjoining room was a large space in the wall where a family altar would normally stand. Framed Noh masks lined the walls. Compared to the cramped apartment he'd grown up in, and even his in-laws' modern house, the *machiya* was a masterpiece of elegance and refinement.

Emmitt leaned toward Kimura to ask if he and Mirai might offer to buy one or two of the Noh masks, and Kimura, despite whispering in reply that they'd be unaffordable, passed along the question more politely than Emmitt could have managed to. Mrs. Kurokawa smiled almost painfully and told him it wouldn't be possible.

She then told Emmitt about her husband's work as a Noh actor and teacher. Like Mirai's father he had been a salaryman, but somehow, he'd found time to pursue theater and had earned numerous accolades. When she asked Emmitt if he knew any-thing about Noh, he said his interest in it was sparked several years ago when staying at Hōshi Ryokan in Awazu Onsen where an old Noh stage jutted into a pond. He admitted never having seen a Noh play, though he'd read a book of Noh plays and vis-ited Kanazawa's Noh museum. Both of his parents-in-law, too, he told her, had a deep affection for Noh. They regularly attended two plays in particular, *Ama* and *Yamanba*, whenever they were put on. "You must go sometime," Mrs. Kurokawa said. "Nothing compares to seeing it performed." Emmitt glanced then at Mr. Kurokawa, but he only continued to look at the Noh masks on the wall. It seemed he hadn't heard what they were talking about.

Two copies of the lease lay on the table before them. Emmitt's cell phone sat atop the one he was to sign, and he reached for it to check his messages again.

Half an hour ago Kimura had reminded him that the lease required only one signature, but Emmitt had said he preferred having Mirai look it over a final time. Kimura explained the contract was a duplicate of what he'd sent them last week and gone over with him on the phone. Even so, he had deferred to Emmitt's concern.

As they waited, Kimura diverted the Kurokawas with stories of his friendship with Emmitt—meeting him for the first time at a Halloween party his language school had thrown; their one attempt at *manzai* comedy, when Emmitt had played the straight man and Kimura the comic, but no one understood their routine;

and how Emmitt had helped him land his current job after rec-
ommending him to the agency president, to whom Emmitt was
teaching the pronunciation of American song lyrics on his kara-
oke machine. But by the time Mirai was forty minutes late the
mood of the room had dimmed. Kimura sighed, stared at his
watch, then turned to Emmitt and frowned.

"I don't know where she could be." Emmitt grabbed his
phone again. He tried calling once more, but in the end could
only leave another message.

"As I explained earlier," Kimura said, "the contract on the
table is exactly what we went over. If you have questions, it's not
too late to ask."

"I'm sorry for the trouble," Emmitt said. "If you don't mind,
I'm going to look for my wife outside."

"Stay inside where it's warm," Mrs. Kurokawa protested, gesturing toward the electric heater in front of them. "I'm sure she'll
arrive soon."

"I'll just be a minute." He stood and walked from the room.

Snow had accumulated since late that morning. Emmitt
trudged through it to the old wooden gate fronting the property
and stood before the narrow street. It was silent here except for
the blowing snow flicking the trees.

He telephoned his mother-in-law to ask if Mirai was home,
and if not, when she had left.

"We just got home from the doctor and then dinner," she
said. "I have no idea where she is."

"Could she be with Asuka?"

"No. Mirai was working when Asuka's friends came to pick
her up. She'll be out late tonight celebrating her job offer."

He was too distracted to inquire about his father-in-law's
condition and what the doctor had said about his leg. "Did Mirai
take the car?"

"No, Otōsan and I needed to use it. Is something wrong?"

"She's supposed to be at the lease-signing with me. She's almost an hour late."

"It looks like she ate this afternoon's leftovers. I assume she went out after that."

She'd had plenty of time to get here, Emmitt thought, even if she'd come on foot. "If she gets home before I do, have her call me right away."

The sky seemed lower somehow, and snow was falling heavily. He was about to walk down the street when he heard someone close the front door of the Kurokawas'.

Kimura jogged toward Emmitt with his arms crossed over his chest. He was wearing his suit jacket but not a coat, and his hair was gathering snow.

"I don't know if you remember," Kimura said, "but the Kurokawas live in Kaga now and will feel it's troublesome to rearrange another meeting, especially if the weather is as bad as this."

"I know what's at stake," he said. "I just wish Mirai would answer her phone."

"If you two don't see eye to eye about this place, I need to know. Are you sure you both agree about the house?"

Emmitt thought for a moment how to explain it. "The renovations will stretch us, but we can afford it. The only thing she opposes is me quitting my job. Once we commit ourselves to the *machiya*, we can get clear of these worries and refocus on our future."

Kimura looked at Emmitt carefully. "Whatever the case is, you'd better decide. Even if Mirai has doubts, I assume you've given the decision the thought it requires." Kimura patted Emmitt's shoulder before hurrying back inside. Before he slid open the front door he called out, "The Kurokawas won't wait forever."

Emmitt fretted again that something had happened to Mirai.

He had already suspected that this was her way of backing out, and he realized everyone in the *machiya* suspected this as well. Did she not worry, if she now second-guessed the arrangement, that he might sign the contract on his own? Was she leaving the choice to him?

Tromping along the street, he called her again but she didn't answer.

With his head bent to the wind and snow he returned to the *machiya*. Echoing inside him were Mirai's plans to enlarge the connecting four- and six-mat rooms and find antique wooden furnishings, to offer to buy the Kurokawas' hanging scrolls, and to renovate the storehouse so she might use it one day as an ike-bana classroom and gallery. What had happened to her vision for it? Where had her earlier excitement disappeared to?

From behind the latticed front doors, soft light filtered outside. To the left was a long window, also latticed, where two generations ago the family had run a rice business. A chain of delicate cast-iron flowers, their upper halves cupped with snow, hung from the gutter so that rain, or winter's meltwater, would cascade down. The second-floor roof, made of baked black tiles, was blanketed in a foot of whiteness. A mossy stone lantern stood unlit before the entrance. Beside the front door a clay *tanuki* animal figurine held a sake bottle in one hand and a promissory note in the other, a turtle-shell hat pushed back on his head, his testicles bulging, his toothy smile flashing at passersby.

Even if Mirai now opposed renting the house, wouldn't she get used to it over time? Once they'd renovated it, he couldn't imagine what she wouldn't like about it.

Re-entering the sitting room, he saw that Kimura and Mrs. Kurokawa had their eyes on her husband. The old man sat cross-legged in the darkness of a connected room, which led past the veranda to the garden and storehouse.

Emmitt saw belatedly the ancient-looking Noh mask on his face. In places the paint had flaked off, but the wood from which it was carved remained pristine.

The face was dark and frighteningly realistic. Although Emmitt couldn't tell if it was male or female—or even if it was meant to be living or dead—it was clearly that of someone long in years. The penetrating eyes stared outward. The smile, if that's what it was, revealed small black teeth, thin lips, and fleshy gums, and stretched the lower half of the mask eerily wide.

Two other masks now lay atop the lease he was supposed to sign. When Kimura reached for one, Mr. Kurokawa raised his hand to stop him—a precise and graceful flick of the wrist. The gesture belonged not to the hidden Mr. Kurokawa, but somehow to the wooden mask, whose mouth at its present downward angle seemed to be silently keening. No remonstrance was uttered, but the gesture made clear the prohibition.

Mrs. Kurokawa started to speak. She seemed both eager and reluctant to tell everyone something.

"As your presence here attests, it's time for us to leave this house. For my husband, it's difficult to part with. Last Saturday was his final performance at the Nōgakudo, though he will continue to advise the theater and its actors, especially the younger ones."

Mr. Kurokawa swiveled his head from side to side, ending with a jerk that left his mask angled down, its expression, it seemed to Emmitt, either inconsolable or delighting in his wife's words.

"My husband feels that letting go of this house, though we haven't lived in it for several years, is like opening a door to see beyond this life. I assure you that he accepts your and your wife's tenancy. We feel indebted to you both."

She placed her hands on the floor and bowed to Emmitt. After a moment's hesitation he bowed in return.

Kimura handed Emmitt a pen and suggested again that he sign the contract. "We've inconvenienced the Kurokawas for more than an hour. They've been exceedingly gracious up to now."

Worried by Mirai's absence, and disappointed that it fell on him to make this commitment, Emmitt leaned forward to sign the papers. He hovered over the page, ready to sign it one moment, then afraid to do so the next. Finally, he set the pen on the table and straightened up.

He bowed deeply for a second time and kept his head lowered.

"I'm sorry. I can't do it without my wife here."

When he looked up, he found Mrs. Kurokawa staring at him, a trace of a smile on her face. Kimura, too, apologized to her and her husband, but she didn't appear to notice.

Emmitt watched her turn to her husband and say, "He couldn't do it. He couldn't do it."

Her husband's mask, glowing in the room's light, seemed to laugh at Emmitt.

Mr. Kurokawa raised himself to his feet and shuffled toward the garden, where he opened the door and stepped outside. Sitting on the edge of the floor there, he stared at the snowy pine tree before him. The house quickly filled with cold.

Kimura led Emmitt by the elbow to the front door. Emmitt tried to apologize once more but Kimura interrupted him.

"I spent hours working on this with you and Mirai, and with the Kurokawas, too. Never in all my years as a real estate agent has someone backed out of an agreement at the last second like this."

He stopped speaking when Mrs. Kurokawa approached them. In that brief interval, in which panic began to hammer inside him, Emmitt saw his dream for the future disappear.

"It couldn't be helped," she said. "A terrible snowstorm like this would keep anyone away. I hope your wife is safe and warm." She paused. "Although the rental income would have been nice for my family, my husband is, as you can tell, relieved."

"Please excuse us," Kimura said to her, and pulled Emmitt into the *genkan* where, below the step leading into the house, everyone's shoes but Emmitt's were neatly lined up. "Look," he told him. "I hope Mirai is okay. If she's not, by all means let me know and I'll pass the word on to the Kurokawas. Otherwise, these negotiations are finished."

Emmitt stared at him, unable to move or speak. Somehow he managed to slip into his shoes, slide open the *machiya*'s door, and without a word to anyone, only raising a hand to his shoulder as if he couldn't commit all the way to saying goodbye, began trudging again through the snow.

He couldn't bear to turn and look for a last time at the *machiya*. He had been a pen-stroke away from acquiring it, from being able to live there with Mirai and eventually their own family—a home that was not just a shelter and collection of modern comforts, but also a place to admire and explore for years, a living reminder of a time he would never stop being curious about.

Emmitt had no idea what to expect when he arrived home. He felt torn between even greater worry that something had happened to Mirai and fury at the possibility she had sabotaged the plans they had staked their future on.

❋

"I'M RELIEVED THAT YOU'RE okay," Emmitt told Mirai when he got home. He trembled as he spoke, a result of the cold outside combined with resentment he'd never felt before. "All this time, I thought you might have gotten into a terrible accident. Or worse."

She was sitting in the living room with her parents, a blanket around her, watching TV. Her mother was reading the final proof of her literary club's translation while her father, his leg in a brace, glanced through an outdoor catalogue addressed to Emmitt.

"If you don't answer your phone when I call, especially when the weather's bad and we have an important appointment together, do you think I won't worry? Also, didn't you have a responsibility to explain your absence so I knew what to say and do at the Kurokawas'? They're almost eighty, and they came all the way from Kaga in a snowstorm."

He noticed Mirai's parents watching her, as if waiting for what she would say. Emmitt derived no joy from seeing the disappointment on their faces.

When her silence continued, he muttered: "I didn't sign the contract. I guess that's what you wanted." When she still said nothing, he added, "I'm your husband. Why would you avoid me?"

Her prolonged silence made him consider walking out and spending the night at a hotel.

"Surely you can't quit your job now," his mother-in-law ventured.

He was unprepared for her to interject. Her words reminded him that more than the *machiya* had been at stake, and his anger rose. He hurried from the room and went upstairs.

From their bedroom he heard what sounded like Mirai's parents talking to her, but she apparently had nothing to say to them, either.

While showering, he couldn't keep from thinking about the *machiya* and the possibility of reversing his decision about a job he was desperate to quit. Having their own house seemed more than ever now a fragile and unreal dream. Until tonight, Emmitt had felt confident that the *machiya* would change that. He thought it would change their lives.

When he returned to their bedroom, Mirai was lying on the floor, staring at the ceiling. Her eyes were rimmed with red when they hadn't been downstairs. He looked at her more closely without wanting to give himself away. The redness penetrated the whites of her eyes as well.

Sitting at the foot of the bed, he kicked at his briefcase. He kicked it harder and several essays he needed to grade by Monday morning tumbled out.

"Have you eaten yet? Can I get you something?" Her voice was shaky, and not like her own.

"I'm not hungry."

Emmitt refused to break the silence that followed. He wanted the awkwardness to compel Mirai to divulge what was on her mind.

"I'm sorry about tonight," she said. "I told you before I was worried about the money. That it was your dream was the only reason I considered that place."

He couldn't believe she'd only been thinking about his dream, and that she'd forgotten her own was once wrapped up in the house, too. "But you left the decision to me. And in the few times you told me you were worried about something, I always reassured you." In his present mood, he was unable to regurgitate his old arguments. "We had a good plan," was all he could say.

"What if I don't agree?" A tremor re-entered her voice. "You never listen when I offer a different point of view, or a different, more conventional plan for us."

He considered what she said. He couldn't recall ever having rejected an idea or plan she had shared with him, unless she meant her suggestion they move to Tokyo. He was left with one question he couldn't answer: Had he pushed her too far over the *machiya*?

He thought he heard the snow falling—not outside but, as before, somehow in the room between them.

"The old man was a Noh actor," he said after the silence between them grew long again. "I'd forgotten. Kimura told me about his background when I first heard about the house."

"Mr. Kurokawa?"

"His father had a rice business but was also an engraver, and his mother came from a long line of Noh actors—back to when the Maeda clan ruled. After hundreds of years, he's the last of that line."

Mirai sat up and stared at the wall.

Why was he telling her this? What little relationship they had had to the Kurokawas had ended, but something pulled him back to when he saw Mr. Kurokawa perform. He wished Mirai had seen it; there was no question that he would have signed the lease with her there.

"He put on a mask when I went outside looking for you," he stammered. "When I came inside, he had it on—an old hag's face. Somehow he brought it to life."

She fell back onto the floor and closed her eyes. "I bought a ticket to Tokyo."

Still thinking of the evening's meeting, he didn't grasp what she said right away. "What for?"

"To help Asuka."

He stared at her a long time. "When are you leaving?"

"In two days."

"For how long?"

"I don't know. For as long as it takes."

There was nothing funny to him about this, yet he laughed.

"What does that mean?"

"I wish we could live in Tokyo, Emmitt. For a few years, at least. Asuka could stand to have me in her life for a while longer. Until she gets married, at any rate. Her life is moving so quickly now."

How was he to make sense of this turnaround? She was suggesting the opposite of what they had been planning for weeks—until tonight.

"The fact is," she said, "I don't think I'm cut out to live in a *machiya.*"

With sorrowful belatedness, he could see they had conflicting ideas about the future. The *machiya* had been a way for them to start a shared life less governed by her parents, one that promised more personal freedom, but it wasn't worth it if she opposed his efforts.

"What about our plan to start a family? Is that not important to you now, or are you saying we do this in Tokyo? I've always said I want us to have our own house first." He wondered if she was reconsidering having children.

"I don't feel any urgency to start a family just yet. Besides, I've always said we could do that while living here."

"And I've always said I don't want to."

Out of nowhere, they seemed to disagree about their entire future together.

"Have you turned in your resignation?" she said.

"I was going to next week."

"It's not much time for the university to find a replacement."

"That's not my concern. Especially after the way they've treated me."

She rose from the floor and announced she would take a bath. He watched her leave the bedroom with the slowness of someone desperately tired or sick. He thought of calling her back, but what more was there to say?

It hit him, sadly and with greater force, that he hadn't merely lost the *machiya*. Worse, Mirai had hurt him in a way he thought her incapable of.

For the first time in his life, he felt they no longer trusted each other.

Though exhausted and not in the mood to speak with Mirai's parents, he forced himself to go downstairs to ask his father-in-law about his leg. He'd seemed fine when Emmitt came home, but hearing this from him directly might unburden him of at least one thing weighing on his mind.

4

ON FRIDAY AFTERNOON, ON his way to the university bus stop, Emmitt stuffed a resignation letter into his department chair's mail slot. He had dismissed his final class early, unable to concentrate on the lesson he had prepared to teach. With the extra time he'd revisited the letter, which he'd drafted halfway through the term.

A colleague in the office next to Emmitt's spotted him from her door. "I thought you had class fourth period. You'd think that by the end of the term I'd know my neighbor's schedule better."

"I dismissed my students early to work on their final essays in the library or computer lab. There's nothing more I can do for them now."

"You deserve the extra time after all the work you've done these last sixteen weeks," she said. "Are you all right?"

"I'm fine," he said, trying to smile. "Why do you ask?"

"You haven't seemed like yourself this week. Also, your coat's inside-out."

Emmitt set down his briefcase and put his coat back on properly. "The end of the term is always stressful," he muttered, not wanting to linger.

At the bus stop, his thoughts crept back to the loss of the *machiya*. He had tried to see the wisdom in Mirai's opposition to it, but he couldn't disregard how she'd handled the situation. She had disappointed him. What was done was done, he told himself; holding grudges did no one any good. In his effort to accept the loss, he admitted to himself that he could sometimes be reckless.

But recklessness didn't equal a considered willingness to take risks, and unconventional life decisions were too often deemed selfish. Until last night he was prepared to risk both money and job—not recklessly or selfishly, but to reach a goal he was certain would benefit them both.

His burnout seeped into the warm space of his former *machiya* dream, filling it from corner to corner.

As the bus pulled up, he wondered if resigning was more reckless than well-considered. But if so, why then did he feel so relieved?

※

THE BUS LURCHED TO a halt before the former Fourth High School, a brick building that now housed a literary museum his mother-in-law sometimes visited. Stepping onto the street, he spotted the entrance to Kenrokuen Garden in the shadow of two old, embracing pine trees. Although it hadn't been in his plans, he now thought to himself: Why go straight home when the park would distract him from the chaos in his mind?

He couldn't remember the last time he'd seen the beautiful shapes that snow made of the large landscape garden, how the piled whiteness framed the winter-black waters of the ponds and streams, and the way Kenrokuen's gardeners protected trees from snow with *yukitsuri* ropes. Nor could he remember having visited during any other season recently, not since the spring wedding photos he and Mirai had had taken along the garden's iris-filled streams, in the tree-shade of its villas, and before its lotus pond and shrine—photos Mirai had arranged in an elaborate album and now kept beside their bed. Had he not been here in the last five years?

After stepping toward the entrance, however, he stopped

at the sight of a monk shuffling in his direction. Stubble speck-led the monk's red face as if he'd been journeying through the cold for days. He wore a conical straw hat covered in plastic, and a dark knee-length cloak of frayed, pilling wool hung from his body. An off-white flannel scarf drooped at his neck; knitted gloves with holes in the knuckles covered his hands; white socks encased his legs; and wooden clogs crusted with snow clad his feet.

The monk shuffled past him, his wooden staff clacking hollowly. His face reminded him of someone, and a name he couldn't recall struggled to loosen itself from his tongue.

The monk continued to the end of the road and waited at the stoplight to cross. When he stepped into the crosswalk, Emmitt followed him from a distance.

Passing through the Katamachi entertainment district, Emmitt was surprised to see so many bar and club touts at this hour lining the scramble intersection. More tenacious than usual, they forced their information cards on passersby. One young man grabbed Emmitt's sleeve and tried to pull him toward a building, but Emmitt shook him off. No one bothered the monk or could even make eye contact with him; he walked through the touts unmolested.

Where Katamachi ended, a bridge spanned the Sai River to Teramachi, the temple district on the opposite side. He expected the monk to cross it; he turned left, however, down a narrow street lined with leafless, snow-laden cherry trees.

As they walked, separated by thirty or forty meters, what had been an almost spring-like afternoon changed to its usual North Country conditions, replacing with long shadows the rays of sunlight that had brightened Kanazawa until now. Wher-ever it had come from, the cloud cover sent a deep chill through Emmitt.

The monk walked on the pavement where the snow became slush. He passed beneath the cherry trees, then cut right at a public restroom, past a memorial to the writer Murō Saisei, and went straight through to some steps that ended partway down an all-white slope. Upon reaching the river, where pedestrians had kicked an uneven path through the snow, he continued toward the mountains.

It began to rain, but soon the rain became sleet, and the landscape lost any semblance of hue. The sky and air were varied shades of gray and white; the river where snow hadn't accumulated was deep black; the city on both sides of it was steeped in frozen dreariness. Except for the cold and wind, it was like being in an old Shūbun painting.

The monk trudged on. Emmitt followed him until the next bridge, even though the wind was in bursts cold and fierce. Shivering, he couldn't imagine how this monk persevered in these conditions. The sleet had turned to snow.

"Daijōji," Emmitt whispered to himself. Surely he was on his way there. Whenever Emmitt had visited the great temple, he had seen a poster near the entrance in which a procession of monks exited the temple gate into a frozen landscape—a harsh winter ascetic practice called Kanshugyō. However, they were exiting as a group, looking as freshly washed as their monks' clothing, and were only venturing into the local neighborhood to collect alms. But Kanshugyō took place in late January. This monk seemed to be on some kind of pilgrimage.

Emmitt had seen monks before near Higashi Honganji temple, not far from Kanazawa Station. But he never saw them here. He also couldn't remember having seen them looking as thin and ragged as this one.

Soon the ground beside the path widened and the houses on the street above it grew smaller with the distance. Ahead of them, traffic rushed across Shimokiku Bridge, beneath which ducks and herons perched on rocks. The monk kept his head down, seemingly oblivious to his surroundings.

For a moment Emmitt thought he remembered why the monk seemed familiar, but as soon as the thought came it disappeared.

The monk seemed to have been plucked from a previous time—thirty years past, one hundred, even four hundred and forty years ago when Kanazawa was founded. For a Buddhist monk, would the passage of time make any difference?

The monk halted at the intersection where Yukimi Bridge started. He waited for the stoplight to change, as if his plan was to proceed straight ahead, over the snow-white hills and into the mountains.

Emmitt came even with him. Clouds of steam pushed from the man's colorless lips. He was younger than Emmitt had assumed, his face of the same aspect as the students he taught. And it was this thought that connected the young man to the mystery that had eluded him.

The monk reminded him of a former student. His parents, farmers in Mie Prefecture, had pressured the boy to pursue an engineering degree and become the family's first university graduate. The boy's name was Michio. He'd been quiet and studious, and though teased for being *inakamono*—a country boy—his peers all seemed to like him. In the two classes Emmitt taught him, Michio started strong only for his efforts to flag in the final weeks of both terms, which was when most of his grade was decided. Emmitt passed him the first time as a nod to his potential, but the second time the boy stopped attending class and Emmitt failed him. When Emmitt inquired with Michio's classmates about his whereabouts, rumors swirled that he had quit school to work a menial job full-time, while others said he had returned to Mie after his parents were in some kind of accident.

Once, Emmitt had assigned a narrative essay and encouraged his students, if they had trouble choosing a topic, to describe their dreams. One student expounded on his Buddhist faith, explaining that if he could travel back in time he would train as a monk, not as an engineer. The student wanted to devote himself to the Noble Eightfold Path, but he'd succumbed to pressure to study at university. Emmitt would never forget the opening sentence: "What I learn in school has no practical value in the religious life I seek." Had the writer been Michio, Emmitt felt he would have remembered. Michio hadn't seemed that type of person, and, looking back, Emmitt thought the essay more developed and articulate than the boy could have written. Yet Emmitt couldn't place this essay with a face or name. He also couldn't recall what essay Michio might have turned in, or if he'd turned one in at all.

Emmitt found his voice. "Are you Michio?" he said. "Michio, Mi-kun, from Mie Prefecture. Do you remember me?"

Although the monk continued to stare straight ahead, his eyes had widened. Violently he shook his head.

"You were a university student recently, no? You had nearly completed your engineering degree but disappeared. You left before graduating."

The monk thumped his staff on the ground, producing a hollow noise. With the snow slanting into his face, he glanced to his right across the bridge.

Had the boy taken a vow of silence? Perhaps Emmitt was mistaken, and his forwardness had embarrassed him. In shame he wondered if he'd shattered some kind of trance.

The monk turned and half-ran to the opposite end of the bridge. He then crossed to the other side, stopped, and looked back at Emmitt, who could barely see him in the distance and through the snowfall.

Emmitt felt the monk was beckoning to him, issuing an invitation.

A moment later, rather than continue up the paved road, the monk descended through the snow to a path alongside the river.

The monk's figure faded to a stain in the white landscape. When he disappeared, Emmitt sensed that he'd lost something or had encountered some unanswerable riddle.

Starting back, Emmitt glanced across the river and considered where the young man might go from there. If not to Daijōji, perhaps there was a temple nearby that would welcome him. Or maybe the mountains of Hakusan were his destination after all.

The mountains were large here, whiter than the wintry sky. The sun slipped through a break in the clouds, turning Hakusan so white Emmitt had to shield his eyes.

He continued walking, eager suddenly to see Mirai, to be home by the time her ikebana class ended and she returned to pack for Tokyo. Overnight he had become worried about his marriage in a way he never had before. The more he thought about it, the more he hated that she was leaving in the morning. But he also knew there was no stopping her.

※

"I SUBMITTED MY RESIGNATION today," Emmitt told Mirai and her parents after dinner. Although everyone knew he planned to quit, surely they assumed the plan had hinged on the *machiya*.

Mirai muted the TV. "What did you say?"

"I told my department chair I was leaving after this term."

Her mouth hung open, as if she couldn't believe what he'd done. "Your department chair didn't try to dissuade you?"

"I didn't speak to him about it directly. This morning, though, he said it was too late to redo the teaching schedule for next term, but then he wasn't willing to do that before, either, when I first complained. My only choices were to be overloaded again or walk away."

"I assumed you'd grit your teeth and persevere a little longer. Until the end of your contract."

"Gritting my teeth takes a toll. At some point, I have to stand up for myself. In any case, I told you my plans before."

Her scornful expression made him think she either didn't consider his situation to be that bad or believed perseverance would solve every problem.

"Couldn't you at least have waited until I returned from Tokyo and we had more time to discuss it?"

"What more is there to discuss?"

She got to her feet as if to leave the room but went instead to the front window and stood there looking outside. No one said anything, and it was as if Mirai's parents were waiting for her to take a stance.

Emmitt hadn't noticed before, but he saw that it was snowing again. "As I told you, I plan to stop working for one year. Only one year. And our savings can support us for longer than that."

"But what will you *do*?" Mirai said. "Your plans obviously aren't the same as they were."

"I haven't decided. But I'm not the kind of person to sit around doing nothing."

"I guess you haven't considered what we're supposed to tell people."

"What business is it of anyone what I do?"

She looked to her parents, who remained silent.

"I'm not the first person who walked away from a job to fig-ure out his life," Emmitt went on. He assured her that there was nothing complicated about his plan. He simply subscribed to the idea that taking a break from working was warranted if you were determined to find meaning in other kinds of life experience. Once you were established in a field and had saved a certain amount, was it so radical to focus on how you lived? Money didn't seem the root to everyone's opposition to his plan, he added. That what he wanted to do was *different* seemed to be the issue.

"That's what it is, isn't it?" he said.

His mother-in-law, perhaps chastised slightly, said, "Is this common in America? And for someone your age?"

Emmitt tried to ignore the implication, in his mind, that his upbringing made him behave in a non-Japanese way—in other words, irresponsibly. But he could think of no more responsible path than the one he'd just committed to.

"It's not unheard of. No one would bat an eye over it if the decision didn't threaten anyone."

"At thirty-six you're taking an unnecessary risk," she went on. "Especially if you want to start a family."

"It's less of a risk than if I did it at forty-six. Especially if we have kids then."

"He's made his decision," his father-in-law said. "The world hasn't ended as far as I can see."

"You approve of what he's done?" Mirai's mother said.

"Why don't we take him at his word? It's not my place to meddle, and I'm not sure it's yours, either."

Mirai left the room. When she returned a few minutes later, she had calmed down. "After the way the university treated you, I don't blame you for wanting to quit. I also support your decision to take time off. But over the next year, if you complain about not working, or if you tell me you miss the university for any reason, I can't promise I'll still support you."

"Thank you," Emmitt said. "And I won't."

"But don't you think what you're doing is selfish?" she added.

"I don't say that to pick a fight. I just wonder if it ever crossed your mind that it might be, and that for that reason alone you should continue on a bit longer. Or look for a better job somewhere else."

"Maybe I am being selfish. But if so, it's no more selfish than not showing up to sign the lease at the Kurokawas' after two and a half months of negotiations."

He supposed it was the wrong thing to say, especially with her leaving for Tokyo the next morning. He expected her to get angry, or at least defensive, but she remained calm.

"I see." She sat with her back against the wall and stared across the room.

Mirai's mother slipped into the kitchen. A moment later she came back carrying a tray with four cups and a bottle of sake from Awazu Onsen. She poured Emmitt the first cup, and when they all had one, they raised them slightly, toasting what was apparently a return to peace.

Emmitt was glad to have cleared the air. Still, the atmosphere in the house had darkened because of his decision. Wanting to give Mirai and her parents a chance to discuss things without him around, he told them he needed to grade papers upstairs.

"But we just opened this Hirohisa," his father-in-law said. "At least come back when you need more."

"Wait until he's unemployed before turning him into an alcoholic," Mirai said. "On second thought, don't encourage him then, either."

Emmitt glanced toward the *genkan* and back to Mirai. "Where's your suitcase? Haven't you packed?"

"It's in my parents' bedroom. Okāsan wants to include some things for Asuka."

He looked down the hallway, toward her parents' bedroom. From where he stood, he could only see a pillow on one of the separate beds they slept in. He promised himself that he and Mirai would never live the same way. Although her parents seemed to love each other, it was a love that lacked intimacy. To Emmitt, this was another reason for him and Mirai to have their own home, where they could make their own rules to live by and not be overly influenced by how her parents were together. He didn't want her to copy their habits as a matter of course, a matter of "culture."

Emmitt turned to look at Mirai until his father-in-law gestured at the cup of sake he was holding. Emmitt swallowed the sake, set down his cup, then picked up his briefcase and climbed upstairs.

5

AT THE END OF the following week Emmitt came downstairs after changing out of his teaching clothes. His mother-in-law, preparing a seafood hotpot her husband liked to eat in the winter, looked up as he entered the kitchen and removed a sake cup from the cupboard.

At the university that day he had found in his briefcase a first printing of her literary club's translation of Izumi Kyōka's work. Its title was *Red on White*. She had bundled it together with some English translations she'd bought him last year. While he was eating breakfast that morning, she must have entered his room and slipped them in his briefcase. Upon discovering them, he couldn't figure out why they were there. A moment later, he'd laughed aloud.

By the time his bus had brought him back to Kanazawa that evening, he had read half of *Red on White*. From the first page, he'd understood his mother-in-law's disappointment. Although there were no obvious gaps or inconsistencies in what he'd read, the English was subpar. His instinct as a writing instructor was to flag choices of diction, ungrammatical sentences, instances of verbiage, lazy repetitions—his fingers had twitched constantly.

The quality of the translation drew attention to itself and made Kyōka and Kanazawa look second-rate. Walking home from the bus stop, he'd regretted not having made time to help. If his mother-in-law gave him a chance to again, he would do so however he could.

Before joining his father-in-law, who was drinking sake in

the living room, he decided to broach the translation with her. He knew she must want to hear about the books he'd found in his briefcase.

"I'm curious," he said. "Why did your group name the story collection *Red on White*?"

Without looking up she said, "I didn't realize you knew the title."

"I didn't until today. I happened to find it in my briefcase at school."

"You found my copy, did you? How odd for me to have misplaced it there."

Emmitt laughed. "I read a few stories at work and on the bus home."

"And?"

"And I'm curious about the title."

"It's not what I wanted. A majority of our members voted for it."

Since the publication had been her idea, and she was in charge of it, he was surprised that the group had voted for something she opposed. "But what is its significance?"

She set down her cooking chopsticks and explained it to him. Kyōka juxtaposed red with white because of the beautiful contrast and their associations with eroticism and violence. Red is the color of passion, of sexuality; white the color of purity, but also death. The colors were for him an aesthetic obsession.

"This imagery appears in every story of the collection, and that accounts for its title," she said. "But it sounds like you didn't notice."

Once he heard her explanation, he remembered several references. Armed with this information, he would now look for it in Kyōka's other works.

"I tried to push for an introduction that clarified these sorts of things. Even for Japanese readers, understanding his writing on its deepest level requires some explanation."

"It might have been helpful, but I enjoyed what I read without it."

"You would have enjoyed it more. Perhaps your feeling for his work would be closer to mine now."

She asked about the translation. "Do you agree with what my friend told me the other day?"

He plucked a salted plum from a bag beside the stove and slid it into his mouth. It was a sweet variety and he chewed it, thinking how to answer without implying he should have helped her.

"The stories I've read haven't been very engaging. I don't blame Kyōka, either, or your group for selecting them. The person who translated them into English doesn't seem to be very good. Her best writing isn't much more than competent."

"I see." She sighed and returned to preparing dinner. "There's nothing we can do about it now. If we're lucky no one will read it and it will quietly fade away. Then we can try again."

"Is that what your group plans to do?"

"I don't know yet. Not everyone in the group likes his work. It may come down to what the city wants."

"I regret not helping you. But I honestly didn't have time."

"I understand. I understood all along. I never should have pressed you like I did. Thank you."

They both laughed at her fumbling remarks.

"Go bother Otōsan, please. I need to finish dinner."

❈

EMMITT'S FATHER-IN-LAW WAS FLIPPING through TV channels looking for a sumo tournament he wanted to watch. Unable to

remember when it came on, he picked up the elaborate drawing kit Mirai and Asuka had sent to help him get through his
recovery. Apparently their mother had told them he'd spent the
entire day after Mirai's departure drawing. He had recreated the
statue of a woman that stood somewhere in Kanazawa, but had
destroyed his work before Emmitt could see it. His mother-in-
law claimed it had been of a quality you might see in a museum.

The kit arrived two days ago, and though his father-in-law
had inspected it several times, he hadn't opened it.

"You don't like your daughters' gift?" Emmitt said.

"They shouldn't have spent the money."

"They did it because they want you to keep drawing. Doesn't
that encourage you?"

"They felt sorry for me. Why should I get excited about that?"

"What does Okāsan say about it?"

"Nothing. Why would she say anything?"

"Mirai and Asuka would be upset if they knew you hadn't
bothered to open it."

His father-in-law shoved the kit beneath the coffee table and
changed the channel again. "Maybe I'll ask Mirai to return it
when she gets home."

He shushed Emmitt before he could argue with him, and
they sat together drinking.

A TV segment began about a monk from a mountain temple who was in Kanazawa to discuss the marathons he'd walked,
every day for a thousand days, seeking enlightenment. His
father-in-law repositioned his leg as the newscaster announced
that the monk would have had to commit suicide if he'd taken a
day off, regardless of sickness or injury.

"Since when does Buddhism require a devotee to take his
own life?" Emmitt said.

"The temple would have stopped him. They say that only to

get donations." He reached for the remote and changed the channel again.

"One thousand consecutive marathons," Emmitt said, impressed by the feat. "There are worse things people do for money."

"It's not the same as working. Look at him now—he's a celebrity."

Emmitt considered the monk's feat at least equal to working, if not superior to it. He wondered if his father-in-law thought a price could be put on enlightenment, then realized with a start he had no idea what religious beliefs either of Mirai's parents held, or for that matter what they thought about an afterlife.

He watched his father-in-law lift his sake bottle from the table as if to study the flowing *kanji* on its label. A friend had dropped off a large bottle of Shun after a trip to Yamanaka Onsen, a nearby hot spring town. Emmitt shook his head when his father-in-law offered him the last pour from it.

"Do you think that monk lied about walking all those marathons?" Emmitt said.

"No. But stories like that get embellished. And I disliked that newscaster fawning over him. What's the use of putting him on TV?"

Emmitt told him about the monk he'd followed last week, and how he'd thought the young man was his former student.

"You followed him all that way in the snow? It must be four kilometers to that bridge."

"Was it actually him?" his mother-in-law called from the kitchen. Emmitt hadn't realized she was listening.

"I doubt someone like him could have changed so drastically," Emmitt said. "He was lazy and unmotivated in my classes. After he dropped out, I imagined him returning to Mie and working on his parents' farm."

"Maybe you misconstrued his nature," she said. "Not everyone thrives in a classroom. He might have only needed to find his true path. Few people ever manage that in their lifetimes."

Emmitt sometimes thought the same thing—he'd seen proof of it at the university every term—and he thought about it again now. Only twice in his life had he felt that he'd taken the right path and found something essential to his existence. Once was when he arrived in Japan for the first time after passing an interview to teach at a Kanazawa language school, and the second was when he'd proposed to Mirai and she accepted. Though each moment had proved life-changing, both now seemed more a combination of good luck and right choices than paths. If he was born to find a path to travel down, he felt strongly that he still had searching to do.

"Have you found your true paths?" he asked.

His mother-in-law spoke first. "My lifetime, I hope, is far from over. In some ways I feel I'm still seeking for something, that life has more in store for me. What about you, Otōsan?"

Emmitt's father-in-law sipped his sake; Emmitt couldn't tell if he was considering the question or ignoring them. He murmured, "If I haven't, then I've wasted a lot of time. But when I think about it, what have I really done?"

The resemblance of the monk's face to that of his former student still seemed uncanny. "To change to that extent so quickly—to become a monk walking through a snowstorm in barely more than rags—seems unlikely. It was even harder to tell if it was him since he'd shaved his head."

"Are you thinking of becoming a monk?" his father-in-law said.

Had he forgotten he'd asked him the same thing less than two weeks ago?

"Of course not. Why?"

"Staying overnight at temples and following monks through snowstorms. Walking away from your job even after your *machiya* plans fell through. It's worrying for me as Mirai's father."

"We decided not to visit Eiheiji," Emmitt said. Not wanting to appear as if he took the criticism lightly, he added: "You don't need to worry about that. I'm tired of working to no worthwhile end, that's all. And of being taken advantage of."

"We're just concerned about your future," his mother-in-law said. "Mirai deserves stability, doesn't she?"

"Of course," Emmitt said, angered by the comment.

With a finger his father-in-law blotted a drop of sake from the table and said, "Most people dislike their work, at least at certain points in their lives, but they don't just quit—especially when they're married. They persevere. They understand their broader responsibilities."

"I know all this," Emmitt said.

His mother-in-law called them to dinner. On the table was a just-opened bottle of Kiku-Masamune. She had set out new sake cups for them to drink from.

As they ate, Emmitt mentioned that he planned to Skype with Mirai later.

"A week's a long time for her to be gone," his father-in-law said. "I thought she'd only be in Tokyo for two or three days."

The last time they Skyped she'd claimed that she still needed to help Asuka. Asuka was stressed about her job training, she wasn't getting enough sleep, and Shin had started to complain that he rarely saw her. Mirai couldn't promise when she'd return to Kanazawa but hoped it would be soon.

"Why don't you go to Tokyo, too?" his mother-in-law said.

Emmitt had already considered this. But if he spent a pleasant weekend with her in Tokyo, he worried it might embolden her to make more trips. Seeing that it also bothered her parents gratified him.

"I'm not finished at university yet," Emmitt replied, though they knew his responsibilities there were over. His department chair had accepted his resignation, and all that remained was for Emmitt to submit his grades and clear out his office.

The table fell silent until Emmitt's father-in-law finished eating. He rose from his chair and, still limping, took his sake cup and the bottle of Kiku-Masamune to the living room sofa.

"Prop your leg with a pillow," Emmitt's mother-in-law called to him.

"My leg is fine. You'd do better worrying about your daughters, not me."

"I worry about all of you."

A minute later Emmitt's father-in-law reached for a sofa pillow and rested his injured leg atop it.

"Next week," he proclaimed, "I plan to start walking every day."

"Don't push it," Emmitt said. "You're a long way from being able to walk one thousand consecutive marathons."

His father-in-law finished his sake and poured another cup. "So are you."

❋

AFTER DINNER EMMITT WALKED along the Sai River, where he planned to Skype with Mirai. Huddling inside his coat, he tried to imagine how she occupied herself in Tokyo. Whatever her reasons for staying there, he wanted her to come back.

He hadn't felt her absence so intensely before they'd married and were living apart. Their relationship wasn't as complicated then, when their biggest hurdle was finding ways to be together, and when they couldn't manage to, they'd Skyped then, too. Mirai's persistence in wanting to be with him was one reason he'd fallen in love with her. After they'd started dating, she had quickly made a routine of visiting him at his apartment, slowly turning it into his first real home in Japan, though he'd already been living in the country for over a year by that time. Her influence on how he ate, dressed, kept his apartment clean (and enlivened with flowers), spoke Japanese, and comprehended his surroundings led him to see how much she cared for him—and him for her. She had always made Japan more accessible to him, and a happier place to make his life. He'd told her this when he asked her to marry him.

When he reached the Shinbashi bridge, he walked in the direction of the sea. A recent rain had melted much of the snow alongside the river, exposing swathes of uncut marsh grass, now wilted and drained of color. By late next month, cherry trees would turn the riverbank white and pink, and the marsh grass would grow green and tall again.

He received Mirai's call as he approached Saigawa Shrine.

"*Moshimoshi*," he said, passing beneath two *torii* gates. He continued through the small courtyard and sat on the wooden floor above the offering hall's stone steps.

Seeing Mirai's face squeezed into his phone's narrow screen made the pain of her absence fresh again.

As she leaned back, Asuka's apartment swept into view. He noticed new furnishings and how the room was now decorated with flowers and Asuka's paintings. They gave the apartment charm, though it seemed too cramped to share, even if Asuka was rarely home.

When he asked Mirai what she'd been doing since they last Skyped, she told him she'd gotten in touch with Koyo, an old classmate from Kanazawa. They had grown up studying Kaga Koryū–style ikebana together and had once taught at the same art school. Mirai had shifted from painting to ikebana largely because of her. Koyo had also married Emmitt's former colleague, a teacher named Avery with a PhD in linguistics and twenty years of teaching experience in Japan and Southeast Asia. Two years ago Avery had unsuccessfully petitioned for tenure as an exception to the university's rule for foreign teachers. Unable to continue teaching there, he had eventually found work at a private university in Tokyo, while Koyo began instructing at an ikebana school a short bicycle ride away.

"Tomorrow night we're meeting at a Vietnamese restaurant in Ikebukuro. Asuka will join us if she can escape from work and Shin doesn't object."

"Why would he object?"

"Because he doesn't spend as much time with her as he'd like."

"So why don't you invite him, too?"

"It was Asuka's decision. I don't know why she didn't invite him along."

"Have things between them soured?"

"Asuka says they've been discussing marriage, yet they're always so busy they rarely see each other. He often blames her for not being available when he comes home early. I think Asuka likes spending time with Avery and Koyo. She knows she can relax with them."

Emmitt envied Mirai's night out with their old friends and appreciated her part in maintaining their relationship. Even so, he was disappointed she wouldn't come home tomorrow and told her so.

"I never said when I'd be back. And you didn't ask me to come back by a specific date. My school is fine with me being away."

"Otōsan thinks you're avoiding me after what happened with the house. But there's no need for that."

She looked away and didn't reply. Not long ago he would have pressed her for an answer, but in her silence, he was aware she'd already given him one.

The headlights of a passing car briefly illuminated where he sat. Mirai asked where he was.

"I'm by the river."

She came closer to the screen, narrowing her eyes. "You're shivering. You should go home and talk to me from there."

He hadn't realized it, but she was right: He was trembling. "Remind Avery that I wrote him a month ago but he never replied."

"Oh, I forgot to tell you," she said, her mood lifting. "I printed out your CV before coming to Tokyo. Today I sent copies to three universities in the city. Koyo said Avery might want to see it, too, so I'll give him one at dinner tomorrow."

Her subterfuge caught him off guard. It took him a moment to grasp what she had done. "Why the hell didn't you ask me first?"

"I thought since I'm here and have extra time . . ."

"People don't inquire about jobs they don't want, you realize."

"What's wrong with having more options?"

Cursing under his breath, Emmitt wandered to a tall, twisting pine tree and two red-and-black *torii*. A light burned inside a smaller structure behind them, spilling over a pair of stone foxes.

"What sort of cover letters did you include? And how did you sign them?"

"I didn't send any."

Anger prevented him from saying anything right away. "Don't ever go behind my back like that again. Do you understand?"

"I won't. But no, I don't really understand why you're so angry."

"You've broken my trust, that's why."

Shaking his head in disbelief, he told himself not to care about what she'd done. After all, what did it matter? It was better she'd done it in Tokyo than in Kanazawa, where people knew who he was.

"By the way," she said softly, "Koyo said she could probably get me a job at her ikebana school."

"You already have a job at an ikebana school. And a very flexible one, too, considering how quickly you left and how long you've been away."

Mirai didn't say anything.

"You seem to enjoy being in Tokyo more than here."

"It feels good helping my sister. I won't always have that opportunity."

Emmitt walked to a wall on which wooden prayer blocks hung, their inscriptions unreadable in the dark. He ran his fingers over them. They knocked against each other hollowly.

"What have you been doing since we last talked?" she said.

He explained that he'd been working his usual hours at the university and at home. He'd also been looking online for houses—those for sale and those listed on a database of long-empty dwellings that the city had taken possession of. He wanted to contact Kimura, awkward though it would be, for any new leads. After he told her this, he wondered if she had been asking something else.

"Have you heard from him?" she said.

"No. After what happened, I wasn't expecting to right away."

A hesitation entered her voice. "It seems impossible we'll find a suitable old house to live in."

He stifled a desire to raise how she'd handled the Kurokawas' *machiya* and instead took a solicitous tone. "We need to be patient."

"But there are few *machiya* in the city center, and those that exist are too small or unaffordable. And I'm not the only one with that opinion. Kimura says the same thing, doesn't he?"

"In the city center, yes. But we have other options."

"If we're going to consider other options," she said after checking herself once, "I want to add Tokyo to the list."

He nearly told her that she could consider moving there by herself, which meant she would have to get used to living apart. But that was the last thing he wanted, and he had no desire to hurt her with anything so ill-considered. He couldn't help being angry, however. Her change of outlook made him feel that, after five years of marriage and eight of being together, he didn't know her as well as he'd thought. Part of him felt that she'd secretly wanted to move to Tokyo all this time.

Looking past the two *torii* at the entrance, where the snowy peaks of the faraway mountains appeared ghostly pale in the darkness, he added, "What accounts for this sudden change in you, anyway?"

Her eyes settled into a tired gaze—not at the screen of her phone, but off to the side, to somewhere he couldn't see. "I think it would be good for us to take some time off."

Her words unnerved him. "From house-hunting, you mean . . ."

She reached for a glass outside the screen and drank from it, then set it down and looked at it for a long moment.

He repeated his question.

"Well, yes," she said. Her laughter sounded unnatural.

"For a moment I thought . . ."

Where his words trailed off, she sighed.

"I'm putting it in your hands, Emmitt."

"What do you mean?"

"Exactly what I said."

It was either an extreme act of generosity to entrust him with finding a house, or she was telling him to do things her way and give it up. He felt vaguely like she had issued a warning.

He asked again when she was coming home.

"I don't know. And I'm sorry, but I'd better go. I want to pre-pare dinner for Asuka."

As Emmitt stood above the Sai, gazing at what appeared to be more snow clouds rolling in from the mountains, the short-ness of their talk dismayed him. The longer she stayed away, the shorter their conversations seemed to last.

❋

WHEN HE RETURNED HOME, his father-in-law was in the living room, dressed in his pajamas and with his hair combed back as if he'd recently taken a bath. Sitting on the sofa, he held an old dishrag and bottle of cleaner. A stack of framed drawings lay before him along with a collection of Noh plays he sometimes read.

"I see you found inspiration while I was out," Emmitt said, sitting beside him.

"I wouldn't call it that. Though these bring back a time when I was creative."

"What were you reading?"

His father-in-law glanced at the coffee table. "Nothing in particular. But as I was reading it, I recalled you telling me about Mr. Kurokawa. Okāsan and I agreed that we must have seen him perform before. If he's the actor we remember, he was as skilled as any we'd ever seen."

Noticing the drawing kit on the floor, still unopened, Emmitt shook his head. Someone—he assumed it was his father-in-law—had pulled it out from beneath the coffee table while he was out.

"Cleaning those pictures doesn't make you want to draw again?"

His father-in-law looked across the room as if considering

this for the first time. After a moment, he resumed wiping the glass frames. "Maybe it's because I'm thinking of climbing Hakusan when my leg recovers. I told you about my friend—and Okāsan's, too—who died before reaching his potential as a sculptor. By then I'd like to have drawn something that would have earned his admiration."

Emmitt's thoughts lingered on the mention of Mirai's mother. Although it made sense, he didn't realize that the man who had died on Hakusan had also been her friend. He watched his father-in-law wipe the frame down again.

"Where did all these pictures come from?"

"They were in a box beneath Mirai's and Asuka's baby clothes. For some reason Okāsan decided to go through their old things tonight."

Emmitt imagined she was eager for them to have children. Either that, or she envisioned her daughters having their own houses soon and space in which to store their old belongings.

Emmitt craned his neck to see into the kitchen, but she wasn't there.

"She's in the bath," his father-in-law said. "She took two books in with her, so she may be a long time."

"It's too bad what happened with the translation."

His father-in-law shrugged. "She's making more out of it than necessary. While you were out, she learned that her literary club received a grant for a second translation. It's another of Kyōka's works, though I'm not sure which one."

"I wonder if she'll ask me to help again."

His father-in-law smiled. "She knows you can't deny her a second time."

The news excited Emmitt more than he expected it to. It wasn't merely for her sake that he wanted to assist with the translation, or even proofread for her someone else's work. Now that he was free of his teaching obligations, he could see more clearly that becoming involved with such a project might lead him deeper into Kanazawa's past, to see it as Kyōka wanted his readers to see it—uncorrupted, like his writing, by Western influences that had become prevalent during his time.

Emmitt observed aloud, "You're not drinking tonight."

"I've been drawing all day. I guess that threw me off my normal routine."

"You drew today?" Emmitt hoped it was the start of something new.

"If you want a bit of sake, I suppose I could have some, too."

"Maybe tomorrow. I should try to get through more grading tonight. Thankfully, it's nearly the last I have to do."

His father-in-law lifted a picture from the table, spritzed it with cleaner, and wiped it circularly from the center to its edges. He repeated this, and where some speck of matter clung, he wiped it again with the rag.

Emmitt peered at the drawing as his father-in-law held it to the light. "A woman on a cliff?"

Returning it to his lap, his father-in-law squinted at it.

"Okāsan and I went to Noto a few weeks after getting married and stayed at an inn. One day we walked to a promontory and she stood there with the sea wind buffeting her hair. I watched her a long time then insisted we return to our room. I spent all evening drawing her."

He had drawn his wife in a short summer dress, and though Emmitt might have mistaken her face for that of either of their daughters, her figure reminded him of Mirai's. He glanced from her to the penciled trees, the rocky ground, the sea with its midshore outcroppings, and the sky. These, too, were carefully drawn, if less bold in tone than his mother-in-law's image. Their edges were rounded, almost blurred, yet the drawing as a whole seemed sharply detailed.

Emmitt, too, had photographed Mirai on their own trip

to Noto after getting married. Though normally she was camera-shy, she had allowed him to take dozens of shots of her as they drove up the coast, exploring empty bays and picturesque fishing villages, and also at different *ryokan* where they stayed. Two of these photos now hung on their bedroom wall, and two stood framed on his desk. He couldn't help noticing that his best photographs paled beside his father-in-law's least sophisticated drawings.

His father-in-law lifted the picture again, tilting it in the light. "I remember when I finished it, Okāsan didn't like it. I suppose that's why it ended boxed up and forgotten until tonight."

"Why did you stop making art?" It wasn't the first time Emmitt had asked this, but he felt he'd never received a truthful answer.

"My model stopped cooperating."

Emmitt had heard this before from Mirai, never from her father. "You could have continued without her cooperation."

His father-in-law smiled a little sadly. "Work also took me away for long periods. And that tends to crush your spirit after a while."

Hearing this excuse again disappointed Emmitt. No doubt it had been a factor, but he was convinced there were others, too. Yet the answer resonated with him more now than when his father-in-law had said this before.

"And why did you wait until now to start again?"

"I didn't 'wait until now.' I remember clearly the last time I tried—just before my fiftieth birthday. I awoke and the first thought I had, like something calling out from a fading dream, was that I could no longer put off what my younger self had always permitted. I immediately understood the importance of that revelation. But although the truth was obvious—that drawing was what I'd always most wanted to do—I turned away from it. I knew I risked losing it forever if I let myself put it off even longer. I'm only now drawing because sometimes I feel this is my last chance. But perhaps it's too late." He had been talking quickly, and he paused to catch his breath.

"But you've come back to it," Emmitt said.

"I've only made a few drawings."

"But isn't what you're doing now worth anything?"

His father-in-law shook his head. "Obviously, what I'm doing now doesn't define me like it once did. Back then, I thought the present moment was the only one that mattered, and that led me to be consumed with each drawing I made. The idea that our lives are spread across time meant nothing to me. When you're young and bogged down, pulled constantly in multiple directions, reaching that sort of understanding is difficult. At my age, though, I've finally learned this." He paused to replace the picture atop the stack before him. "This is one reason I no longer oppose you quitting your job, though I don't consider it good news, either. I'm confident that you'll figure things out over time."

Emmitt couldn't remember what his father-in-law had done before retiring, only that his company had been near the sea. He might have managed a dozen employees before rising to section chief his last few years. Emmitt looked around the living room for some sign of his work life but couldn't find any. It was as if no one wished to be reminded of whatever had sustained them over the years. Emmitt thought of the university work he brought home every night, and how anyone could guess what he did by walking into his room.

Emmitt's eyes fell back on the stack of pictures. "What about these others?"

"More of the same. I once tried to hang them around the house, but Okāsan pulled them down. I shouldn't have bothered framing them."

"If Mirai and I ever get our own house," Emmitt said, "maybe we could display some there."

His father-in-law laughed. "Mirai won't want these. And Okāsan would refuse to visit if she had to see them on your walls."

Together they re-boxed the pictures, separating each with pieces of cloth.

"Youth leaves us too quickly," he said, gazing at a drawing. "Years sneak up, leaving us with less than what we think we'll always have."

At thirty-six, Emmitt had felt sometimes that his youth was already behind him. He realized that his father-in-law, who was nearly twice his age, must feel this loss more deeply.

His father-in-law placed the drawing with the others inside the box. "Help me set this back in the closet, will you?"

Emmitt lifted the box and followed his father-in-law to the end of the hallway, where he opened the closet and pointed to the back of it.

Emmitt's mother-in-law opened the bedroom door and looked out at them.

She had already bathed, and her face without makeup revealed shallow wrinkles around her eyes, an occasional age spot, and sparser eyebrows than she wore in public. He was surprised to see her in a nightshirt in which the outline of her breasts was visible, and he thought she didn't look old so much as weary. "What are you doing in there?" she said.

"We were just discussing how much I'd have to pay to buy all his drawings," Emmitt said. "One day they may have great value."

"*Baka wa sugu ni kane wo nakusu.*"

Recognizing the Japanese idiom about fools and their money, which was the same as in English, he laughed.

"It's getting late, Otōsan." She held the door open for him.

"Good night," Emmitt said.

"Good night," they both said as she shut the door.

Emmitt climbed upstairs to grade his final batch of essays for the term. As he pulled them from his briefcase, however, he noticed again the books his mother-in-law had put there. Having read enough of *Red on White* for now, he set it aside.

He was about to do the same with the other books when he picked up an older collection of translated Kyōka stories and started reading.

6

AS MIRAI DESCENDED THE escalator from the Shinkansen platform, Emmitt approached the turnstile. Amidst scores of passengers scanning the exits and checking their phones, he took
her suitcase as she passed through.

"It's strange to see you like this," she said. As if to address his
perplexed look she added, "This is the longest we've been apart
since getting married."

They were standing and talking in the busiest part of the station, and he preferred not to linger. "Do you want to eat something before we go back?"

"I want you to take me home."

He wrapped an arm around her and she hugged him.

He felt himself holding something back from her; he wasn't
sure if it was from frustration at her overlong absence or only
something that was slow to make itself clear to him.

For a moment it seemed like he was meeting someone other
than his wife.

They steered her luggage to the taxi stand before the station.
A cold wind swirled around them as a taxi pulled up and they
climbed inside.

On the short ride home she told him she'd received a job
offer that morning.

"Doing what?" he said, taken aback.

"Assisting at Koyo's ikebana school."

He wondered what she had in mind by sharing the news with
him this way. Had she wanted to test his reaction?

"Yesterday Koyo introduced me to the school's owner. After

the woman watched me complete two arrangements, she said my skill and my ability to explain what I was doing impressed her. She offered me a job on the spot."

"Were you applying for a position or did she make the offer when she saw you working?"

"A little of both, I guess."

When he regained his composure he said, "You kept busier in Tokyo than I imagined."

She smiled at him. "I had a good time there."

He didn't ask what answer she gave the woman.

As they neared their house she said, "I'm sorry you couldn't come to Tokyo. It would have been nice to stay there together. Maybe we can visit in a few weeks to see the cherries bloom."

As it was only early March, he hadn't yet thought about the upcoming *sakura* season or its festivities. Spring still seemed far away, though the snow had let up, the temperatures were warming little by little, and Kanazawa was turning greener.

"There are plenty of places besides Tokyo where cherry blossoms are worth seeing. Someplace closer to home would also be less expensive."

"But Tokyo's special. It would be nice to see them there together at least once. Maybe next year would be better."

Passing Seirei Hospital, Emmitt spotted a statue of Jesus beside a large rock engraved with Japanese. It somehow reminded him of Mirai's father, who'd been drawing a statue he'd photographed yesterday.

"By the way, Otōsan finally opened that drawing kit you sent him. He was sketching in the dining room when I left."

"What's he drawing?"

"A sculpture overlooking the Asano River. His rendering was extraordinary."

The statue was called *Dream Flight* and showed a nude man

and woman hovering horizontally over a rectangular plinth, their arms outstretched and left legs intertwining. To Emmitt, the figures appeared to be underwater, the woman suggesting to the man beneath her that they rise to the surface together. Emmitt had asked his father-in-law why he'd chosen this sculpture, but he'd only said, "Why are your eyes green? What do you put peanut butter on bananas for? Do I need reasons for what I do?" Emmitt had left him alone, happy to let him draw.

As soon as they got home Mirai repeated the story about the job offer at Koyo's ikebana school. Her mother let out a shriek and asked what answer she'd given.

Mirai glanced at Emmitt, as if curious why he hadn't asked her this in the taxi. He turned away, unsure whether he wanted to stay or leave the room.

"Asuka thought I should have accepted it. In the end I asked the school owner to keep me in mind for the future. She insisted that I tell her if I reconsider."

"But you couldn't work there unless you lived in Tokyo."

Mirai laughed. She started to respond, but her father cut her off. "I didn't think we'd raised you to be so disrespectful," he snapped from the dining room table, where he continued to draw.

"What are you talking about?" Mirai said, her tone exasperated. "What did I—"

"You were selfish, staying away for two weeks and applying for a job. Did you forget you have a husband and home here?"

Mirai looked to Emmitt and then back to her father. She opened her mouth but no words came out. What seemed like frustration in her a moment ago now seemed tinged with fear.

"You were irresponsible, chasing whatever Tokyo fantasy you concocted."

"Otōsan . . ." Mirai's mother said.

"Tokyo fantasy?"

"That's what I said."

She turned to Emmitt, her eyes tearing. "This isn't fair. I might have found Emmitt a job, too. What's going on here?"

"Come with me," her mother said. "You can tell me about your trip." She led Mirai from the room.

Emmitt's father-in-law turned back to his drawing.

"Thank you," Emmitt said as the women's voices filled the kitchen. "But you don't have to be angry on my account."

He waved off Emmitt's words. "Sometimes I have to remind my daughters that I'm not as blind as I seem. One day you'll have children and do the same thing."

Emmitt didn't know how to respond.

"What's this about her finding you a job?"

"Nothing," Emmitt said. "Just another fantasy of hers."

His father-in-law dropped his drawing pad on the table, turned it over, and stood up. "I'm going for a short walk," he said. "If Okāsan asks, tell her I won't be long."

Although his father-in-law had started walking regularly, tracking his steps on a watch he recently bought, this was the latest he'd ever wanted to exercise.

"It's almost ten o'clock," Emmitt said.

"There's a statue I want to see. I should have photographed it when I walked past it this morning."

"Can't it wait until tomorrow?"

"An idea for a drawing just came to me. If I don't go now, by tomorrow I may forget it."

After his father-in-law left, Emmitt flipped over his sketchpad. The first three or four pages had been ripped out uncleanly, but the next three were different versions not of the statue he thought he'd been drawing, but of the framed drawing he'd made of his wife over thirty years ago, standing on a sea cliff with the wind tugging her dress and hair. He had changed his wife's appearance to look as it did now. He had captured perfectly how time had etched itself into her features.

It was hard to understand why his father-in-law had let so much talent lay dormant for half his life.

Emmitt turned the drawing pad over and arranged it as it had been before.

His father-in-law returned half an hour later. Neither Mirai nor her mother had commented on his absence. They were still in the kitchen, talking about life in Tokyo.

✳

IN THE MORNING MIRAI awoke early and rolled out of bed. Emmitt lay huddled under the blankets, however, for last night she had tossed and turned, keeping him awake. Once she had dressed and left the room, he closed his eyes and thought of her suggestion that they travel to Tokyo at the end of March to see the cherry blossoms.

Although he agreed it would be fun, he could only take being in Tokyo in small doses. It was too big, too crowded and noisy, bursting everywhere with concrete and glass. Once, at the top of Tokyo Skytree, he'd peered out over the city and had the startling illusion he could see half of all human civilization below. He had hoped to see Mount Fuji, but that day smog had veiled it. When he and Mirai had once eaten lunch on the top floor of the Hotel Nikko, Kanazawa's tallest building, what he most remembered seeing was the clear blue ribbon of the sea a few kilometers away. He wondered if only a long daytrip to Tokyo would satisfy her.

An hour later he came downstairs. The house was quiet except for Mirai's pen scratching on a drawing pad and starlings chirping outside. She was at the dining room table, a small blanket wrapped around her.

"Where are your parents?"

"Otōsan's out walking. Okāsan just went to the library."

"I guess we don't have to worry about Otōsan's leg any-more. He seems to be taking his doctor's advice about exercising seriously."

"There's coffee for you in the kitchen."

He went to pour himself a cup, then came back to the dining room and slid into the chair opposite her.

She was diagramming a flower arrangement. Although she was expert in classical Rikka, Nageire, Seika, and Moribana styles, she preferred making freestyle designs, that is to say Jiyūka, and he didn't always know what he was looking at when she diagrammed a plan, or even afterward when she'd finished an arrangement.

Until he met Mirai he had encountered ikebana only on the periphery of his life in Japan. Flower arrangements were ubiq-uitous, and people tended to take them for granted. Even now, he felt sometimes that she was devoting herself to an art that most people never see. But that was the problem with most art, she'd told him, pointing him to a truth he'd never considered. People didn't allow themselves to see art in their everyday lives, and this diminished her chances to communicate with a poten-tial audience.

Mirai had changed his perspective about ikebana and taught him much about flowers: how they changed seasonally, their col-ors and patterns, the varying textures of their leaves and blos-soms, numerous details from the world around them. She had told him once that the challenge for her was to compel people to rest their eyes on her arrangements, even more than she wanted her arrangements judged beautiful. How could her work have value if people weren't compelled somehow to *see* it?

Had he not been constantly busy, he would have liked to

study a traditional art. He had no drawing or painting skills, and he'd failed many times trying to make pottery. The tea ceremony was something Mirai often did, and Noh theater, which was popular in Kanazawa, and which her parents sometimes saw, struck him as esoteric. His mother-in-law used to encourage him to write, but he'd never had enough time, though in college he'd penned poems and stories. Having seen so much of their work, he'd learned to appreciate what Mirai and Asuka created.

"It's been a while since you worked at home," he said.

"This? It's just a small arrangement for Kimura. After I'm done I'll write him a short letter."

"Why?"

"To get back in his good graces."

"You think we're not?"

She shrugged. "It doesn't hurt to do this."

Emmitt wondered what she planned to write.

"Are you going to ask him to keep helping us?" he said.

She looked past him, as if thinking it over. "Do you think he took what happened personally?"

"I've hardly talked to him since then."

She seemed surprised by this. "He's welcome to take this as an apology if it helps."

Half an hour later her mother returned with a bag of books, and Mirai left for her ikebana studio to make Kimura's arrangement.

After getting dressed, Emmitt came across his mother-in-law at the dining-room table with an old copy of Shiga Naoya's novel *An'ya Kōro* in her hands. He had read the English translation, *A Dark Night's Passing*, before becoming fluent in Japanese, and they sometimes talked about the ways its protagonist fought against conventional Japanese life and how he couldn't escape the loneliness it made him feel. He knew she rated Shiga almost as highly as Kyōka and reread his work regularly. Behind her, on a table beside the window, lay a detailed sketch her husband had made after Emmitt went to bed. Emmitt recognized the figure: a statue near Ōmichō Market that his father-in-law must have visited last night. Based on Emmitt's memory of it, his father-in-law had rendered it with exactness. Only the face was different. Emmitt moved closer to it, then pulled back upon noticing the resemblance to his mother-in-law. The drawing was much too successful in its artistry to be a joke, but he couldn't help wonder what his father-in-law was striving for in it.

He was about to ask what she thought of it when he spotted Mirai's card for Kimura. It lay open on the table for its ink to dry. Unable to read calligraphy well, he asked her what it said.

Her lips moved silently as her eyes crossed the page. "She asked your friend to accept her flower arrangement as an apology for her absence at the lease-signing." After a moment she said, "Does it seem inappropriate to you? I suppose it's rather late for an apology."

"It's not that. I'm just not sure what it means."

His mother-in-law lowered her gaze as if to read her book again. Emmitt wanted to know what she thought of her husband's drawing. He asked if she had she seen it, and if so, was she struck by the resemblance between the statue and herself?

"Yes, I saw it. But any resemblances you speak of don't interest me. All he did was conflate two figures."

"Don't you think it's beautiful?"

"I don't see how that matters."

"What matters then?"

She smiled patiently. "He's able to convey beauty when he wants to. But from my perspective, the drawing is grotesque."

"You don't think he's only being playful after so many years of not drawing?"

"Ever since retiring, all he's done is watch television and drink sake, so seeing him rediscover his art is satisfying. Even if I don't find beauty in what he's doing, I support him more than you realize. I only wish he'd draw something else. Doesn't his focus on me seem unhealthy? I find it disturbing. But that only seems to encourage him."

"When you put it like that, yes, it seems a little odd. But maybe this is only his way of getting back into the habit of drawing. In a month or two, he may move on to different subjects."

"I wish his creative urges were . . ."

Suddenly she seemed to find something worth examining in her book. She looked at the front and back cover and then weighed it in her hands. "I told him many years ago that I'd divorce him if he ever drew me again. He finally called my bluff."

It was hard to believe that her love for her husband had ever been so tenuous. Her smile made him think she was joking.

"You dislike that the woman is nude?"

"I dislike that he asked me to pose that way for him and I said no, and he did it anyway."

Emmitt smiled. "I'll let you get back to your novel. I'm sorry to have interrupted."

His mother-in-law looked at him as if she wanted to say something more. When he hesitated to step away, she raised her book toward him and spoke again.

"The hero of Shiga's novel has just left his wife and baby to go into the mountains. To me he's unlikable, yet I can't help hoping he finds what he needs. You're different from him, Emmitt—a better person by a long shot—but somehow he reminds me of you. Maybe it's that I find myself rooting for him in the way I always root for you. One tends to want the best for people who struggle in their lives."

"But I'm not struggling."

She continued as if she hadn't heard him. "I think you'd like the novel, and it would help your Japanese to read it. Shiga was a master of language like Kyōka, but his writing is more accessible. Shall I give it to you at some point?"

"I'd like that. But I still plan to read Kyōka first."

"Oh, yes. Yes, you should."

Mirai returned home before lunch. She had finished the flower arrangement and wanted to go with Emmitt to Kimura's office.

She had wrapped the arrangement in cellophane and decorated it with bows and paper flowers she was also skilled at making. Beneath all of that was a preponderance of white on one side and green on the other. She had enfolded white eggplants in paulownia leaves, while a paulownia stem extended to one side, offsetting the unfilled space in the glass *suiban* basin.

"It's a simple arrangement of winter passing to spring," she said.

As soon as she told him this, his appreciation of the arrangement grew. He took it from her carefully and brought it to the car.

On the way, Emmitt remembered to ask her about Otōsan's drawing.

"Okāsan showed me it this morning," she said. "It's the third time he's done that with the statues he's drawn."

"When you were in Tokyo, I found him cleaning some framed drawings he'd made when he and Okāsan were newlyweds. Have you seen them?"

"I might have at some point. What were they?"

"They were of Okāsan."

"Then they must be old. It's been years since she's let him draw her."

"They were in a box deep in the back of a closet. You never came across them?"

"Not that I remember."

"You told me he was talented, but I didn't realize he was that good."

"But what does talent mean if his ideas and vision fall short?"

Emmitt wasn't sure what she was saying. "Isn't it unfair to expect he'll have a vision for his art? He seems just to enjoy drawing."

"He's always drawn my mother to the exclusion of anything else. That's the problem. Because for years she's forbidden him to draw her, he's found a different way. According to her, he thinks she modeled for several statues the local government installed around the city, and so in his drawings he's turning them into her. I wouldn't call that a very interesting vision. Or a healthy one, anyway."

In eight years of knowing Mirai, Emmitt had never heard that her mother might have modeled for some of the statues around Kanazawa. Was it some kind of family secret? He asked if it was true.

Mirai shrugged, and he couldn't tell if the question held no interest for her or if she was trying to hide her pride. "She modeled for some sculptors whose work the city bought. But she's not sure if she modeled for any statues the city installed, for it commissioned most of them later as part of an urban beautification project. She says it was so long ago she doesn't remember."

Emmitt thought about this for a moment. "But it is a vision."

Mirai laughed at what could have been the absurdity or truth of Emmitt's words. "The only person interested is himself."

"Isn't that enough? I don't think he wants an audience for his work. Well, maybe just Okāsan."

It was almost noon when they arrived at Kimura's office. Although the sun was shining, a hard rain pelted them as they ran to the agency's entrance.

A receptionist told them that Kimura was showing an apartment near Ōmichō Market, after which he would probably take lunch. Mirai explained why they'd come. The receptionist complimented her on the arrangement and said Kimura would be pleased by it.

For some reason Emmitt was relieved that Kimura wasn't there. He didn't expect him to be angry with them for what had happened at the Kurokawas', but he thought things might be awkward, and he didn't want to learn that Kimura had found new interest in the *machiya*.

As Mirai and the woman talked, Emmitt fingered through a box of laminated property specs. These modern houses, or the land on which they could be constructed, cost more than he and Mirai could afford, and more than they would have had to pay to renovate the Kurokawas' *machiya*. Kanazawa was one of the few cities in Japan where property values were rising. Had he started before the Shinkansen between Kanazawa and Tokyo began running two years ago, their options would have been better.

Not wanting to wait for Mirai, he stepped outside. The light shower from before had ended, and he bathed himself in the new sunshine. The smell of spring imbued the air.

When Mirai joined him outside, she seemed relieved to have finished her errand.

"Let's go home," she said. "I want to help my mother with some things."

"Before we leave, maybe we could make an appointment with Kimura to talk about other houses."

Mirai looked at him with a pained expression. "But that's not what this was about."

"Then what was this about?"

"Kimura's your friend. I wanted to do what I could to set things right again."

But by saying she no longer wanted to look for a house, she was doing him no favors at all.

"So you're done looking for houses? I thought you were putting it all into my hands."

They sat in the car and buckled their seatbelts. Emmitt started the ignition and turned to her, waiting for her to answer him.

"Until you've figured out your future and our financial situation is more stable," she finally said, softly, as if she didn't want them to argue about it, "I don't see the point. It's a waste of time and energy."

"What's different about staying on at your parents' house?"

"Nothing at all. It's a short-term solution."

He shifted the car into gear but didn't pull out of their parking space. "But you just said you don't want to look for a house."

"In Kanazawa . . ."

Emmitt's frustration nearly boiled over. If she didn't want to look for a house in Kanazawa, where *did* she want to look for one? The answer dawned on him a moment before she spoke: Tokyo.

"I have a job offer there, and Avery said he was confident he could find you work at his university. Kanazawa will always be here if we want to come back."

On the drive home he promised himself to continue the search on his own. Their savings were partly his, and if he could find someplace that made sense for them, he would push again for them to pursue it.

By the time they arrived at his in-laws' house, however, he was unsure if he had the fortitude to fight with her over this.

7

KNOWING HE'D BE UNLIKELY to encounter any colleagues or administrators on the first Sunday after the term, Emmitt chose that day to clean out his office.

Rather than go to the university by bus, he drove his in-laws' car to the campus in the foothills.

In late March the university was empty of people and verdant, with stately brick buildings sitting amidst recently mown grass, beds of flowers in early bloom, and cherry and ginkgo trees leafing.

As dusk spilled over campus, he crossed the quad to the Foreign Languages department and let himself inside. In the long hallway past the entrance, the only sounds were of his footsteps on the tile floors and the double-hum of fluorescent lighting and massive vending machines.

Reaching his office, he gazed at the announcements, photos, and posters he'd taped to the door and the walls on either side. One by one he tore them down, then walked into his office.

He stood in the room looking around. Out his window, crows materialized from a band of pink clouds, then flew from the neighborhood below to the forested hills ringing the campus. Kites circled above them, their wings outstretched, like origami birds fastened to an invisible helix. How many times had he viewed such a scene from this window as he worked into the night?

For over a year the atmosphere of his office had turned oppressive, and somehow, only now, he decided that it was because of the books, papers, and standing whiteboards swimming in red marker that he'd neglected to put in order. Half-heartedly tidying up, he came across several open boxes he'd set inside his door two terms ago. The boxes had been full of final essays he'd asked his students, multiple times in class and by email, to retrieve before he threw them away; he had then placed each box, marked by class, on a separate chair in the hallway. Inside each box, dust covered the essays on top. He carried them across the room and dumped them onto his desk.

He flipped through some of the essays before settling down in his chair to inspect them. The lack of effort they showed struck him as forcefully as ever. Most students, he guessed, had found Japanese essays online, fed them through a translation program, and submitted them without checking the English. He had given his students poor grades almost universally. He had been powerless to fail them all, though many deserved that. What was the point in devoting more than sixty hours of his life every week to a system that enabled students to pass without trying and, worse, never learn anything? His students had been studying English for ten years and yet, when introducing themselves, couldn't communicate their names and where they were from— and couldn't even do that without first checking with classmates, in Japanese, to see if they'd understood Emmitt's questions.

A common expression these days described young Japanese men as "grass-eaters," or "herbivores." "Herbivorous men," according to the many newspaper articles about them, had no desire to engage intimately with women and abhorred the idea not only of procreation but also of sex itself. Sexuality was the context in which the epithet was most often used. They were sexually neutral and would be the ruin of Japan, already in a demographic implosion caused by longer lifespans and plummeting birthrates. Emmitt felt the appellation heaped the blame in the wrong place, as if "grass-eating" was a deliberate choice—a lifestyle based on the worst laziness—and not the result of a lack of sex education for young people, of a society that stigmatized mental disorders, and, often, of parents who encouraged asocial behavior in their children. Nonetheless, there was a kernel of truth in the description. On the whole, the young men in Emmitt's classes had become more passive over his tenure at the university. But they weren't "grass-eaters" merely with respect to the opposite sex. Their passivity affected every aspect of their lives. They had never learned to deal with discomfort, physical or emotional, yet this didn't bother them. They lived in a bubble. Parents, teachers, and friends never pushed them to do otherwise. Despite their ages, they were coddled. Protected. And he didn't blame them, but felt that anyone in their shoes, living at such a time in a society they had been unable to shape to fit their values, would be the same. They were rotten English students, but there was a certain idealism, a certain purity, to which they clung, and in this they were almost refreshing to have in his classes. Beneath his frustration over their "grass-eating," he felt a certain admiration for them.

He tossed out the essays, fingering through each one as if to affirm that he'd wasted years at this university. His margin comments, stretching for something positive to say amidst all the red marks he had made, elicited a wry smile.

In the last batch of essays he combed through, he read several in their entirety. He had assigned this class a final essay in which they were to compare and contrast their dreams of the future with those of their parents when they, too, were college aged. Assigning such an essay hadn't been a bad choice, but Emmitt wondered now what had prompted him to. He guessed that he'd been curious to understand why so many of his students saw no benefit in learning a foreign language. When Emmitt first came to Japan, learning Japanese had been a priority; it helped him get closer to the local people he met and understand on a deeper level the rich culture that supported his life. And he wasn't finished yet. Literacy was the next step—to reach the point where Mirai would never have to explain her culture to him again. He had tried to communicate to his students his own interest in language learning, but his message only ever encountered apathy. It was a hurdle he'd never surmounted.

Flipping through the essays, he saw that most of them focused on the importance of finding a job with a good salary, getting married, and starting a family—in other words, conforming to expectations rather than dreaming of something even slightly different from the norm. Only a handful talked of traveling or working abroad, or of backpacking around the world, or of leading a "slow life" in nature, whereas their parents had been much more conservative and also hadn't had the same opportunities—perspectives similar to those of Emmitt and his peers at the same age. The essays reminded him of Michio, his student who had quit university and might have become a Buddhist ascetic.

The final essay he glanced through, startingly more assured than the rest, stated in its introduction (after Emmitt's corrections):

> The biggest difference between me and my parents when they were my age is that they had dreams, many dreams, whereas I have none. But I think I'm not alone. Most of my friends are the same as me. Perhaps we are a generation without dreams. But if we are, I think people are wrong to think this is a problem.

The essay concluded three pages later with the words:

Not having dreams in life is better than having any. Life should be straightforward: sleep, wake up, eat, work (but not too much), go home, eat again, and sleep. To do the same every day until I die is my dream. I can imagine no better way to attain happiness.

The essay had lacked logical development and support, but the student had taken more care in writing it than most and the essay had strayed far from conventional sentiment. For those two rare qualities alone, despite Emmitt's disagreeing with the message, he had given the student the highest grade he could. Regretting that he hadn't challenged the student in his written evaluation to strive for a bolder vision for his life, he tossed the essay back atop the pile. Any challenge he'd attempted wouldn't have mattered, however; the student never bothered to claim his graded assignment.

He looked for the students' names on the essays, and yet after finding them they failed to bring to mind faces or even where the students had sat in his classrooms.

It felt like another sign that it was time for him to leave.

He spent the next three hours cleaning and arranging on his desk what he wished to take home. When he left, he took nothing.

He wrote a short note, wrapped it around the key to his office, and stuffed this into an envelope. On his way out of the building he pushed the envelope under the department secretary's door. He imagined she would find it on Monday morning and not think twice about it. In his four years at the university she had been there for the last two. Although they had said hello to each other nearly every day, he knew nothing about her other than her first and last name and that at thirty-five years of age—one year younger than Emmitt—she had lost her husband to cancer.

She had been at work on the day he died, and it shocked Emmitt that she had prioritized work over her husband's last moments. When he told Mirai this, she suggested his death might have happened suddenly, perhaps from some complication. But Emmitt never found out. People in the department rarely opened up to each other, and in any case, it wasn't his business.

It was dark when he stepped outside. The campus, on holiday now, and at the close of a weekend, seemed to be conserving electricity; his walk back to the parking lot was through darkness. When he reached it, he pushed a button on the key ring to the car; its flashing headlights instructed him where to go. Turning around, only the shadow of the Foreign Languages building was visible. It was as if a power outage had spread through campus.

He started the car and turned on its high beams. Pulling toward the exit, he felt relieved leaving the university. By the time he arrived at his in-laws' house he realized, with disappointment, that nothing in him had changed.

Neither Mirai nor her parents said anything as he announced his return and climbed upstairs. With all the thoughts running through his head, many unwanted and unexpected, he appreciated their silence.

8

KOYO'S IKEBANA SCHOOL HAD invited Mirai to a flower-arranging exhibition in Tokyo. Its director had asked her to create a free-style arrangement representative of Ishikawa Prefecture in winter, and with six weeks to prepare it she was enthusiastic about the opportunity.

Sitting beside Emmitt on their bed, she handed him a tourist brochure she had picked up from the train station that afternoon. It was for the Nakaya Ukichiro Museum of Snow and Ice.

"They have photographs of magnified snow crystals I thought I could incorporate into the arrangement. I've already contacted the museum's director about them."

Emmitt opened the brochure. The museum, on Lake Shibayama an hour south of Kanazawa, was dedicated to the life and work of a Katayamazu Onsen–born physicist and glaciologist who in the early twentieth century had invented a way to create artificial snowflakes.

"The school will cover my travel expenses and pay a stipend. This could be the start of something new for me."

Emmitt congratulated her. He thought this might be an arrangement she could sometimes make, taking part in the school's events now and then while living in Kanazawa.

"How long will you be in Tokyo?"

"Three days. The event is on a weekend, then I want to see Asuka before I return."

He didn't like it coming on the heels of her last trip to Tokyo, but it was important to him that she follow her way as an artist. And "three days" sounded like a promise.

He glanced again at the brochure. The snow crystals in it looked diamond-like, flawlessly cut and polished. Recalling Mirai's interest in them, he saw them as almost floral, but more angular, delicate, and symmetrical—like skeletal structures of magnificent flowers (if flowers had bones). He saw right away the possibilities of incorporating snow-crystal morphology into ike-bana. If she were successful with this, he knew it could open new avenues for her. It was an appealing prospect, yet he viewed it as another factor that might pull her toward Tokyo.

"How does it feel being free from the university?" she said, standing up to change her clothes.

"Except for the luxury of catching up on sleep, it's a little strange adjusting to a new routine."

"Is that all you feel?"

He watched as she tied up her hair at the back of her head. "No," he said when she turned to him. How was he to explain it?

The first thing he'd felt was a kind of emptiness, a loss of something that had long been part of his life and who he was—like where he was from, or the color of his eyes and hair—but he didn't tell her this. It was also true he felt a sense of relief, and of freedom, similar to how he'd felt when he first came to Japan. He didn't want to waste his newfound time. It was as precious to him now as air or water. This is what he told her.

"Then you're happy?"

He wasn't sure how to answer. Although he'd been unhappy with how his work had taken over his life, outside of that he'd never *not* felt happy. "Most of all I'm glad for the chance to find my way again."

She smiled as she finished fixing her hair. "I'm excited to see what the rest of this year brings. I have a feeling things will be good for us both."

That night at dinner Mirai shared with her parents the news about the ikebana opportunity and her plan to visit the museum at Lake Shibayama.

"I've heard of Dr. Nakaya," her father said. "He once said that each snowflake is a poem written by the gods. The notion that nature's beauty originates beyond the realm of human life is interesting, don't you think?"

"It's a bit sentimental. . . ."

He straightened, his expression serious. "But couldn't 'poems from the gods' be useful to consider in an ikebana design?"

Mirai looked up at her father. "Yes, I guess you're right."

Her father grunted as if satisfied with her agreement.

"While you're there," Mirai's mother said, "try to visit Iroha Sōan, the former residence of Kitaoji Rosanjin. It's in Yamashiro Onsen, close to where you're going. I've never managed to visit."

"Who was he?" Emmitt said.

"He was an influential artist last century. I remember reading he was interested in only one thing throughout his life—discovering beauty. Of course, he had talent and intellect, which brought him renown, but he dedicated himself fully to the artistic life. He never stopped searching for beauty. It seems rare today, to devote yourself to such a high ideal."

Mirai seemed skeptical. "Perishability is a central theme in traditional Japanese art. Every ikebana artist will tell you that beauty is ephemeral."

"What's the point of embarking on an 'endless search for beauty'?" her father said. "It's more important to have food and a roof over your head."

"Few people nowadays will risk what he did," Mirai's mother said, almost defensively. "They don't question the importance of beauty to their lives—Izumi Kyōka was another who did. They were both rare for their times. Now, the whole world conforms to a shallow, material culture. It may even be why the world seems so divisive and dangerous now."

Emmitt's father-in-law glanced at Mirai. "It's good that you and Emmitt live in Japan. It may be the only country right now worth living in."

Emmitt only half-heard the comment. He was thinking of his failure to visit Eiheiji last winter with Mirai. Instead he had gone alone to a Buddhist meditation class at a temple in the Shoei-machi area of Kanazawa, a fifteen-minute walk from their home. He regretted not having gone to Eiheiji. He thought to himself: What's the point of living anywhere if you never make chances to experience it?

"If the weather is good when you go to the museum," Emmitt's father-in-law said, "you'll be able to see Hakusan across Lake Shibayama."

"You remember the view, Otōsan, but you forget our family stayed on the lake three years ago. In Katayamazu Onsen. We've seen it before."

As if contemplating his rice bowl, he was quiet for a moment. "Well, some things are worth being reminded of."

Mirai looked at him strangely. "What else should we see?"

"I'll have to think about it," he said. "Right now nothing comes to mind."

Mirai and her mother turned away, trying to hide their laughter.

❋

THE NEXT MORNING EMMITT met his father-in-law in the kitchen. Dressed in his walking clothes, his father-in-law was lifting a plastic bento box up and down as if to weigh it.

"You made yourself lunch already?" Emmitt said, looking around for signs of cooking.

"Okāsan made it for me yesterday."

"You forgot to eat it?"

"I don't remember."

Emmitt glanced out the window. It had been sunny when he woke up half an hour ago. It was raining now, though, and the kudzu vines on the neighbor's house were greener and darker with the wetness. He continued to gaze at the kudzu-covered wall as his father-in-law spoke again.

"I can't decide whether to go out now or later."

Emmitt was sure his father-in-law would hear the patter of rain on the house and stay home, but he seemed deaf to it. "It's raining."

"Is it? Ah, I guess it is." He opened the refrigerator and, hesitating for a moment, replaced his bento on a shelf inside. "Okāsan will kill me if I forget to eat it again today. Or maybe this is yesterday's after all."

Mirai and her mother entered the kitchen as Emmitt prepared coffee.

"What are you two talking about?" Mirai said, opening the refrigerator and looking inside.

"Otōsan didn't realize it was raining," Emmitt said.

"It should clear up soon. When it does, I thought we could take a stroll through the city. It's been such a long time since we've done that."

"I'd like that," Emmitt said. "Where do you want to go?"

"Anywhere. But at some point, I need to stop at a gallery on the Asano River. I want to check on a flower arrangement I made for a gallery opening there."

"Which gallery?" her mother asked.

"I already told you. You said it was where the mother in

Kyōka's *Kechō* story used to collect fares from people crossing the bridge."

Her mother turned to Emmitt. "That reminds me: In my club's meeting today, we'll discuss how to use our grant for a translation. I may want to talk to you later. You have more free time now, if I'm not mistaken."

"More than I've had for a long time."

Standing in the doorway she smiled and said, "Mt. Utatsu is right nearby and should be worth seeing today. I'm happy you two can go there together."

"I expect that it's changed since I was last there a few years ago," Emmitt said. "It could be because of all the tourists these days, but when I first came to Kanazawa—how should I put it— that part of the city felt older."

"You're too sensitive," Mirai said. "You see the past floating away wherever you look."

Emmitt disagreed with her, but it was true he felt more strongly than she about what was worth preserving from Kanazawa's past.

"When I was a girl," his mother-in-law said, "Mt. Utatsu was much different from now. It even had a zoo and an aquarium, if you can imagine. Before that, as you may know, only the Maeda lord's closest retainers were allowed to climb it because of the direct view it gave of the castle. Shortly before the Meiji Restoration, seven men were executed for climbing the mountain to protest rice prices. Just think: In only eighty-five years, climbing Mt. Utatsu went from being a death sentence to how people reached the city zoo. I guess the changes were more noticeable when I was growing up."

Her husband had already left the kitchen, and at a noise down the hallway she looked in that direction. Before she went to check on him, she suggested that the cherry blossoms should be in full bloom on Mt. Utatsu.

Her prediction of cherry blossoms pleased Emmitt. It would be nice to see *sakura* there again.

❋

BY EARLY AFTERNOON THE rain had cleared. Following a late lunch, Emmitt and Mirai walked east through Korinbō and past the intersection at Ōmichō Market, turning at the Asano River toward Mt. Utatsu. They proceeded through Kazuemachi to Higashichaya, through one former geisha district to another, stopping at flower shops, small museums, and shrines and temples they hadn't visited together since before the bullet train began running between Kanazawa and Tokyo.

Over the last year Mirai had commented more on small changes she saw in both districts, how things she remembered were no longer there—old miso stores, traditional sweet shops, gold leaf and antique purveyors, *machiya* and traditional *kominka* wooden houses and stone *kura* storehouses, some dating as far back as the mid-1800s. Her parents seldom visited these areas now, but when they did, they noted similar things. When Emmitt asked about vestiges of old Kanazawa disappearing, they only shrugged and said, "*Shō ga nai.*" It can't be helped.

On a backstreet in Higashichaya they climbed a staircase to Kannon-in temple. Before getting married, they had come here for the annual Forty-Six-Thousand-Day Festival, an auspicious day in August when the Goddess of Mercy conferred forty-six thousand days' worth of merit on visitors. On that day the temple had sold individual ears of corn purported to be lucky charms. He and Mirai had brought home two ears, prompting Mirai's mother to fuss over the silk that escaped from their husks; the longer it was, she'd said, the greater the buyer's luck. She'd followed the custom of hanging the corn outside their home. Crows had pulled them down in mid-September.

As Mirai stepped to the entrance, deposited a coin into a collection box, and bowed to the Goddess of Mercy inside, Emmitt waited outside. He checked his cell phone and saw an email.

"Kimura thanks you for the flower arrangement and card," Emmitt said when Mirai returned moments later. "He says he'd still like to help us find a house."

"Do you think he's being sincere?"

"Why wouldn't he be?"

"It would be good for you to explain our situation."

"Our situation?"

But she didn't answer him, and he soon realized she was referring to their impasse about where to live.

They backtracked toward Higashichaya before turning and climbing a steep set of steps, to where the trees greening Mt. Utatsu greatly outnumbered the houses. Coming upon an open area, they found picnickers sitting on plastic sheets beneath a row of cherry trees. They were eating barbecued food cooked on small braziers, drinking beer and sake, and singing songs of the cherry blossom season, out of tune and as loud as possible. Pink and white blossoms swung on the air, carpeting the ground where they fell. Emmitt thought the revelers' noise had shaken them from their branches.

When they reached Hōsenji temple, they decided to climb one hundred meters further to a larger road leading down Mt. Utatsu's southern slope.

On their winding descent, Emmitt saw a small park he had never visited lying beneath them, between where they walked and the traditional black roofs of the houses below.

Pointing to the far end of the park Mirai said, "Do you see the monument over there? It's dedicated to Izumi Kyōka."

The monument was a tall slab of rock at the end of a path and covered with the needles of surrounding pine trees.

When they reached the end of the path, Mirai read aloud the engraving down the monument's face.

Haha koishi
Yū yamazakura
Mine no matsu

"How would you translate this into English?" she asked Emmitt.

For a poem so short, and despite his fluency in Japanese, he couldn't render it into a coherent whole. "I understand each word, but I'm unsure how to put it all together in English."

"I'm sure it's difficult to convey in another language," she said.

"I can see it's a haiku about longing," he added, perhaps a little too quickly.

"He was supposed to have longed all his life for his mother, who died when he was young. But that longing motivated his works. It gave his writing distinction."

They left the park, and in a few minutes found themselves approaching the Asano River.

As they crossed Tenjin Bridge, Emmitt glanced downstream and saw a wooden footbridge—in May people hung carp streamers from it and stretched others out in the river beneath; in June they rinsed dyed Kaga Yūzen fabrics there, and at night, on the eve of the Hyakumangoku Matsuri, the city's biggest festival, floated lanterns with candles burning inside them. Now that he had more time, Emmitt looked forward to seeing all these things again.

At the end of Tenjin Bridge Emmitt surveyed the side from which they'd come. It was the more beautiful side of the mountain, he thought. He recognized beeches, river birches, ginkgos, and Japanese maples. A monochromatic quality imbued the bridge-crossed river, and perhaps because of it the mountain's beauty seemed rooted in the past.

Mirai pointed up the road and said, "The gallery's over there."

The gallery was in a small, renovated *machiya* beside Tenjin Bridge. Where the river wound into the distance, Emmitt glimpsed the Hakusan range to the east.

Reaching the gallery Mirai wanted to visit, a translation of Kyōka's haiku occurred to him and he went over it in his mind.

Longing to see my mother
A cherry tree on the mountain at dusk
A pine tree on a summit

Though the nostalgic images lacked a device to properly unify them, he was pleased that a coherent translation had come to him.

As they entered the gallery, wiping the sweat from their necks and faces after all the walking they had done, a man about their age looked up from a corner table and hurried over. Mirai introduced him as Hotaka.

"Your flower arrangement goes well with the colored photos over there," he said, pointing to an ikebana display beneath photos of a mountain town. "Every visitor has remarked on it."

Emmitt looked at Mirai's work, which he was seeing for the first time: a shallow water tray of intertwining peonies framed by climbing pampas grass and white, star-shaped flowers—an array of subdued, natural colors that blended together simply, infinitely soothing to look at. Surrounding them were photos—old wooden homes, clean rows of cedars towering over two stretches of river, a leaf-strewn hiking trail through a forest, old Buddhist temples and Shinto shrines, wooden sculptures shrouded by incense smoke, and the snow-capped mountains, much more detailed than he normally saw.

Emmitt asked if all the photos were of the same place.

Hotaka nodded. "They're all of Shiramine."

Emmitt pulled out his cell phone and, on a *kanji* app he often used, tried to write the town's name: "white" combined with "peak." Mirai corrected the second character, which combined the radical "mountain" with "winter" and another she thought meant either "abundant" or "grass."

Hotaka asked Emmitt if he'd ever visited Shiramine.

"Not yet, but maybe later this year I will. I plan to climb Hakusan this summer."

"People visit without climbing Hakusan. It's barely an hour from Kanazawa and has a few *ryokan* and restaurants and a large *onsen.* After the cherry blossoms in Kanazawa have fallen, you can go there to see them bloom again."

"I didn't know such a beautiful place existed so close to Kanazawa."

"The photographs don't capture being there in person, surrounded by trees and in the shadow of the mountains. People there live differently than in the city, too, close to nature and observant of village life. Many old people there cling to the traditional ways of doing things. What I like about the photos is they suggest an atmosphere of *shinpi* that's uncommon in Japan today."

Hotaka had used a word he didn't understand. Pulling out his phone again he found the word meant "mystery." But the two *kanji* that combined to form the word seemed to get at its meaning more: *gods* and *secret.*

Hotaka pointed again to Mirai's flower arrangement and asked where she had found peonies so colorful this early in the year.

Emmitt stepped toward the photographs. He stopped before one that showed the town from a bird's-eye view. The hills and mountains, covered with trees, sloped toward the town from all directions, forming a narrow valley. Sparkling in the sunlight alongside the town, a river wound toward Hakusan, which loomed in the distance like an ancient, hoary god. The town seemed to have been born from the natural scenery, its houses clustered like a garden of black and white roses.

He moved toward the gallery's window. Outside, the sun had nearly set, and the trees and wooden houses across the river seemed freshly lacquered or rained on.

More than once Mirai had said she didn't like the idea of living on Mt. Utatsu. She feared landslides that heavy rains or earthquakes might trigger, and its narrow, winding roads that became treacherous when it snowed unnerved her. That cemeteries bestrewed it also put her off. He'd thought her attitude was too cautious—or perhaps she'd only been trying to dissuade him from ever raising the idea.

His mother-in-law had said this gallery could be the setting for Kyōka's *Kechō*, he remembered. He remonstrated with himself for not having read the story yet.

Emmitt's gaze fell on a young woman in a bright, cheap-looking kimono—the kind that tourists in Kanazawa sometimes rented from shops—with elaborately fixed hair. She was kneeling on the bridge beside a man seated on the walkway, hugging his knees, his head pillowed on his arms. A jacket lay on his shoulders, and he wore black leggings similar to what tourist rickshaw drivers in the city wore. The contrast in their appearances couldn't have been greater. The man got to his feet and looked at the woman as if he didn't recognize her. When he strode to the end of the bridge and lit a cigarette, the woman hurried after him. Emmitt heard her wooden *geta* clogs ring faintly with each step.

In the reflection of the window he saw Mirai come up behind him.

"I know it's short notice, but would you like to visit Shiramine tomorrow?" she said, leaning into him.

Surprised by her suggestion, he turned to look at her. "Did the photos convince you we should?"

"They're beautiful, of course. But no, I thought it would be a nice chance to spend time together alone. Also, Hotaka asked me to consider a regular commission at a silk factory there."

"Oh?"

"There's no harm talking to them if they're looking for someone new, is there?"

Emmitt wasn't sure if she was asking the question rhetorically, but in case she expected him to answer, he said no.

"It's too far away to make it a priority, and I'd have to visit often just to select flowers that are in season there, but I'm willing to consider it as a favor to Hotaka. It also seems to be the kind of place you might like, especially after being so busy for so long."

Emmitt appreciated her thinking of him in this way and he told her again he'd like to go.

"I can stay overnight, but I have to go to my studio the next day."

"Whatever works best for you," Emmitt said. "I'm just happy you suggested it. It's been a long time."

The lights on the bridge turned on, scaring up a giant egret from beneath the bridge. A white streak against the dusky trees of Mt. Utatsu, it flew upriver. In the shallows, what looked like two giant inkcap mushrooms stood well over a meter tall, their stems bright white under the light. Suddenly one moved, and the other did the same. The mushrooms were two fishermen in the river wearing conical hats—a common enough sight, but not one he had seen at night or in such dreamlike lighting.

"One must see strange things living beside a bridge. . . ."

"That's a funny thought. But yes, it's probably true."

Mirai stood on her toes to get a better look at the river. She seemed to be peering at where the light from the bridge made the stone walls underneath it glow.

"One summer when I was a child, I saw a monkey tied to a tree beside that bridge." She pointed to where she meant. "An old man had brought it to a festival nearby, and he was sitting there staring into the river while passersby descended the embankment to give the monkey food. Even I tossed it a tangerine I'd been carrying around. My mother felt sorry for the old man, who seemed sick, and persuaded him to accept some money. As soon as he did, he stood and walked away. My mother called him back, worried about the monkey, but he said it would be fine without him. We watched him cross the bridge and disappear into the mountain."

"What happened to the monkey?"

"We saw it again later. It was still tied to the tree, but someone had built it a shelter and it had more food than it could possibly eat. I don't remember seeing it after that."

Another couple entered the gallery and Hotaka approached them.

Mirai suggested leaving. They crossed the room to the front door and nodded goodbye to Hotaka. He bowed to them as they walked outside.

❋

ALMOST AS SOON AS they left the gallery, Emmitt received a phone call from Kimura. He apologized for calling Emmitt after having recently sent him an email, but he wanted to know if Emmitt was free for a drink.

"Actually, I'm out with Mirai and she wants to get home."

"Where are you now?" When Emmitt told him he said, "I'm not far from there. At least come have one drink."

Emmitt checked with Mirai. She agreed to meet Kimura if only to say hello, but she wanted to leave after that to prepare for their trip. She told Emmitt he could stay as long as he liked.

Kimura gave him the name and address of a place in Kazuemachi.

They turned down a flagstone road with a sign on a lightpost that read, Izumi Kyōka no Michi: Izumi Kyōka Road. A hundred meters further on they stopped at a monument of a geisha holding a paper fan: Taki no Shiraito, a character in *Giketsu Kyōketsu*, Kyōka's first novel.

At Asanogawa Bridge they cut through traffic to where Kazuemachi's riverside *machiya* were lined in a row. Through the vertical wooden slats over the windows of sake bars and *izakaya* they heard talking and laughter. The plaintive notes of a *shamisen* drifted from one of the old houses along the river, or perhaps from the narrow street of *machiya* behind this one. For all the revelry contained within these *machiya*, they had the footpath nearly to themselves.

The neighborhood would soon erect summer restaurants over the water, with geisha performing for customers. It seemed a missed opportunity not to build these restaurants when cherry trees were in bloom, turning the river pink with their reflections. Even so, the atmosphere, following a long, harsh winter when pedestrians were at a minimum, was that of a celebration.

Before they reached where the river-wall curved and a wooden bridge crossed the water, they turned into a narrow side street.

"There it is." Mirai pointed to the bar's small sign, glowing in the darkness. They went inside.

Kimura sat at a polished counter by himself. He stood up when he realized Mirai didn't plan to stay.

"Thank you again for the card and flowers. You didn't need to go to such trouble on my account."

"It was the least I could do after not appearing at the Kurokawas.'"

"It wasn't as upsetting as you might think. They realized it was a big commitment and not a particularly normal lease."

Mirai thanked him for his understanding. "I don't mean to be rude, but I should leave you two to talk. I have things to do tonight."

After exchanging bows with Kimura she squeezed Emmitt's hand and left.

Kimura asked the owner to bring him and Emmitt sake.

"Do you know this place?" Kimura said.

"Only in passing."

He pointed to a woodblock print on the wall. In various shades of blue and indigo, it depicted a bar similar to the one they were in. *Evening Doorway* was penciled along the bottom of the print.

There was something odd about the picture. Emmitt finally realized what it was. "Why is the title written in English?"

"The artist was American."

What stood out were the bold, bright colors of the picture. The style and composition were distinctly Japanese.

"Clifton Karhu . . ." Kimura said, adding that the bar in the painting was around the corner from a gallery devoted to Karhu's work. "The bar closed down two years ago," Kimura said. "Its owner sold the place, and Kazuemachi lost a piece of its history."

It was impossible to live in Kanazawa without encountering Karhu's name, for Kanazawa had been his home for a decade until he died in 2007. Before that he had lived in Gifu, where he sold Bibles door-to-door, then moved to Kyoto, and over the next thirty-five years learned the techniques of *shin-hanga*, a style of woodblock print, and made his reputation. That was all Emmitt knew about the man.

"Karhu interests you?" Emmitt said.

"My wife and I visited the gallery around the corner once. We spoke at length with the owner, and he brought us here for a drink. He knows a lot about Karhu, as you'd expect."

"The artist's life seems ideal, doesn't it?" Although they were talking about Karhu, Emmitt was thinking of how Kanazawa was replete with artists and craftsmen. In Mirai's family, everyone had a creative outlet but him.

"Your plan to stay in Japan reminds me of Karhu."

"Why? All I've been is a teacher. And I feel I've wasted a lot of time—time I could have spent better learning to live a different way."

Kimura chuckled. "How many ways are there to live? You make it sound like an open market."

"Who knows? But don't we have the freedom when we're young to reshape our lives? Do we have to live one way without the possibility of change ever?" When Kimura didn't say anything, Emmitt added, "Karhu died one year before I arrived. It's hard to believe I was twenty-six then."

Kimura shook his head as if he disapproved of Emmitt looking back. "At your age *now* Karhu and his family were almost starving. They survived on spoiled milk begged from neighboring dairy farms. He had no choice but to find a way forward. And he did so working in an unfamiliar art form and in a country he hardly knew. He climbed out of a deeper hole than you're in and accomplished more than you even seem to be dreaming of."

Feeling as if his inability to decide on his future was on trial, Emmitt welcomed the approach of the woman at the counter. As she set before them a wooden tray with a *kutani*-ware sake carafe and cups, Kimura said, "I apologize if I came off too strong, but my point was that you should take inspiration wherever you can. If you can't see it in Karhu's life, you're on your own."

Emmitt waited for the woman to finish pouring them sake and return behind the bar before replying. "It must be strange to you that I want to stay in Japan, in a small city like this where few foreigners settle down."

"It's not strange to me at all. What I find strange are the foreigners who live here but never learn Japanese. Who settle into lives doing the easiest thing they can to get by, and when that proves unsatisfying, complain about the country, not their own shortcomings or lack of effort. Of course, it's the same anywhere, including with Japanese who choose to live in other countries but never try to adapt. I'd probably be no different if I were them, but I have no desire to leave. I'm just a normal Japanese, after all. You're different from people like that. You appreciate your life here, like Karhu did. They called him 'the green-eyed Japanese,' you know." He leaned toward Emmitt and looked at him closely, then turned to the woman behind the bar and said, "Do you know what color my friend's eyes are?"

"His?" she said, nodding at Emmitt. As she considered this, an uncertain smile came over her face and she blinked quickly. "Blue?"

"Green," he said, laughing.

Turning back to Emmitt he said, "That's another thing you share with Karhu. You could be called a green-eyed Japanese, too."

"I'm not Japanese. I doubt Karhu considered himself Japanese, either."

Kimura shrugged. "You may be right."

"Mirai and I once planned to leave Japan, you know. We

would have come back, but we were never able to take that first step. We couldn't manage to uproot ourselves."

"Why not?"

Reaching for his sake cup, Emmitt thought back to why they couldn't, and realized he'd misspoken. It hadn't been "Japan" they were unwilling to uproot themselves from, for their lives together had taken shape nowhere else but Kanazawa. It was Kanazawa they had foreseen themselves regretting leaving behind. Aside from America, they had never considered moving anywhere else.

"Leaving seemed the wrong thing to do. Back then, life in America felt like something we were supposed to want, but we both realized that what we had here was better."

Kimura pointed at Emmitt, as if to extend the meaning behind what he'd just said. "You don't have a choice but to stay."

"Why don't I have a choice?"

"Because you're happy here. You've learned the language, have serious interest in the culture, have family here now. You have dreams for your future in Japan. Why give up so many good things? As a Japanese myself, I'm happy knowing you want to live here. I know it's not always easy. Sometimes it's not easy for Japanese to live here, either."

Emmitt tried to wrap his thoughts around what he and Kimura had been talking about.

They continued drinking, listening to the old Japanese music the bar's owner put on. Behind her was a vintage gramophone, and the record she set beneath its needle was sometimes scratchy. The song's nostalgia and the bar's atmosphere reminded him of the happiness he felt when he first came to Japan, of being immersed in a foreign culture—it was a romantic feeling, with infatuation on the edges of it, his existence suddenly dependent on this previously unknown source of fascination.

"There must be some beautiful houses in the mountains,"

Emmitt said when the record ended, remembering the photographs at Hotaka's gallery and the trip he and Mirai would take tomorrow. "If not for sale, then abandoned."

"Where were you thinking?"

"I don't know. Shiramine, for example."

Kimura looked surprised by Emmitt's suggestion. "Every year in the countryside, more houses become empty. They blight the landscape, and are fire hazards, and the situation will only worsen as the population declines. It costs money to tear them down. Because the owners have to pay for that, they choose instead to sit on them. They don't mind paying property taxes because usually they don't amount to anything. Two million yen is a far greater expense than one percent of that every year; people carry that much around in their wallets." He reached for the *kutani*-ware carafe. "A square meter in Shiramine might sell for what this sake costs. Many owners would be happy to sell for a pittance, especially if their heirs don't want the properties. Still, it's mountain living, and the reality of that deters a lot of people."

There was no getting Mirai on board with living in the mountains, or probably anywhere outside the city. If Kanazawa felt too small to her, there were few places they could agree to live.

Emmitt would have liked to stay longer, but he didn't want to be out late. He thanked Kimura for the talk and, despite Kimura's protests, paid for their drinks.

On the walking path outside the bar, Emmitt turned the corner. There, before a cherry tree that continued to shed its delicate blossoms, and which half-hid from view the stone staircase Kyōka as a boy secretly used when visiting the geisha districts along the Asano River, was the Karhu gallery he and Kimura had spoken of. Emmitt approached its sliding door, which was adorned with carvings of rabbits. Beside it was the late artist's self-portrait and a small plaque in English about his life. Framed pictures hung inside, their bright colors visible in the moonlight. Emmitt had passed by here before but never entered.

Karhu, Emmitt reflected, had come to Japan during an era he wished he could have known, when Japan retained a stronger connection to its past than now, the country was still poorly known beyond its shores, and, following the end of World War II, the world seemed simpler and more forward-looking. Karhu represented an earlier era. Emmitt had arrived here too late.

9

ON THE FOLLOWING MORNING Emmitt and Mirai drove the thirty or so miles to Shiramine. Approaching where Kanazawa expanded outward, he tried to ignore the blight of new developments as well as older ones whose deterioration showed less their age than the poor quality and regularity of their construction. Kimura had recommended suburban properties like these as affordable alternatives to those in the heart of Kanazawa. Pockets of old *machiya*, *kominka*, and *kura*, cultivated garden plots squeezed between houses, and more and more open space—distant, water-filled rice fields, many with herons and egrets feeding in them—eased the strain on his eyes.

A range of low, fog-strewn mountains appeared, curving like a sickle, cutting away the last vestiges of the city. Eventually they came to a brick hydropower station and the steep narrow gorge on which it sat.

Mirai slept beside him, leaning against his arm. When they turned deeper into the mountains, she opened her eyes and looked around, as if she couldn't imagine how they'd gotten there.

They'd rarely had time in their busy lives to branch out in their travels. Although they had gone as far away as Okayama Prefecture for Mirai's ikebana, they had come home the same day. And when they had wanted to get away for more than a day, the farthest they'd gone was to Wakasa Bay in Fukui Prefecture. Most of the time they stayed in Ishikawa. It was disappointing to admit, but Wajima, Suzu, and Yamanaka Onsen were the only places they had spent the night outside of Kanazawa without her parents and sister. His excitement about this trip seemed incommensurate with how close to home their destination was.

They arrived in Shiramine eighty minutes after setting out. As they left the mountain road and turned into a narrow street leading to town, Emmitt pointed to two ski slopes peering over the valley. According to Mirai, they had closed around ten years ago.

The mountainous scenery made the short journey, and the notion he hadn't come here before, seem impossible. But here they were, not even mid-morning yet, surrounded by cedar forests and sandwiched between branches of the Tedori and Ōmichitani rivers. Another forty-minutes' drive would have delivered them to Bettō Deai, a popular base station for climbing Hakusan.

They arrived at their *ryokan*, in the center of town, several hours before they could check in, but the receptionist, who stood inside the entrance behind a row of paired slippers, said they had few guests that day and could give them their room early. She asked them to come back later that morning.

At Mirai's request, the woman handed them a town map. She laughed when Mirai asked if they were usually fully booked.

"At this time of year we're fully booked only when there's a funeral in town."

Outside, the sound of water was almost deafening—it barreled down the streets through covered trenches. The few shops they saw were not yet open. One or two had their doors ajar, their signs advertising mountain vegetables and fresh *wasabi*. A handful of people worked in their small gardens, which were covered in netting to keep out crows.

Emmitt paid special attention to the houses here. Many were old and constructed of dark brown wood, larger and wider than Kanazawa *machiya*. More traditional houses had mud walls painted ocher or gold, with oblong windows and wide doors on the second floor for loading firewood in the winter. Stacked kindling and ladders used to clean snow from the rooftops leaned against nearly all of them.

They came to the edge of town, where the Ōmichitani River unfurled below. The other side of town offered a view of the Tedori River, but here one could see, below and across the water, abandoned ski lodges and ski equipment buildings, and the shells of old clubs and restaurants. The lettering on their signs had faded, the signs themselves left dangling from frontispieces. Parking lots overflowed with weeds and rotting leaves.

Emmitt asked Mirai what she thought had happened to the former ski runs.

"It was probably a combination of things: not enough quality snow to sustain them, and developers in other places made their ski facilities more attractive."

"Shiramine fell out of fashion?"

"Something like that."

It was like saying nature could lose its magic in people's hearts. But how could people turn their backs on a setting as beautiful and pristine as this?

The Ōmichitani rushed by, through rocks and small boulders. In places it was shallow enough to walk across, though a modest bridge traversed it downriver. Mirai said she had no desire to go to the other side.

"It's sad here with all these shuttered buildings on both sides of the river."

"We've just caught it between seasons, newly awakened from the long winter," Emmitt said. "Up the mountain there's still snow. It must be spectacular here in the middle of each season. I can almost hear cicadas droning in the forests in summer. And imagine the mountain's green walls turning crimson in autumn, then white again after a heavy snowfall."

"It's so quiet it's almost eerie."

"What's wrong with quiet? It's unpleasant imagining this place filled with tourists and cars."

Shiramine covered only a few short blocks, but it had more than enough charm to retain his interest.

Consulting their map, they noted several places that seemed worth visiting: an Edo-period merchant house, a large *onsen* overlooking the Ōmichitani River and mountains, a well-known tofu shop, various temples, a museum of mountain folk houses, and the silk factory where Mirai had an appointment later that morning. Farther afield were an insect museum, a dinosaur museum, and a sacred 1,800-year-old cedar tree.

"Let's start with the silk factory and get my business out of the way," Mirai said. "I don't want it hanging over our time here if I can help it."

"What time is your appointment?"

"We didn't settle on one. They told me to come whenever it's convenient."

According to their map, the factory was a wide, two-story building between the prefectural road and mountainside.

Water flowed below where they walked, in a rocky channel between garden plots. They could hear it as they approached the silk factory, though they couldn't detect its source. It seemed to come from the mountains—a distant, endless rumble.

A minute later they reached the entrance, where a white silk *noren* curtain fluttered. It sounded as if hail was drumming the roof, but Mirai said it was only women working at their looms.

Mirai informed the ticket desk worker that she had an appointment.

"The director just stepped out, but he'll be back soon," the woman said. "Please, have a look around until he returns."

They passed through an exhibition space with silk kimono

stretched across lacquered frames, into a room where antique spinning looms, baskets of silk cocoons, unspun silk, and old kimono stood behind glass cases. They moved on to an old spinning workshop, then into a dyeing studio where two women sat pushing and pulling at their antique machines, the pounding sounds of their weaving filling the room.

On the second floor, looking through its windows, Emmitt was struck by the vivid green of the mountain forest that enveloped Shiramine. The treetops reached halfway up the sky, left to right in a gentle curve.

Along a road in the distance—he couldn't place it on his mental map of the town yet—extended a row of what appeared to be cherry trees. He remembered what Hotaka had said about the *sakura* season here, and realized he hadn't seen any blooming as he had in Kanazawa. It was clear they would bloom soon, though. Their canopies glowed like the coals of soon-to-rage white and pink fires.

He turned away when Mirai said, "I never expected to find a place like this. My family rarely came here on our ski trips."

Behind them an old man climbed the stairs from where they'd come. When he found them, he introduced himself as Matsumoto, the factory's public relations director. He thanked Mirai for coming and they exchanged business cards.

As Mirai followed Matsumoto to his office, Emmitt returned to the lobby to wait for her.

Although she seemed hesitant to accept commissions in Shiramine, he hoped she would agree to a trial period. Tokyo was far away for regular work, whereas Shiramine was closer, and they could both come here together sometimes. The more commissions she found in and around Kanazawa, even if they were in the mountains, seemed like a development that would make her goals as an ikebana artist more attainable.

When she returned twenty minutes later, Emmitt asked how her meeting went.

"He was nice, and his interest flattered me. But I told him I didn't want to overextend myself now. He left the door open for me to help."

"How would it overextend you?"

"I'm starting a handful of commissions from the ikebana school in Tokyo, and because of the school's reputation I can't refuse what they offer. That takes priority over what Mr. Matsumoto might ask me to do."

"You're already doing commissions for Koyo's school?"

"I have one now, and I'm lining up others. Sometimes you have to turn away a sure thing to chase a greater but less likely success. Maybe this is how people change their lives."

It was the first time Emmitt had heard her suggest she had a plan for changing her life.

As they walked down the path back to town, several folk houses came into view beyond the trees. They hadn't been visible from the direction they had come.

"Walking through an old mountain town," Mirai said, "I feel like we're walking into an earlier time. I haven't seen thatched roofs like those since I was a child and we drove through the countryside to visit my grandparents. They're magnificent."

Her enthusiasm surprised him.

In a few minutes they were back in the center of Shiramine.

When they returned to the *ryokan* they rang a bell atop the check-in counter. The woman they'd spoken to before hurried over from a rear room and handed them their room key.

"The men's and women's baths are on the fifth floor. And dinner will be served at six on the second floor. If your *yukata* robes aren't the right sizes, please call me and I'll bring you different ones."

They went upstairs. The room felt worn, and it lacked amenities—only a small TV on a shelf in the wall. Although it had a low table, and two futons rolled up beneath the window, there was nothing but the tatami flooring to sit on, not even a floor cushion.

Mirai made tea from a thermos of hot water the inn had provided. While it steeped, they listened to the water under the town's streets rush down and away from the mountains.

Mirai lay on the floor. "It's going to rain," she said. After a long pause, in which Emmitt thought she'd fallen asleep, she added, "I can smell it blowing over the mountains."

The only thing he smelled was the room's tatami and a woodiness either from the *ryokan* or from the cedar trees that dominated their view out the window. He wondered if someone in a house nearby had lit a fire.

"I don't mind if it rains," he said. "I brought a collection of Kyōka stories in case the weather turned bad. If you want to stay here, I can start reading it."

"Let's see more of the town before it rains. If possible, I want to find reminders of my family's skiing trips."

"I thought you were eager to try the tofu."

"I am. But that's what lunch is for. It's only ten o'clock."

When they got to the lobby, Emmitt asked for two more maps of the town.

"We already have a map," Mirai said.

Meeting her glance he said, "In case your parents want to come back sometime. To see how it's changed."

❈

THE RAIN BLEW PAST, and their walk turned into a full day's outing to the folk house museum, a tofu restaurant, a *kominka* café, an *onsen* they found after walking above one of the rivers in town, and an overlook where they fell asleep on wooden benches. They returned just in time for dinner.

As they passed through the lobby to the *ryokan's* second-floor restaurant, a man at the counter stood facing the receptionist's room in back. There was something odd about his appearance: His head was long and heavy, almost melon-shaped, and he wore a black *yukata* with a sleeveless brown *haori* jacket over it, not the white-and-blue ones the inn issued to guests. In one hand he held a walking stick. Spotting the whistle around his neck, Emmitt remembered having heard its piercing sound as he and Mirai were walking. Unexpected and unidentifiable, it had sent a shiver through him. Mirai, too, hadn't known what it was.

Turning to them, his eyes were rolled up and only the whites of them showed. The man said, "Are you the guest who requested a massage before dinner?"

"He's blind," Mirai whispered.

"You must be looking for someone else," Emmitt said.

As they were about to continue to the second floor, the receptionist hurried from the back room and told the man, "The guest is in the annex, not here. Room 204. He says he's left the door open for you."

Tapping his walking stick before him he made for the exit.

After the masseur crossed the street the receptionist told Emmitt and Mirai, "He makes his rounds every evening. He usu-ally comes by three times before giving up for the night. He's a self-taught musician, too, and quite a decent one."

"What does he play?" Mirai said.

The woman laughed. "Not what most people your age care to hear, I'm afraid. He sings Noh librettos to the accompaniment of a hand-drum. He's always ready if guests want to hear him. And he charges next to nothing." The woman seemed to be making an offer on behalf of the blind man.

Mirai looked at the clock on the wall. "We're going to be late," she said, pulling Emmitt to the stairs. "Perhaps another time."

✳

THEY SAT ON THE dining room's tatami floor, loosening their *yukata* as they ate the dishes laid out for them. It relieved Emmitt to see Mirai relaxed.

Dinner consisted of local char, mountain vegetables, tofu, and a bottle of Manzairaku sake, brewed from Hakusan's waters. The old woman serving them explained each dish and came back often to refill their glasses.

A clatter arose outside and lasted several minutes. It sounded like drumming, but without a regular rhythm. When Mirai inquired about it, the woman explained, "On moonlit nights otters climb the stone walls above the river and cause trouble at our inn. They used to chew the electrical wires here so that lights in the annex toilets went out. Now we put small drums out for them, and luckily they seem to prefer them."

"That's two things I didn't know," Emmitt said. "There are otters in the rivers here, and they know how to drum."

"They're only small gourd-drums," the woman said. "It's a kind of amusement for them. They're not musical, as you can tell, but guests enjoy seeing it."

Emmitt and Mirai said they would look for them later, but the woman told them they stopped playing after ten or fifteen minutes. Indeed they had already stopped. "By now they'll be returning to the river." After a moment she said, "Is this your first time in Shiramine?"

Mirai set her sake cup down. "I used to come here with my family when I was younger. But it's my husband's first time, yes."

"What does he think of it?"

Emmitt answered for himself. "I like it here very much."

"And what do you like about it?" She quickly apologized for the question, as if she'd been rude to ask it. "I'm curious why foreigners would like a place like this. There's nothing much to do here."

"I like everything about it."

She turned to Mirai and said, "I suppose you would never consider living here, would you? Shiramine needs an injection of youth."

Mirai smiled and shook her head. The woman laughed as if to recognize some absurdity behind her question.

An hour after dinner they took their white *onsen* towels and headed for the fifth floor, to the men's and women's baths.

Emmitt stuck his head inside the men's changing room. "Except for the guest in the annex, we're the only ones staying here. Let's go in together."

Mirai peeked inside the women's changing room. Finding it empty she said, "There's no one there, either."

She followed Emmitt inside the men's changing room. She checked the bathing area to make sure Emmitt hadn't missed anyone, then undressed beside him. Together they entered the bathing room. They took turns washing each other, and after rinsing themselves they stepped into the hot bath.

The town and surrounding mountains were visible through a long window before them. Below, a car's headlights illuminated the road as well as the houses on either side. As if from the mountain, a whistling pierced the window. A moment later they heard it again and Mirai groaned.

"That sound is creepy beyond words. I hope I don't hear it in our room tonight. I won't be able to sleep."

"It's part of Shiramine's charm. Isn't it better to think of it like that?"

She sighed and closed her eyes. "Today wore me out."

For a moment he thought she meant she hadn't enjoyed herself.

"Maybe the air in Shiramine is thinner than I'm used to."

"We're not that high up."

"Does one need an excuse to be tired? Maybe I've been working too hard. . . ."

"That's one reason I wanted to come here with you. It's important to get away sometimes."

"But I enjoy my work. It's the most relaxing thing I can imagine doing."

The mountains had left Emmitt feeling uplifted. If Shiramine were closer to Kanazawa, he could imagine living here. And if he were in Japan on his own, he might well want to settle down in a place like this.

"Was coming to Shiramine part of your plan for the next year?" she said.

"Seeing more of where we live is."

After a short silence she said, "Why don't I feel that need, I wonder? Perhaps I would in Tokyo."

Emmitt didn't reply.

"Living there would be enough for me," she went on. "I wouldn't feel I had to see every corner of the city."

"Are you opposed to what I'm doing, then? I can't figure out where you stand."

"No, just as long as you're moving toward a better situation than what you walked away from."

She leaned into him. "It would be nice if the *ryokan* had an outdoor bath, don't you think? I'd like to be with you like this in a darker place." Holding him, she twisted to look behind them. Emmitt turned around, too, but he was certain no one had entered the changing room.

Despite her worry at being caught in the men's bath, she reached across Emmitt's thigh and started to touch him. At a voice calling on the street below she quickly pulled back, however.

"What is it you dislike about Shiramine?" he said when the voice disappeared. "Or is it just because you know I'm fond of it?"

"I like it here," she corrected him. "But it feels dangerous. . . ."

"Shiramine?" He couldn't imagine what she meant.

She stepped out of the bath. He trailed behind her to a hot water spigot and sat beside her.

"It feels dangerous," she went on, struggling to find the words, "to embrace these things from the past. It's not that I don't appreciate them—as an ikebana artist, I think I appreciate tradition more than most people in Japan—but it feels like a pattern you're following of going backwards. I don't like experiencing that with you."

"I see nothing wrong with how I am."

"There's nothing wrong with you, Emmitt. And I still love you. But I can't help think that our happiness together—even at this moment—comes at the expense of living a normal life."

"There's nothing wrong with what I'm doing, either."

She went on as if she hadn't heard him. "Since what happened with the *machiya*, you've changed somehow."

"What if I'm changing for the better?"

"I don't think you're becoming bad, Emmitt. But you're unemployed. And you feel no urgency to find a new job. Can you not see how I might consider this . . . dangerous?"

"No," he said. "We have savings, enough for me to figure out a different path for the future. I'm not hurting you. I'm not hurting your parents or your sister. I'm not hurting the environment. I just want a chance to find a better way to live."

"What does that even mean? Is it more than just finding a new livelihood?"

"It's more than that, yes. But I'm not sure how to explain it. I just want you to trust that I'm doing something that will benefit us both."

She shut off the water and stood up. Stepping toward the changing room she said, "I just think there's a less selfish way."

"But it's not selfish, Mirai."

She dressed quickly and returned to their room.

When he got there it was cold, and the wall heater was preset to a temperature that seemed would never warm the room.

He opened the book he'd brought, but as if she didn't see that he was trying to read, she turned off the light and burrowed under her blanket. They were quiet a long time in the darkness.

Emmitt looked out the window. If not for the stars between the clouds, and the light from the hot spring reflecting off the windows and roof tiles of the houses below, he couldn't have discerned a thing. Even now he could barely distinguish the night sky from the forested mountains.

When the moon came back out, he looked down at Mirai, who already breathed as if she were asleep. A trail of moonlight divided her body into left and right parts. He wanted the light to slip further onto her face so he could study it. He liked to see her in these fleeting moments before sleep when her skin was scrubbed clean, her muscles were finally at rest, and the edges of her face seemed transparent. The movement of clouds dimmed the light on her face.

A moment later, the trail of light down her body was gone.

✳

HE AWAKENED FIRST FROM birdsong flowing out of the forest, and then, after drifting to sleep again, from the sun streaming through the thin curtains.

There was a quality to awakening like this that he wished he could experience every day. The morning atmosphere made him feel virile. He wrapped himself around Mirai, sensing that the air, or the altitude, or the sunshine—whatever the source of his new vitality—was present in her as well. He kissed her neck and shoulders, and then her mouth, and soon they were sliding off each other's *yukata*, she with even more urgency than he. Atop the thick futon, washed in a blue-backlit glow from outside, they merged. A temple bell rang out as they climaxed together. The timing made them laugh.

They slipped into their bathrobes and went upstairs to bathe, this time in separate areas.

As he stepped into the bath and, through the window he faced, looked over the town in the morning's swelling light, a possible way forward dawned on him. By the time he left the bath a new possibility consumed him—a paradox of moving forward in reverse—buying a second house prior to a first one. He expected Mirai to dismiss the idea, but if they could find an abandoned house in excellent condition that hardly cost anything to buy, then later, when they had more money, they might look for a permanent dwelling in the city. Shiramine seemed like a perfect place for a second home: Only thirty miles from Kanazawa, it was easy to travel to. And since Mirai might have already found a commission here, she could build on that if she wanted to. The thought drilled itself deeper inside him as he toweled off and dressed, but by the time he reached their room he realized the timing wasn't right. He had no intention of acquiring a home in the mountains with how things stood between him and Mirai.

Even so, there would be no harm in inquiring with Kimura about the possibility.

When Emmitt stepped inside the room Mirai was drying her hair. He was glad they had come to Shiramine and spent the night. He was glad, too, that she liked this small mountain town. It had been too long since they felt positively about the same things.

"What time is it?" she said.

"Not quite seven." Unable to let go of the idea that had occurred to him in the bath, he ventured, "Isn't it beautiful here?"

She lowered the hair dryer and thought a moment. "The air tastes good here," she said, as if to herself. "And the sunlight has a different quality. It's purer than in the city. It would be nice to come back one day, maybe in late summer or fall."

Sunlight parted the clouds. It washed over Emmitt, warming him.

10

ON SATURDAY, ASUKA TOOK the earliest Shinkansen from Tokyo and arrived in Kanazawa at eight-thirty in the morning. Last night, she had called Mirai to say she and Shin had broken up. He still insisted on spending time with her, however, only to accuse her of never having been committed to their future. She'd said she needed to escape from the verbal abuse he kept heaping on her.

When she came through the front door, carrying a bag of small gifts as big as the daypack on her shoulder, her father had already gone walking. Emmitt told her not to expect him back until mid-afternoon.

"Is he training for the Senior Olympics?" Asuka asked, slipping off her shoes at the *genkan*. Laughing at her comment, Emmitt noticed that her face was thinner, and her clothes hung loosely from her frame. She had easily lost ten pounds since he last saw her.

"I dare you to ask him that when he comes home," Mirai said. "He walks six hours every day, four in the morning and two after dinner. His feet have swelled, but it doesn't stop him from getting his steps."

Asuka looked around. "Where's Okāsan?"

"She's out buying fish. She'll be back soon."

They sat in the living room and Emmitt offered Asuka an open package of sweets from the coffee table.

"Where does Otōsan go when he walks?"

"He won't say," Mirai told her. "The rain doesn't bother him, nor does this unseasonable heat we're having."

"The doctor must have instilled great fear in him at his last check-up."

"Wait until you see him," Emmitt said. "He's lost weight from all that walking. He's in better shape than I've ever seen."

"Otōsan doesn't seem to know what to do in his retirement. I feel bad I'm not here to help."

"You've lost weight, too," Emmitt remarked.

"Stress is unbeatable for losing weight." She laughed unconvincingly.

"Enjoy your life in Tokyo and don't worry about anything here," Mirai said. "Once you marry and settle down, you'll realize that now is when you were freest. You have a lot to look forward to."

Given Asuka's recent breakup with Shin, Mirai's comment about marrying and settling down struck Emmitt as insensitive. Asuka, however, seemed unfazed. She got up and walked to the window. Looking out at the gray day, she seemed to be thinking she might spot either of her parents returning home.

"Do you miss Kanazawa?" Emmitt said.

"Maybe I'm a little homesick. Living in Tokyo by myself, life is more complicated than I'm used to. It's hard to deal with everything on my own."

"It's natural," Emmitt said. "Don't beat yourself up about it."

"I know," Asuka said, turning around to face him and Mirai. "But with all the time I spend in the office, I don't have much of a life."

"There are limits to what you can get used to," Emmitt said. "Over time you'll come to understand what that means for you."

Asuka looked at him as if she wanted to hear more.

"You'll be fine," Mirai said. "Even if you spend all day in an office, is that so bad?"

"I don't know yet."

Mirai looked at her incredulously and shook her head.

"I heard a university in Tokyo might offer you a job," Asuka said to Emmitt, coming back from the window and sitting before the coffee table, where her father usually sat. "If it's a good opportunity, I hope you take it. It would mean a lot to me to have both of you there, too."

"That's not really how it is," Emmitt said. "We have no plans to leave Kanazawa."

"You may still get an offer," Mirai said. "It's easy to say no before anything happens, but when an opportunity comes you won't be able to dismiss it so easily."

"It won't change how I feel."

Emmitt saw Asuka's face fall hearing his reply.

Apparently not keen to push the matter, Mirai told Asuka that Koyo and Avery had decided to visit Kanazawa next weekend. Mirai had suggested they stay overnight with her and Emmitt in Katayamazu Onsen.

"I wish I could join you," Asuka said, sounding as if she hoped for an invitation.

"I don't think I'd want you there. Not when you're like this, anyway."

Emmitt thought Mirai couldn't have hurt her sister more had she slapped her. Inhaling shakily, Asuka was unable to speak up for herself.

Uncomfortable witnessing this side of Mirai, Emmitt left them to talk. He returned to reading Kyōka, whose early work he'd finally begun to put a dent in.

※

ASUKA RETURNED TO TOKYO the next morning. She had planned to stay until Sunday evening after dinner, but Mirai convinced her to go back early.

Mirai and Emmitt drove her to Kanazawa Station to catch her train.

As they approached the drop-off area, Asuka started crying.

"It's hard to go back," she explained, "with all the things happening in my life and also when Otōsan's still recovering from his injury. I worry about Okāsan and Otōsan more now than ever."

"You're only two and a half hours away," Mirai said. "It's not difficult to come back, and anyway there's nothing to worry about. Our parents are fine."

"I can't help it. It's natural to worry about them when they're getting older and I've moved away."

"That's not what this is about. There's nothing you can do, Asuka, but continue with your life. Everything is under control here. Okāsan and Otōsan would say the same thing."

"I miss Kanazawa. Part of me wouldn't mind moving back, but maybe that's the homesickness or separation anxiety everyone supposedly goes through." Turning to Emmitt she said, "I have a newfound respect for you. You must have experienced worse moving to Japan."

Emmitt hadn't wanted to force himself into a conversation between Mirai and her sister. Now that she had addressed him, he wanted to ease her mind. "It's okay to feel how you do. I never felt that way myself, but I know people who did. For most of them, things got better with time."

"You never felt homesick?" Asuka persisted.

Emmitt hadn't thought about that time in his life in ages, and it didn't come back to him clearly. He shook his head. "As soon as I arrived in Kanazawa, I knew it was where I wanted to be."

Mirai hardly gave Asuka a chance to hear what Emmitt said. "I don't believe what you're saying. And after all the efforts people made to help you."

"My life has become complicated. And Shin won't leave me alone; it's ironic that I see him more now than before, but it's only so he can criticize me." She paused before adding, "I didn't have so many obligations here."

"You're in Tokyo working for a top design firm," Mirai said. "What is there to complain about?"

"I'm grateful, of course. But that doesn't make things easier."

Emmitt pulled up to the curb. Tsuzumi-mon, the giant vermilion *torii* gate before the station, and the "Hospitality Dome," arching behind it in a graceful latticework of aluminum and glass, towered over travelers hurrying past. Knowing he couldn't stay at the drop-off point if his wife and sister-in-law continued talking, he was about to circle back through traffic when Mirai reached behind her seat and opened Asuka's door.

"The longer you stay, the harder it will be for you. So just go."

"Why are you getting angry with me?"

Mirai shooed away her words. "You've been away for less than two months, and already you're talking about moving back. I'm disappointed to hear you talk like this."

Behind them a taxi honked. Asuka yanked her daypack out of the car with her. Her face wet with tears, she bowed abruptly to them both, then turned and ran toward the station.

"You were unfair to her," Emmitt said. "She's young and inexperienced, and her breakup with Shin makes things harder. She only wanted assurance that things would be okay. It was wrong to get angry like you did."

"She needed to hear what I said. Where you see youth and inexperience, I see cowardice and selfishness. I see my sister throwing away her dreams."

"Are they really her dreams?"

Mirai's eyes seemed to fill with spite. "Whose would they be if not hers?"

Concentrating on turning across traffic, he didn't answer. After inching out someone finally let him through. The light before him turned yellow, and he accelerated through it.

※

LATE THAT MORNING A package arrived by courier. Emmitt signed for it while Mirai and her mother drank tea in the dining room.

"Who's it from?" Mirai said as Emmitt brought the package to them.

"The name says Takahashi. And the address is somewhere in Ibaraki. Tsukuba City, isn't it?"

"Yes, yes," his mother-in-law said. "Mrs. Takahashi was part of our literary club until she moved. She's in the hospital now."

Two weeks ago she had received news that Mrs. Takahashi had been rushed to the emergency room for surgery. Mirai had spent the next day preparing a flower arrangement for her and, at her mother's request, shipping it by special delivery.

"What kind of surgery?" Emmitt asked.

"It was her heart," his mother-in-law said. "Ever since I've known her, she's never touched meat, and she's a serious runner, too. Last year she placed twelfth for her age in a national marathon. She's only fifty-five. Her doctor says that otherwise she's healthy. It's just rotten luck."

Mrs. Takahashi's daughter had reciprocated for the flower arrangement with a package of seasonal fish: Pacific Ocean monkfish, abalone, and oysters.

Emmitt's father-in-law entered the room to see the fish and shellfish. "It's a shame Asuka went back," he said. "She'd claim all the oysters for herself."

"The abalone, too," Mirai said, crumpling up the packaging to throw it away.

Before she could, her father took it and scanned the label on the package. "It was processed in Oarai City." He gave a low, questioning hum.

"You don't think we should eat it?" Mirai's mother asked.

"You and I can. We're old enough not to care if it's contaminated. But Mirai and Emmitt might want to skip it."

"Contaminated?" Mirai said, bringing the packaging to the kitchen and putting it in the wastebasket there. "You mean with radiation?"

"Oarai is close to Fukushima, you know," her father said. "Several seafood companies there sued TEPCO a few years ago for damages to their industry. The courts sided with them, from what I recall."

Mirai stepped back into the dining room. "They couldn't sell seafood if it wasn't safe."

Something in her voice made Emmitt look at her.

"Who knows?" her father said. "But since you and Emmitt plan to have children, why take the risk?"

"It's not contaminated, Otōsan. And even if it was, one meal won't affect us."

"There's a reason we only buy fish from the Japan Sea."

Mirai's voice grew heated. "I ate fish all the time in Tokyo. Now Asuka is living there and doing the same thing. All the testing says the seafood there is fine. At least among what's being sold to the public."

"The public are sheep," Otōsan said. "And the media—the government-controlled media—leads them by their collective nose. Here, take this into the kitchen, too, if you don't mind. It needs to be kept refrigerated." He held out the seafood, in vacuum-packed plastic, to Mirai.

She made no movement to take it, however. "So everyone in Tokyo is eating contaminated seafood? That's completely unreasonable. How could you let Asuka move there if you're so worried?"

Her father sighed but said nothing.

"Tokyo is *not* contaminated the way you suggest. I'm not saying that Fukushima isn't a potential danger, but you're trying to sow fear. If you don't want to eat the seafood Mrs. Takahashi's daughter sent, then I will. Or you can throw it away; I don't care."

"You're making too much of this, Mirai," her mother said.

"No, I'm not." Mirai's voice grew shriller. "But I won't be ruled by fear or the stupid things Otōsan says."

Emmitt pulled her out of the kitchen. "What was that about?" he said when they were upstairs in their bedroom.

"My parents," she said. "They're—"

"No, I mean with *you*. Why are you so angry about what Otōsan said? I'm sure he planned on all of us eating it together."

"He was being paranoid about all of Tokyo. He was drawing a circle around it and suggesting it was poisoned, it was off-limits. I felt like he was trying to discourage me, even criticize me."

"But for what? If anyone sounds paranoid . . ."

His words seemed either to injure or shock her. "I'm not paranoid at all. It's just that he's always been that way. He's always taken digs at me to show when he doesn't like something I represent."

He stared at her for a long moment, unsure of anything anymore. "And what do you represent?"

"His failures." When Emmitt looked at her in confusion she turned away. "Maybe I overreacted, but I'm certain about what he meant."

As Emmitt was about to return downstairs, she asked him to drive her to her ikebana school. He reminded her that the family planned to eat lunch together soon, but she said she wasn't hungry.

"You can take me there and be back in time to eat with them. I have to prepare for tomorrow's classes."

"I didn't know you taught tomorrow."

"The school exhibition is coming up, and they've asked me to teach an extended class. We could also use the extra money."

He calculated what she would earn; it didn't seem possible that the money could be so important. Even so, he respected her commitment to the school and her students.

He waited for her in the *genkan*. He heard her running down the stairs before calling out to her parents that she was leaving.

"What will you do about lunch?" her mother called back.

"Otōsan ruined my appetite," she answered while slipping into her shoes.

The front door closed behind her as her father chuckled from the kitchen.

"I'll be back soon," Emmitt said. He waited in the doorway for a reply, but when Mirai's parents started talking to each other in low voices he shut the door.

✳

THE FOLLOWING AFTERNOON EMMITT waited in the ikebana school lobby for Mirai to finish teaching. Beyond the window of the enclosed room, roseate in the late-day light, was the studio where she instructed her students.

The silence in the building made it easy to overhear her, though it was difficult to tell if her students were listening.

"Ikebana goes back fifteen hundred years," she said. "I practice it every day, and teach it, as a way to keep the tradition alive. You must recognize that what's beautiful is eternal, and what's merely fashionable has no meaning—in flower arranging, too. Although perishability is central to ikebana, we need to make arrangements using what we've learned from the past—even if just to wonder at it. 'Why do these flowers combine so perfectly?' 'How does space affect our reaction to an arrangement?' 'What kinds of flowers did people use long ago?' 'What would someone fifteen hundred years ago think of what you arranged today?' 'How different is our sense of beauty now compared to then?' Looking at what our predecessors accomplished, it's hard to argue that our appreciation of beauty now is superior, and that makes our task a greater challenge. Understanding what came before feels like a quiet space into which we can unfold ourselves—to feel and to think. Besides art, what else allows this?"

The students had raised their eyes and were watching her, waiting for her to go on. For someone who often opposed his interest in Kanazawa's past, Mirai's reverence for a fifteen-hundred-year-old art form seemed improbable. He wondered what it would take for them to find a middle ground.

When she finished speaking, she projected arrangements from different schools of ikebana onto a screen, stopping to explain each picture. Tomorrow, students would put on an exhibition involving calligraphy and flower arrangements.

Over the last several days he'd noticed she'd become more stressed. Not only were her exhibition preparations never-ending, but she also worried about Asuka, who either didn't respond to her messages or responded only briefly.

Before arriving at her school he had visited a bookstore near the station. Wandering down an aisle stuffed with certification materials for various subjects, on an impulse he'd bought three translation practice tests.

He now removed an insert from behind the front cover of a booklet and skimmed the dates listed of when certification tests would be administered nationwide. The next one was in June. After that, September.

When he looked back to Mirai's studio he saw she had turned the lights on and was writing on a whiteboard.

Fifteen minutes later she spotted him and came over. She apologized for not being ready to leave.

"Take your time," Emmitt said. "I can study *kanji* while you work."

"Go home if you want. I'll take a bus back or ask someone for a ride."

"It's all right."

"But I thought I told you before not to come. I had a feeling we'd have more to do this afternoon than usual."

"It's okay. You were on my way."

She glanced toward her studio. "I'm afraid that tomorrow's exhibition will be disappointing. Maybe I'll let them go early. Are you sure you want to stay?"

"I'm sure."

His phone vibrated on the seat beside him. The notification at the top of its screen said he'd received an email. It surprised him to see it was from Avery.

When Mirai left, Emmitt opened the message. Laughter surged from another classroom down the hall, and the students inside—junior high school girls by the looks of their uniforms— poured into the hallway and remained there, chatting noisily, sometimes shouting so loudly he expected Mirai to scold them.

Emmitt went outside to read Avery's message.

> *Dear Emmitt:*
> *It's been a long time, and I apologize for not replying to your emails before now. This isn't an excuse, but Koyo and I have been busy with our lives in Tokyo, which sometimes still feel new to us.*
> *I'm eager to hear about your life these days, and I also*

want the chance to convince you to visit us here sometime. I know you've been to Tokyo before, but not since we moved here. Tokyo isn't the asphalt jungle it sometimes seems, you know. It's enormous, true, and yes, commuting by train isn't always pleasant, but the city compensates for its hassles in ways you can't imagine. Trees and koi ponds surround our campus, and from the floor of our department you can hear a wide canal. Where we live, there's a park across the street, the Sumida River is a short bicycle ride away, and in between are shrines and temples I've gotten to know. Tokyo is easy to fall in love with if you view it with an open mind.

By the way, the department at my university will soon post public advertisements for instructor openings. I could get you a position with little more than a whisper to my department chair. Maybe we can discuss this when we see each other. I merely ask you to humor an old friend.

It's hard to believe that Koyo and I will soon be in Kanazawa again. It's all she talks about these days. Both of us look forward to seeing you again.

Avery

Avery's generosity moved Emmitt. Tokyo didn't sound bad the way he described it, but Emmitt reminded himself that he could write a similar letter that might sway Avery, encouraging him and Koyo to move back to Kanazawa.

Tokyo was only two decades younger than Kanazawa, which was founded in the 1580s, but so much of it had been destroyed in earthquakes, fires, and near the end of World War II that vestiges of its history were few. Now, however, it was a miracle of design and engineering, and no city even half its size could compare with it for safety, cleanliness, law and order, and many other things. But it had also felt claustrophobic, especially during rush hours. Its bus and train systems were no less confusing to him than a detailed diagram of the human nervous system. And people were everywhere. No matter where he went, he felt the city encroach.

Kanazawa felt like home to Emmitt in ways Tokyo was too modern and sprawling to rival. With its manifold paths back through time, what Kanazawa offered was enough. Until Asuka moved to Tokyo, Mirai had almost never questioned their plan to live here.

Emmitt returned to the lobby, which was quieter now that most students had gone home. He approached Mirai's studio and from the doorway observed his wife help three students put finishing touches on their flower arrangements and calligraphy.

Without Mirai noticing, he stepped inside and swept up the cuttings on the floor, then collected and brushed clean the small saws, floral scissors, branch hatchets, and *kenzan* flower holders her students had used during their lesson.

When the students left, Mirai asked him to straighten the tables and chairs and throw away a bag of trash. When he had, and she still wasn't done, he said, "You're coming in before the exhibition, aren't you? Do the rest then. You're exhausted, so let's go home."

As they walked to the car Emmitt told Mirai what Avery had written.

Mirai faintly smiled. "I didn't ask him to recruit you, I hope you know."

He pulled into the road and, before he could reply, slammed the brakes as two schoolchildren cut across in front. Although he felt nothing, he saw one of them jerk to the side and nearly fall to the ground. He had hit the boy, though apparently not enough to hurt him. The children remained standing in front of the car, and Emmitt jumped out. With one foot on the road and one still inside the car he called out to them.

"Are you okay? Are you all right?"

The children darted to the other side of the road. They were lucky not to be hit again in the open lane beside him, but traffic lagged behind them. When the children made it to the other side, they turned to stare at Emmitt open-mouthed, straightening their yellow school caps. The boy Emmitt had hit bowed quickly to them, but when his friend didn't also bow the two boys laughed, as if it had all been a complicated joke they belatedly saw the humor in, or as if they had realized with relief that the accident hadn't been worse. Emmitt watched them run away with their backpacks jostling behind them.

Traffic caught up and a car beeped its horn. Emmitt felt Mirai grab a fistful of his jacket and pull him back into his seat.

"Are you okay?"

"Sure," he said, slowly moving forward again, "except that I nearly killed two children."

Mirai rubbed his shoulder and said, "But you didn't. Those kids are fine, and so are we."

In front of them a traffic light turned red. When he slowed to a stop Mirai attempted to peel his fingers off of the steering wheel. He released his grip, let his arms fall to his sides, and screamed into the windshield.

"Forget it," Mirai said. "It's in the past now, where it belongs."

They didn't speak for the rest of the ride home. Emmitt was thinking about what she'd just said.

11

AFTER LEAVING THE UNIVERSITY, Emmitt established a routine he intended to be temporary: studying *kanji* and attempting to read in Japanese the Kyōka books his mother-in-law had given him. He considered the routine temporary because he hadn't decided how to use his newfound time. Even though he was a fluent speaker, becoming literate in written Japanese had always been a goal. It would take time, but he had as much of that now as he'd ever wanted.

And although Kyōka's Japanese was famously difficult, Emmitt welcomed the challenge of reading him. The stories were unlike anything he'd ever encountered: a startling fusion of fantasy with realism, full of sensual imagery that heightened his feeling of being present in another person's dreams. But they had another quality that set them apart, which was their power to stir within him a longing for the past, no matter what kinds of stories he wrote.

By mid-April Emmitt's language study and reading merged into a new interest. While his father-in-law drew, his mother-in-law directed her literary club's activities, and Mirai undertook more commissions, he tried to translate *Kechō*, the Kyōka story his mother-in-law had told him was set at Tenjin Bridge and which her literary club planned to publish next in English.

Despite his interest in the story, about a young boy's imaginative view of the world he encounters along the Asano River—a magical world in which humans are no better than what he finds in nature—Emmitt never expected *Kechō* to be easy to translate. Still, it proved more difficult than he imagined. Much of the difficulty involved voice and sentence rhythms as well as overall tone, and its lack of proper nouns made important locations in the story confusing at first. The grammar posed few problems, or none he couldn't solve with a little effort, but the vocabulary was old and sometimes nearly impossible to look up. An archaic *kanji* character might take an hour to find, and then longer to understand how it combined with other *kanji*, which might also no longer be in use. His mother-in-law promised to help him understand characters with nuanced meanings.

Translating proved to be pleasurable, however, and every day once he'd resumed where he'd left off he was reluctant to give it up.

As Emmitt learned more about Kyōka, he grew fascinated with how the narrative of his own life in Kanazawa intersected with the author's, one hundred and twenty years ago. And after reading a story like *Kechō*, Emmitt saw the city in a deeper, more intimate light. Many places that were seminal to Kyōka's youth in Kanazawa could be found if one knew where to look. When Emmitt succeeded in doing so, it not only gave more meaning to his efforts, but also impelled him to look for more.

"Since quitting your job you've been spending your days like a scholar," his mother-in-law remarked, picking up the copy of *Kechō* she had given him.

Like her, Emmitt found his interest in the story unexpected. Part of his motivation to translate it stemmed from a desire to dedicate himself to an intellectual, creative task; part came from wanting to push himself toward a mastery of Japanese; and part, he supposed, was because it was the first story he'd read that was set in Kanazawa. The city as it was during Kyōka's boyhood exploded in Emmitt's imagination.

"Are you finding Kyōka easier or merely skimming his work?"

"For a long time, what people told me about his writing

intimidated me—his sentences and diction were too complex, his Edo-period allusions were unrecognizable today, his whole aesthetic was too old-fashioned. But you get used to these things and come to savor his style and language. *Kechō* is a good starting point for me. Perhaps because it's a children's story, it's easier than other things he wrote."

She glanced at the draft of his translation. "If there's foreign interest in his work, it might spark more interest among Japanese readers. The greater part of his work remains untranslated. With the time you now have, you could help preserve something that's in danger of disappearing."

"It would take me a long time just to read them all. Translating any of them could take years."

She didn't seem to hear what he'd said.

"Why not expand your purpose and translate *Kechō* for my literary club? At our next meeting I can propose it. It would give us much-needed direction."

"But I'm sure you could find someone better qualified to do it."

"Nonsense. Are you going to take the same tack with me as last time?"

"I'm just being honest," he said, smiling at her exasperation. "I'd like to try, actually."

"Then it's settled. I wonder how much we should pay you." She laughed as she said this. "In any case, leave that to me and spend your time on the translation."

A wave of anticipation surged over him. With enough time, he felt he could give her a translation of *Kechō* they could both be proud of.

Mirai called out from upstairs. "Okāsan, does the *takkyūbin* company still do home pickups?" She'd been preparing to send a delivery to Tokyo all morning.

Her mother left Emmitt in the dining room where they'd been talking and walked to the foot of the stairs. "From what I understand, they're cutting staff but not services. Why?"

"I wanted to send a suitcase to Tokyo before my exhibition there. I thought I might keep some clothes and cosmetics with Asuka from now on."

"But your exhibition's not for another month."

"The earlier I can get organized, the better I'll feel. I have a lot to do between now and then."

When Emmitt's mother-in-law returned to the dining room, Emmitt said, "It sounds like she's moving down little by little."

"I don't think it's anything to worry about. Do you disapprove of her working in Tokyo when she has the chance?"

"Her leaving for a few days every month or two isn't a problem. Actually, it seems like a good compromise."

"And if it's more than that?"

Emmitt wondered if she knew something he didn't. "I don't want us to live apart. I would never start a family with her if we did. Or if it seemed like eventually that would happen."

His mother-in-law stared at him as if he'd uttered something she'd never dreamed him capable of. And perhaps he had, he thought.

They turned toward the stairs as Mirai dragged her suitcase from the bedroom. Emmitt went to help her.

At the top of the stairs, she stood behind a suitcase that came up past her waist. For a moment he mistook it as one of the two he'd brought with him from America ten years ago.

"Can you help me?" she said, brushing a strand of hair from her face.

He grabbed hold of the suitcase handle. The suitcase was so heavy he had to bring it downstairs one step at a time.

Could clothes and cosmetics possibly weigh this much? He

tried to recall what he'd seen her packing, but nothing came to mind. He would have paid more attention if he'd realized what she was planning to do.

※

ON THE WEEKEND OF Avery and Koyo's visit, Emmitt and Mirai drove to Kanazawa Station to pick them up. When Emmitt saw them approach, he got out of the car to hug their friends.

"It's great to see you," he said after resituating himself in the driver's seat.

"After all the fun we had in Tokyo with Mirai, we wanted to see you, too," Avery said.

"It's the first time we've returned since the Shinkansen route opened," Koyo said. "It's brilliant how the trip takes only half what it used to."

"Still, it's expensive," Mirai said. She thanked them for coming all this way.

"You feel no resentment toward Kanazawa after the way things at the university ended?" Emmitt asked Avery.

"For a long time I resented being forced to leave. I don't feel it now, but maybe that's because Koyo and I are doing well these days. It's nice letting go of old grievances."

Koyo asked Emmitt to take the Hokuriku Expressway. "I haven't seen the Japan Sea since we left Kanazawa. When Avery and I first met each other, we used to snorkel in some cove all by ourselves. Where was that, anyway?"

"Up the coast around Noto. Not around here."

"That was ages ago. Before you and Emmitt knew each other."

Emmitt continued driving until an expressway sign appeared. He turned in that direction and the traffic soon thinned out.

Whenever Avery or Koyo spoke, he glanced at them in the

rearview mirror. In person they looked different from the photos Mirai had taken of them in Tokyo. Koyo's hair was shorter than she'd worn it in Kanazawa, giving her a younger, more boyish look, and she had filled out as if from regular exercise. In a word, she looked robust. Avery, too, had changed—bigger now in the chest and waist, but from sedentariness, Emmitt guessed, not physical activity. And though his hair had receded, it remained almost bushy on top, without a trace of gray. Somehow, the atmosphere they exuded was of settledness and success. There was no question but that moving to Tokyo had brought about these changes.

When they reached the sea, the embankment and densely clustered trees beside the highway obstructed their view. Only as they crossed a narrow estuary past Lake Shibayama did the highway offer an open vista. They passed the closest turnoff to get an extended view, which came and went as the embankment rose and fell.

Small waves unsettled the sea here. The beach, sloping to the gray-green water through patches of tall grass, was unpeopled, and offshore lay long cement pilings meant to protect the shore from erosion. Four or five fishing boats floated on the horizon.

Emmitt suggested looking for a way to reach Amagozen Cape, where they could leave the car and make their way to the water, but Mirai protested gently.

"I don't want to be late to the museum. You and Avery can drive back while we're there. Or we can stop there tomorrow when we return to Kanazawa."

At the next exit Emmitt turned toward Katayamazu. He had overshot it by several miles.

✳

THE MUSEUM ENTRANCE WAS reached via a short walking bridge, in a hexagonal structure patterned after a snow crystal. Beside it, a canal lined with cherry trees extended into Lake Shibayama.

Despite the sea's proximity, the image of Hakusan beyond the lake's placid waters drew their attention. It rose like another world, its upper half still frozen, its long ridges still draped with snow.

"Would you like to come in with us or head off on your own?" Mirai said when they arrived.

"I was hoping Emmitt and I could take a walk and see what this town offers at ten-thirty in the morning," Avery said. "I could use a cup of coffee."

"Funny how we spent a decade in Kanazawa yet never came here until we moved away," Koyo said. "Tourists to Kanazawa probably see more in a weekend than we used to in a year."

Her comment echoed what Emmitt had felt when he worked at the university. The difference between them was that they'd both found something in Tokyo similar to what they'd had in Kanazawa, whereas he wanted to stay to discover something new.

After Mirai and Koyo disappeared inside the museum, Avery said, "Hakusan looks majestic reflected in the lake." With his phone he snapped a photo.

"Did you ever climb it?"

Avery shook his head. "It was one of many things I never got around to."

Nearly three thousand meters high, Hakusan's jagged, snow-peaked top rose above the lesser, forested slopes of fore-grounded mountains. It seemed especially broad-winged from here, stretching laterally for a greater distance than he normally saw. It astounded Emmitt that the appearance of a mountain Hakusan's size could change so much depending on the season and from where one viewed it. The phenomenon made the mountain seem alive.

They set out along the lake's perimeter. Ducks lifted from a ribbon of reeds nearby and flew, squawking, farther out on the mirror-like water.

A few minutes later Emmitt and Avery found a ramen shop that had just opened and took a small table inside. They ordered ramen, fried rice, and *gyōza*, and Avery asked for a beer.

"I thought you wanted coffee."

"I'm on holiday. I'm free to eat and drink however I please. Isn't that the rule when you travel?"

"It certainly should be."

Two waitresses approached their table, one carrying Avery's beer on a tray, the other carrying *gyōza* and fried rice. Emmitt mixed soy sauce with hot oil for the *gyōza*. The waitresses returned immediately with their ramen, setting their bowls on the edge of the table. Emmitt steered one to Avery, then pulled the other toward himself.

"There are some incredible ramen shops in Tokyo I want to take you to whenever you visit—Koyo and I have brought Asuka to two already. I miss the seafood in Kanazawa, but it's a loss I've come through unscathed. Lately Koyo and I have been splitting our time between Japanese and Vietnamese restaurants. Koyo never had Vietnamese food until we moved there."

"Did I tell you that I applied for university funding to present at a conference in Hanoi last year? It didn't work out, unfortunately, and I didn't bother trying again."

"That's too bad. I heard that the department doesn't have the same funding it used to."

"I was told that, too."

They paused to eat. The ramen nearly scalded Emmitt's tongue, and Avery passed Emmitt's water glass toward him.

"Tell me," Avery said, "what prompted you to quit the university? I remember the politics being ugly, but you always seemed to steer clear of them."

"University politics had nothing to do with it. Maybe that would have entered into it when I approached the end of my contract next year. It's hard to explain."

"I'm only asking because I didn't want to put you on the spot in front of Mirai. Maybe I'm wrong, but the way the two of you acted together on the ride here, you seem to be doing just fine."

Hearing this relieved Emmitt, though an hour together in the car hardly meant anything. "I like to think she's giving me space to figure out what I need. I've assured her it's not true, but I think she's worried that I'm withdrawing from life."

"Are you?"

Emmitt looked up at Avery in surprise. "There may be times I wouldn't mind that. But no, I just need more time for myself. To figure out what to do next in my life. And in our life, too. It's been impossible to find anyone who can relate to what I'm doing."

Avery nodded, staring at his spoon, on which he'd heaped noodles and a slice of *chashu* pork. Dumping it back in his soup he looked up and said, "I completely understand the impulse. She probably does, too. When she was in Tokyo, she seemed upset most of all by the ease with which you risked your career."

"Maybe that's where she and I differ. To me it's not a risk."

"What about teaching part-time?"

"The thing is, I want nothing to do with teaching. Not now, and maybe not in the future, either. I want to branch out into something new, where I can test myself in a way I never have before. I don't mean just a new livelihood, which is part of it, but a new way of living. I didn't realize how dissatisfied I'd been with the way things were, and it started with work. I sometimes think teaching to an empty classroom would have been more satisfying

than the teaching I actually did. I see you smiling, but it's true—
an empty classroom wouldn't have generated so much extra work
for me to do at home every night. Everyone needs a sense of purpose. I had none until I quit. Risking that was no risk at all."

Avery nodded again thoughtfully. "If you want, I can try to
tell Mirai what you just told me. Her hearing this from a third
party might help."

"I'd prefer that my words sink in with her after hearing them
from me. I think we just need more time to get used to the situation. And for her to consider my needs in a way she might not
have done so before."

"To be fair, maybe you could use this time to consider her
needs, too."

"I'm happy to do that. But I could use her help to learn what
they are if I've been wrong about them until now."

"If there's anything I can do," Avery said, "let me know."

He called to the waitress for another beer. Sipping a spoon-
ful of broth he said, "This is better than I expected. But I still
want to give you a ramen tour of Tokyo."

❊

AT THREE O'CLOCK, HAVING picked up Mirai and Koyo, they
checked into the *ryokan*. A pair of inn workers led the four of
them upstairs and down a long hall before introducing them to
separate rooms. Avery and Koyo were staying next door.

Inside their own room, Emmitt peeled away from Mirai as
the inn worker explained the layout and amenities. He walked
to the large window at the far end of their bedroom. Lake Shibayama spread out in all directions. From close to shore a walkway
led to a temple built over the water, beyond which a fountain
spouted high into the air, partly obscuring the mountains.

When they were alone, Emmitt and Mirai changed into their inn-issued *yukata* and, carrying what they needed, went to find the baths.

"I didn't have a chance to ask you before," Emmitt said. "Was your meeting at the museum productive?"

"I think so. I learned a lot about snow- and ice-crystal photography. What most impressed me was how these tiny crystals have been enlarged so clearly. The details and pattern variations are inspiring. I can already imagine how useful they'll be to me."

Before parting at the men's and women's changing rooms, Mirai said, "They have a private bath here. If you want, I can make a reservation for tonight."

"Dinner's at six. Why don't we go at nine?"

"It costs four thousand yen. Do you mind?"

"Of course not."

"I'll call the front desk from the changing room."

They met in the hallway after their baths. Toweling her wet hair, Mirai said she had reserved the private bath for nine-thirty.

When they returned to their room, she called Koyo to inform her of the private bath. After hanging up, she told Emmitt, "She said they prefer the general baths downstairs."

"Why?"

"It sounded like they didn't want to spend the money. Maybe we should be more careful, too. Do you think we should cancel our reservation?"

"No," Emmitt said, his voice more forceful than he intended. "Good for them for being so careful. Their priorities aren't the same as ours, that's all."

Avery and Koyo soon came to their room. At some point Koyo turned the TV on, though she kept it muted while they talked.

A bit later a short news brief came on. In Atami, a resort

getaway outside Tokyo, a pair of bright red objects tumbled in frothy mid-shore waves. They were round, and big enough that they wouldn't fit on the *ryokan* table around which all of them sat. Two young boys, their bodies blurred to disguise them, lay on a stretch of white sand near the water, their feet pointed to a crimson horizon.

"What are those red things in the waves?" Emmitt said.

Avery said, "It's strange. They look like lion masks."

Koyo twisted around to see the TV behind her. "Lion masks?"

"Like you'd see in a Chinese lion dance. But I saw no sign of the rest of their costumes. Assuming that's what they were."

"You think those boys were wearing them while swimming?"

"What does it say at the top of the screen?" Mirai said.

The TV was small and the Japanese characters difficult to decipher. Emmitt, who was closest to the TV, leaned forward and said, "It says two boys went swimming wearing costumes from a lion dance. The currents pulled them out and they drowned."

Koyo and Avery complimented Emmitt on his Japanese reading ability.

"Wasn't anyone supervising them?" Mirai asked.

Avery shook his head. "Not enough to save them."

"We went to Atami last summer," Koyo said. Turning to Avery she added, "That looks like the beach where we swam, doesn't it? I remember the water being just as green."

"It's hard to say. The currents were strong, though, wherever it was."

Avery reached for the remote and turned off the TV. "You really should come to Tokyo sometime, Emmitt. We could take you to Atami on a day trip. Or to any number of places. The good thing about living where we do is you can get out of the city in an hour in any direction, and you feel like Tokyo's far away."

Emmitt found the comment odd, particularly as the drownings of the two boys had triggered it.

With that the conversation changed to Tokyo. After half an hour it trickled to a stop, and Avery and Koyo lay down beside the table as if to nap.

Before going downstairs to eat, Mirai called the front desk to cancel their reservation for the private bath.

❋

AT DINNER, MIRAI MENTIONED that her family had stayed at Katayamazu Onsen three years ago. She looked at Emmitt. "Do you remember where we stayed? We were here the weekend the emperor and empress came."

Emmitt couldn't remember the name of the *ryokan* either. He thought it had been on the opposite side of the lake.

"Why were the emperor and empress in Katayamazu?" Avery said.

"They participated in a tree-planting event in Komatsu, not here—at Kibagata Park, I believe. We caught a glimpse of them on our return to Kanazawa."

"I've always wanted to see them in person," Koyo said.

"It was in May," Mirai explained, "and I had an ikebana event at a culture center in Kaga City. My mother learned that the imperial family would be in Komatsu at the same time, so after my event we hurried over there."

"Your mother was keen to see them," Emmitt said.

"It's her literary background," Mirai explained, laughing. "She said the emperor and sea were motifs that Mishima developed in several novels. And Hakusan is a sacred mountain. For her there was some kind of bundled symbolism in their visit."

"Your mother reads Mishima?" Koyo asked.

"She reads everyone as long as they're dead."

Avery laughed. "How close did you get to them?"

"Not very. They were among a crowd gathered in the park.

The ceremony was broadcast on a big outdoor screen—only important dignitaries could observe the ceremony firsthand— but afterward we spotted them in the distance."

Their waitress came to add several dishes to those they'd finished. She refilled Emmitt's and Avery's sake cups before leaving. Mirai and Koyo were drinking oolong tea.

When the waitress left, their conversation drifted. Asuka came up again, and so did two mutual friends from Kanazawa, one of whom had recently launched a clothing brand in Tokyo and another who had become a minor TV celebrity there. Emmitt felt they were trying to impress him with what kind of lives people could make for themselves in Tokyo.

During a lull in the conversation Avery said, "I was sorry to hear about Natsumi. I didn't know her well, but I had no idea she was struggling so much."

"What about Natsumi?" Mirai said.

Avery looked at Emmitt as if he might explain why Mirai didn't know. But Natsumi wasn't Emmitt's friend, and he knew nothing, either.

Koyo spoke up, her voice trembling. "I'm sorry, Mirai. I thought you'd heard. I didn't talk to you about it because I thought it was still too painful for us both."

Mirai turned pale. "I haven't heard a thing. She acted peculiar when I saw her in Tokyo two months ago, but she was doing really well at her job. Why would anything be painful?"

Only when Mirai used the word "peculiar" did Emmitt remember who she was.

Natsumi was an old classmate of Mirai and Koyo from Kanazawa. After graduating from high school at the top of her class she had attended Waseda University in Tokyo; in her senior year, a famous company there had recruited her. Mirai had told Emmitt of a particularly odd conversation she had with

Natsumi the last time they'd met. Alarmed by Mirai's story, he thought Natsumi needed psychological help, but Mirai only said she was overstressed.

"I've heard nothing," Mirai said again. "Please tell me."

"I wish there was a gentler way to share this," Koyo said, "but there isn't. She killed herself last week."

"What? You're wrong, surely."

Koyo couldn't manage any words right away.

"That's impossible," Mirai went on. "She wasn't suicidal when I last saw her. Are you certain?"

The news shocked Emmitt, too. Recalling a colleague who had overdosed on sleeping pills after his fiancée left him, he said, "Did someone jilt her?"

Koyo didn't answer for a moment. "She never had a romantic relationship."

"But it's impossible."

"Your last conversation with her . . ." Emmitt didn't want to imply what its significance might have been.

"What conversation?" Koyo said.

Mirai stared at the table without speaking. Finally she answered, holding back tears.

"We met at Tokyo Station on my way back to Kanazawa. She took a late lunch—her first lunch in over a month, I remember her saying—to meet me at a café."

She stopped talking to collect herself.

"It's true she complained that the city had become too much for her. I didn't take it that seriously, but even so I asked what she meant. And she said her feet hurt living in Tokyo, that the pain was so bad she often broke down in tears. I asked if she'd seen a doctor, but she said there was no point, she only had to get used to it."

Koyo wiped at her eyes. She was nodding as Mirai spoke, as if Natsumi had told her the same story.

"'Get used to what, exactly?' I asked her," Mirai went on, her cheeks streaming with tears, "and she said it was from walking on concrete all the time.

"'I fall asleep every night after massaging them and crying from the pain,' she said. I wondered if she really walked all that much, but it couldn't have been more than anyone else in Tokyo. Again, I didn't take her seriously, but I also didn't want to brush her off. Then she said something that shocked me. She told me that she did go to a doctor once for the pain. She told the doctor that slivers of concrete had penetrated the soles of her feet through her shoes, but the doctor only laughed at her. He examined her and found nothing wrong.

"Even though we were in a café, she removed a shoe and sock and, lifting her leg above our table, demanded that I feel the sole of her foot. People around us stared at her, and I couldn't do what she asked. When she realized how embarrassed I was, she slipped her sock and shoe back on and abruptly left the café. And she was limping, though I didn't remember her limping before. I was so unsettled that I didn't call her back. I watched her disappear into the station. That was the last time I saw or spoke to her."

Mirai lifted her eyes and looked at Koyo. "She didn't complain about her work conditions. Only that her feet hurt. I remember feeling like she thought I was part of a conspiracy to deny a source of distress in her life. But I didn't think more about it. I should have."

"She told me a similar story," Koyo said. "Personally, I was annoyed by what she said and that she wouldn't let it drop. I always felt she was lonely in Tokyo, but that her work compensated for it. School and then work seemed to mean everything to her. She was the most ambitious person we went to school with. I had no idea she would . . ."

"Why didn't anyone tell me?" Mirai half-shouted. "Every

morning my parents read the newspaper, but they must have seen nothing about it."

Their waitress came back with small dishes of fruit for dessert. Koyo and Mirai, both crying, waved theirs away. Emmitt helped Mirai to her feet, and Avery did the same with Koyo. They thanked the waitress, who seemed confused by their departure, and walked out of their private dining room.

＊

THAT NIGHT, IN THE men's hot spring bathing area, which had both an indoor and an outdoor bath, Emmitt headed to a stool in front of a mirror and spigot and washed himself. Afterward, he settled into the steaming water where he had a view through the windows of the lake and mountains. Across from him, Avery was submerged past his shoulders.

"I drank too much tonight," Avery said. "Koyo sent me here to sweat some of it out."

Behind Avery, through the half-steamed window, houselights across the lake outlined the arc of the shore. Further on, above the string of lights, was Hakusan, the last of winter's snow on its peak glowing beneath the moon and stars. Setting his small washcloth on his head, Emmitt gazed at the mountain, which periodically disappeared behind the steam.

"Did Mirai tell you about the apartment we're trying to buy?" Avery said.

Their financial situation surprised him, but more than that he found himself envious of their opportunity. It was difficult to respond to Avery's news. He had wanted to bring up with him the idea of finding an abandoned house to buy in Shiramine, but it felt foolish in comparison now. "You're buying an apartment in Tokyo?"

"We're waiting on news about a loan. But Koyo and I both

came into small inheritances last year and we're pooling what we have to get a home."

The apartment they were buying was small by Kanazawa standards, he said, but it was in Akabane, where they had been renting. "We planned to buy a place in Kawaguchi, one stop outside of Tokyo. But the apartment we found in Akabane was cheap. The owner's husband died there, and as you know, Japanese want nothing to do with that kind of place. The woman's eager to get rid of it."

"How'd he die?"

"Choked on a piece of *mochi* on New Year's morning."

"Koyo doesn't mind?"

"She's not eager to live where someone died, but the deal was too good to pass up. She insists we hire a Shinto priest to purify it before we move in. By the way, what was your reaction when Mirai visited those real estate agents in Tokyo? We discouraged her from doing it without talking to you first. Don't think it was our idea."

Emmitt looked past Avery to the window. The fog on its glass had thickened, and the lights above the *rotenburo* bath outside were like a row of blurred yellow moons. He felt a smile come over him, though there was nothing particularly funny about what Avery had said. "I had no reaction. She never mentioned it."

"I'm sorry, I just assumed . . ."

"It's fine," Emmitt said, letting himself sink to his chin in the hot water. "She can't move there without me."

Avery splashed his face with water then rubbed it with his hands. "I understand you wanting to stay in Kanazawa, Emmitt, but Koyo and I are both happier in Tokyo than we ever dreamed, and there's no place we'd rather be now." With the towel he'd set at the side of the bath he wiped his face. "Spending time with you and Mirai here has been unexpectedly good for me. It's been almost healing coming back to where I used to live, especially since I left the university on bad terms. Now that I'm back, I feel I took for granted the beauty of this area."

"I'm glad you came back, too."

"I know I've said it before, but I hope you manage to come to Tokyo soon. When you do, I'll make sure I can spend all my time showing you around. Or as much time as you'll let me. Despite our differences, I'm certain I can plant in you a seed of possibility about having a good life there. I'm starting to think you believe this, too, but don't want to deal with the complication."

"But I've been there before. A few times now. You seem to forget that."

"I haven't forgotten. But one day you'll have to work again, and this period of not teaching, if it drags out, may become prob-lematic. There's a lot of competition for good teaching jobs—or good jobs in general, if you never teach again—and you're not helping yourself by quitting and doing nothing."

"Who says I'm doing nothing?"

"Sorry. I didn't mean to imply that you were being lazy." He paused to suggest moving to the empty bath beside the one they were in. Several old men had just entered their bath and their voices made it hard to hear each other.

When they had moved to the other bath, where the window wasn't as fogged over and the lake and Hakusan came back into view, Avery said, "Is there anything in particular you plan to do over the next year? Or do you just want to recharge yourself for the future?"

"I've been mulling over the idea of translating. Mirai's mother has asked me to help translate Izumi Kyōka for her liter-ary club. If it goes well, they may ask me to do more translating. And it's paid, though I don't know how much. I also want to find a home for us to live in. To start a family in. Someplace with a lot of history, that I can spend my life taking care of." When Avery didn't say anything, Emmitt added, "There have to be other ways for me to live here, and I want to explore them unfettered by teaching."

Avery grew thoughtful. "I hope you don't take this the wrong way. . . ."

"What's that?"

"You can build a dream only to find out soon afterward that its foundation is too soft to stand on."

For the first time, a shadow of a doubt wrapped itself around Emmitt.

"I know I told you that I lived in Southeast Asia once," Avery said, "but we've never really talked about it. It was a long time ago, before I moved to Japan."

Emmitt had long been interested in this part of Avery's life, which he rarely talked about. He nodded for Avery to continue.

"It was in the early nineties, shortly after college. I went there to teach in the countryside. Back then Vietnam blocked the Internet, so I had no way to use my email account. I also didn't have a phone, or a television, or access to foreign newspapers or magazines. I could receive letters, but many were confiscated or had their contents inked out. For one year I lived with almost no connection to the outside world. In some sense it was like returning to a more innocent time. I was a hermit from Western life, but not from the Vietnamese community that had accepted me. I can say without qualifications it was the best year of my life. The joys far outnumbered the stresses."

Wondering why he'd never heard this before, Emmitt listened with interest. Still, he wasn't sure what had prompted Avery to share this.

"There was a river researcher in Cambodia I got to know.

He told me something about the Mekong River I never forgot. In the 1970s, when the Khmer Rouge took over Cambodia, they banned people from fishing in the country's lakes, rivers, and tributaries. You need to know that in Cambodia more than eighty percent of the country fishes for daily food—or they used to, anyway. Because of the ban, which if broken usually resulted in execution, in only one year the Mekong River went from being depleted of fish to being abundant with them. All it took was one year without human activity for the river to recover. And I see a parallel between that fact and the year I spent in Vietnam.

"The world has changed a lot since those times, and I'm not sure my experience in Vietnam could be duplicated anywhere now. And I wonder if that's what you're trying to do. But you have obligations that I didn't have back then. I think you can improve the life you have here, but you can't turn your back on it and walk away. Maybe at one time Japan was like the Vietnam I experienced—but back then the world wasn't as interconnected as now. And that's what I'm saying: You can't go back; you can't retreat from the world and still be fully part of the human experience."

After thinking about the point Avery had come around to, Emmitt said, "Everything seems out of reach in a way it didn't a few years ago."

"The fundamentals can be hard to agree on, but when you and Mirai do that, I think things will fall into place. They did for Koyo and me. Life for us now is the best it's ever been."

Emmitt tried to think of when his and Mirai's "best" had been. Certainly it was before they planned to rent the *machiya*. And now, only a few months later, they faced a major crossroads.

Avery lifted himself out of the bath. "I think I'll head back now. Koyo won't like it if I turn myself into a prune."

"Good night," Emmitt said. He wanted to thank him but somehow the words wouldn't form.

After Avery disappeared into the changing room, Emmitt slid the door open to the outside bath. He settled into its hot water and, trying to empty his mind, peered toward the lake. Looking past the faintly illuminated fountain and temple jutting into the water, his eyes came to rest once more on the mountains.

As he contemplated what Avery had told him inside, he asked himself why staying in Kanazawa was so important to him. For a long time, he tried to answer the question. He was surprised by the difficulty of articulating the reason to himself. The reasons themselves were simple, however.

Kanazawa was his home. It had given him everything he'd ever wanted, and he'd only scratched the surface of what he could learn and experience here. Maybe it was true that Tokyo could offer him more, but he felt rooted in Kanazawa like never before, connected here in ways he could never feel about Tokyo. If something forced him to leave, he thought, he would die as pitifully as a fish laid out on a chopping board.

Kanazawa was his home.

❋

AFTER DROPPING OFF AVERY and Koyo at Kanazawa Station, Mirai's spirits flagged. Emmitt asked gently about Natsumi, but Mirai said, "Not now, please."

As they approached the Nagamachi district, consecutive red lights slowed them down. Starlings in the sidewalk trees were screeching. It was early afternoon, several hours before they normally grew loud. They reminded him of the shores of Lake Shibayama, which they'd strolled along that morning. What was it that

Koyo had said about the herons among the reeds? He turned and asked Mirai.

"She said she'd forgotten how big herons were."

But Emmitt was thinking of something else. After another moment he remembered: Koyo said she hadn't seen a heron since they'd moved to Tokyo, but that she'd seen them almost daily in Kanazawa, either on the Asano or the Sai.

When they got home Mirai told her parents about Natsumi. Her father couldn't remember who she was, but the news made her mother cry out. Emmitt didn't realize that his mother-in-law had known Natsumi, but she announced, as if to Emmitt or her husband, that Mirai had sometimes visited her family's house as a child.

"I'll send her family something tomorrow. Our condolences, and an appropriate arrangement."

"Please make it from all of us."

Emmitt glanced at his father-in-law, who hadn't reacted yet to the news. His face wore a blank expression.

"Did Asuka know her?" Mirai's mother said.

"Not well. They didn't overlap in school, and their neighborhoods in Tokyo were far apart."

"It would be terrible if she did, being there on her own."

Mirai sat with her head down and said nothing.

Emmitt's father-in-law turned toward the window. He pointed to the glass and said, "Well, well."

Everyone looked to where he had pointed.

In a corner of the window, three geckos clung to the outside of the glass. Emmitt expected them to scramble away as his father-in-law approached, but none of them moved.

"I thought they only came out at night," he said. He tapped the window and two geckos scurried off. The third one didn't budge.

Emmitt saw its heart beat quickly through its leaf-brown skin. A second later its tongue shot out as if tasting the air.

Mirai stood and left the room. Her father turned to watch her go but seemed to see nothing strange about her departure.

When Emmitt returned his attention to the window, the third gecko had disappeared.

12

"I'M PLANNING TO GO away next weekend," Mirai's mother announced one afternoon after returning from her literary club. "It was a last-minute decision, but it was the only time our members could agree on."

"Again?" her husband said, not looking up from his sketchpad. "Where are you off to this time?"

"What do you mean 'again'? Some years we make three or four trips together. This will only be our second in the last twelve months."

"Fine, but I asked where you were off to."

"Yashagaike."

Emmitt turned at the sound of the sketchpad falling to the living room floor. Rather than reach to pick it up, his father-in-law stared out the window in front of him, where the bright, blank sky made him squint.

"What on earth for?"

She laughed at the dismay in her husband's voice. "It's the source of several famous legends, some of which date back to the ninth century. More importantly, Izumi Kyōka set one of his best-known plays there."

"Kyōka again?" Her husband's tone was derisive.

Having heard *ike* at the end of the place name, Emmitt asked if her club planned to visit a lake.

"A mountain pond, actually, in Fukui, on the border with Gifu Prefecture. There's a 1,200-year-old legend about a dragon that married a landowner's daughter and brought her to the pond. Local people and travelers still offer items that the dragon's wife might covet—cosmetics and hair implements, for example—placing them in the pond's clear shallows. I've heard that, at 1,100 meters, it's a difficult but exhilarating hike."

Her husband shook his head, as if he wanted to hear no more about it.

"Since Mirai will be here," she went on, perhaps to lighten her husband's mood, "I won't have to worry about the house only having you and Emmitt to look after it."

Her husband mumbled something under his breath.

"I've been to Fukui many times," Emmitt said, "but I haven't heard of Yashagaike."

"It's a bit remote. But not as remote as when Kyōka traveled there. Some people say he never reached it, but I think he must have."

She told him that Yashagaike meant "Demon Pond," which was also the title of Kyōka's play. Because of the literary associations with the pond and mountain, she'd long wanted to visit the area. Considering it too troublesome to travel there on her own, she was relieved that other members wanted to go, too. That they wouldn't travel together this summer as they had in the past had worried her.

Since Emmitt had married Mirai and moved into her parents' house, he could recall the literary club having traveled to Nara to visit the house of the writer Shiga Naoya; Dazai Osamu's house in Aomori; the Takahan *ryokan* in Echigo-Yuzaka, Niigata, where Kawabata Yasunari wrote *Snow Country*; a Tanizaki Jun'ichirō museum in Ashiya, Hyōgo; the former residence of Natsume Sōseki in Kumamoto; a park in Echizen, Fukui, where Murasaki Shikibu, the author of *Tale of Genji*, once lived; and a museum to Matsuo Bashō in Yamanaka Onsen, a short drive from Kanazawa. And of course she'd visited many times the museums, monuments, former houses, and gravesites associated with Kanazawa's four most famous writers: Izumi Kyōka, Murō Saisei, Tokuda Shūsei, and Fukuda Chiyo-ni. Yashagaike, then, was to be another literary pilgrimage like these others.

On the morning she left, she invited her husband to accompany her. She called from the kitchen into the living room.

"You only need to bring a change of clothes and a toothbrush." Turning to Mirai and Emmitt she said, "You two don't mind if he goes with us, do you?"

"Not at all. Emmitt and I can take care of things here."

The front door opened and closed, surprising all three of them. Emmitt went to the living room window, where he saw his father-in-law in his exercise clothes walking down the street. None of them had heard him announce his departure.

Half an hour later, as a taxi pulled up to take Emmitt's mother-in-law to the station, her husband still hadn't returned.

"What a child he is to act like that. When he gets home, tell him as much. Do you suppose he's jealous of a writer who's been dead for nearly eighty years?"

"I think he doesn't like the idea of you leaving him," Mirai said. "Enjoy your trip and don't worry about things here."

The following night, after dinner, Emmitt's father-in-law went out again in his walking clothes without a word to Mirai or Emmitt. When two hours had passed and he still wasn't home, Mirai called him on his cell phone, only to discover that he'd left it on the living room windowsill. At ten o'clock she made up an excuse to buy something at a convenience store, but Emmitt knew she was going out to look for her father. She returned forty minutes later, her anger at him replaced by concern.

Emmitt was reading Kyōka in bed—a play-within-a-story that somehow reminded him of *Hamlet*—when the front door downstairs slammed open and shut. It was 11:35 p.m.

He and Mirai found her father propped against a wall in the

genkan, his eyes closed as if he were planning to sleep standing up. Mirai pressed him about where he'd been, but he wouldn't say. He reeked of alcohol.

"Where's Okāsan? Is she home now?" He stomped through the house, stopping more than once to balance himself against a wall with his hand. When he lurched past them, they saw the back of his pants was dirty, as if he'd fallen or sat down for a long time on the grass.

Mirai helped him take them off, removing from their pockets his house-key, wallet, and a slip of paper the color of a robin's egg. Emmitt saw a handwritten, five-figure number starting with a two, which meant that wherever his father-in-law had gone he spent around two hundred dollars.

"Where is Okāsan?" His father-in-law rocked back and forth in his sweatshirt, boxers, and socks as if someone were tugging him from behind.

Mirai said, "She'll be back in two days. At the end of her trip."

Her father stumbled back to the living room and collapsed on the sofa. He rolled onto his stomach and closed his eyes.

"Where were you tonight?" she asked, exasperated. "Did you go back to that *sunakku* bar in Katamachi with the Russian and Filipina girls?"

Without moving his face from where he'd smashed it into the sofa, he grunted affirmatively. Mirai handed Emmitt the wallet. "Don't give it back to him until Okāsan's home. Having it will only encourage him to cause more trouble."

Mirai had drawn a bath for her father an hour ago, and though she'd covered it with a plastic board to keep it hot, she said she would reheat it now.

"Keep an eye on him," she told Emmitt. "Don't let him fall asleep. He'll be impossible to deal with if we need to wake him."

"Won't he fall asleep in the bath?"

She stared at her father resignedly. "I'll have to sit there with him. I'll just rinse him down and wash his hair, and if he doesn't want to get in the bath, I may ask you to help me put him into bed. At least Okāsan doesn't have to be bothered by this."

"Let him sleep as he is. He couldn't possibly expect you to do all that for him."

"It's what Okāsan would do."

"She's his wife, not his daughter. Get him to brush his teeth and go to the bathroom. Then leave him alone to sleep."

Mirai wiped her tears with her fingertips and left the room.

Emmitt stood over his father-in-law. He was breathing heavily with his eyes closed again, as if he'd fallen asleep already.

"Had a few drinks tonight, did you?" Emmitt said, poking his shoulder to make sure he stayed awake.

"A few," he mumbled. "One or two."

"Was it worth all that money you spent?"

"What does it matter?"

His father-in-law grunted and rolled onto his back. "There was a Russian girl there tonight. She was tall, and I thought at first she might have defected to Japan from a Russian volleyball squad, but she denied this repeatedly."

Emmitt smiled despite himself at the image of his father-in-law, drunk, insisting on such an absurd premise for the woman being in Japan.

"She was older than the foreign girls who usually work in those places," he went on. "She was so blond it hurt to look at her. Very attractive, too, but she couldn't speak Japanese. When she tried, I kept looking to see if her mouth was full of nuts, because that's how she sounded when she talked."

"Why did you go?"

"Maybe I was thirsty. It makes no difference, does it?"

"We were worried about you."

His father-in-law fell quiet, and in the background Emmitt heard Mirai reheating the bath. His father-in-law's voice, too, when next he spoke, was softer. "I showed her your photo; I'm not sure why. Then I asked her what the chances were of you and she being related. At first she laughed, but after a while her sense of humor disappeared. Actually, it was a photo of you and Mirai. I wonder if I got it back from her before I left. It's possible that she stole it."

"I'm sure she didn't steal anything."

"Then I told her how Okāsan went to Yashagaike to worship a dead writer. She didn't think it was selfish of her at all, and I couldn't control my anger when she said that. I felt she was being inconsiderate, that she said that on purpose."

"Why would she have wanted to upset you?"

His father-in-law raised a hand to his face and, screwing shut his eyes, pinched the bridge of his nose. Recalling these events seemed to agitate him.

"I lost my patience with her and called her an idiot. She wouldn't talk to me after that. A few minutes later a Filipina girl came to pour me drinks, but I didn't want to talk to her. I wanted the Russian girl."

He was slurring so that Emmitt could hardly understand him.

Mirai returned to the room. Standing in the doorway, she frowned at her father. "Are you really so lonely, Otōsan?"

He turned partway toward her. "Why would I be lonely?" He shut his eyes and this time it seemed he would fall asleep immediately.

Mirai came over and with Emmitt's help led him into his bedroom.

"I've drawn a bath for you, Otōsan."

But as soon as he hit the mattress he fell asleep. Shaking him did no good.

"Wake up!" Mirai yelled at him. "Why are you being so selfish? Look at what kind of person you are! Selfish! Selfish!"

Emmitt had to pull her away two times.

Mirai hurried from the room and disappeared upstairs.

Emmitt made his father tea in case he woke up in the middle of the night and found his mouth dry as sand. Afterward, as a precaution, he drained the bath.

❋

EMMITT AWOKE EARLY THE next morning, feeling keener than usual to translate *Kechō*. Last night he had dreamed scenes from the story of his own imagination, although the setting had remained the Asano River and Mt. Utatsu, and it followed the same character, the boy Ren'ya. Emmitt had merely observed the scenes initially, as if from afar, but was soon drawn into them, interacting with the story's characters—the King of the Boars, Mr. Monkfish, the beautiful winged lady, various animals, and even the flowers. They'd seemed to know he was translating them into English and were grateful, urging him to give every possible effort.

His mother-in-law had shared with him something interesting about Kyōka's belief in the power and sacredness of language. For Kyōka, language possessed a supernatural life force, and he considered letters and words not only to be alive, but also to possess the capacity to "live on." She told him that Kyōka used to cut printed words from shopping bags and burn them. He then ate their ashes believing they would protect him, particularly against cholera, which was a scourge during his lifetime. He sometimes sprinkled water droplets on his manuscripts, too, as an act of sanctification.

The idea that writing could be sacred made Emmitt approach translating with a deeper sense of purpose. More importantly, working with Kyōka's writing helped Emmitt feel he was evoking the past, even keeping it alive. And in doing this he realized he was finding a place for himself.

He perused the manuscript during breakfast, keeping one eye on his father-in-law's bedroom. All morning he stayed in bed, only venturing downstairs in the afternoon—for a hard-boiled egg, clear soup, and rice, and also to draw in the living room, which he kept nearly dark.

For dinner he prepared only rice and a few pickled vegetables, and ate alone in the living room among photographs of statues he had taken and printed out.

After dinner Emmitt put off working again on *Kechō* to sit with him. His father-in-law had photographed not only various sculptures in Kanazawa, but also their titles, artists' names, and the years they'd been cast and erected. Emmitt read through the titles he could understand: *Fulfillment of Life's Desires; Waterside Poem; Wall; Dream Flight; Pure; Sound of the Tide.* His father-in-law had scratched notes for each photo, but Emmitt had difficulty making them out.

The next day, too, his father-in-law stayed home. If Emmitt hadn't known he was still sick, he might have guessed he felt repentant. But by late afternoon he was well enough to go walking. As he left, he told Emmitt not to wait for him to have dinner, and that he'd get something when he came home.

Mirai returned early from her ikebana school to make dinner and clean the house before her mother got back from Yashagaike that evening.

"All those photos of statues . . . ," Mirai said, hovering over the coffee table. "I suppose I'd better not touch them."

"What do you think motivates him to study them?"

"I don't know, but he can't keep doing this. What's wrong with him, anyway?"

Emmitt thought his father-in-law's interest in the statues mysterious, but nothing to be upset over. "Don't statues exist for people to gaze at and admire? If Otōsan sees beauty in them, surely what he's doing isn't abnormal. As an artist yourself, I'd think you'd find what he's doing acceptable."

But she only shook her head and said, "It's good that Okāsan wasn't here to see him two nights ago, or to watch him spend all day with these photographs."

Emmitt had looked up the name of the sculpture his father-in-law sketched today. It lay on the floor beneath the coffee table, and he showed it to Mirai.

She read the title aloud: *Mizube no Uta.* Waterside Poem. In the photograph, three statues stood together under a stone wall fronted with trees, facing the Sai River. "The title is more appropriate for a flower arrangement than that sculpture."

"It seems fitting for either one."

Mirai smiled. "Most men would probably say the same thing: There's poetry in the sight of three well-endowed nudes. I'm curious to know how the women who modeled for it feel when they see it."

"Okāsan might have something to say about that. Of course, I have no idea what kind of modeling she did. It's not the sort of thing I'm about to ask her, either."

"I'm not sure myself."

"You never asked?"

"She doesn't like to talk about it. And Otōsan isn't forthcoming, either."

Emmitt recalled the pictures his father-in-law had shown him while cleaning their frames in the living room. It was true that it seemed an uncomfortable subject after all these years, though Emmitt still couldn't guess why. Mirai's family wasn't what he would describe as secretive, but he knew that stories from the past had been buried and weren't to be dug up.

In the sketchpad, his father-in-law had scribbled what appeared to be a title in the upper right corner. The *kanji* differed from the original, and he'd written it so hastily Emmitt couldn't make sense of it. He asked Mirai to read it for him, but she said it was unimportant.

"It probably just means he's trying to make it his own. That he has a different vision for it."

"Isn't that good? That's what you did with Dr. Nakaya's snow-crystal photographs, after all."

"It's not the same thing. In any case, it depends on what he does with it. Hopefully he'll have the sense not to paint them in Okāsan's image again."

Before Mirai's mother came home, Emmitt finished translating a difficult paragraph in a latter section of *Kechō*, when Ren'ya toppled from Tenjin Bridge and almost drowned in the Asano River. Having read the story in its entirety many times, he knew how the boy was saved, and how the experience led him later to nearly turn into a bird one night on Mt. Utatsu, but he didn't want to rush the translation—he didn't know how to present it in English as Kyōka had done in Japanese, both with its imagistic richness and its colloquial narration. What Emmitt had translated up to now still needed much work, and he wanted to make sure he hadn't missed certain nuances in Japanese. Still, it was better than he'd hoped. He expected to finish a draft in several weeks, but looking at the translation again now he thought it no better than what he'd encountered in *Red on White*.

✳

"I'M HOME!" EMMITT'S MOTHER-IN-LAW called from the *genkan*. As she shut the door, Mirai took her small suitcase and a bag of gifts she'd bought in Fukui. Her mother looked tired but happy.

"Are you hungry?" Mirai said, but her mother didn't answer. She walked into the living room and sat heavily in a chair. Her husband was on the floor before her, drawing in his sketchpad.

"I'm home," she said again. "If you welcomed me back, I didn't hear you."

"I didn't say anything," he said. "Welcome back."

She fanned herself with a handkerchief and smiled at him as Emmitt brought her a glass of cold tea from the kitchen.

"Thank you," she said, and drank half the glass.

"How was your trip?" Emmitt said.

She told them that although the weather had been good, in the mountains where they hiked storms had arisen out of nowhere and then disappeared just as quickly. It was cold when they came to the pond, she said, and a strong wind battered them once they ascended five hundred meters. But the pond was beautiful, surrounded in places with orange day lilies, and they had indeed found offerings in the shallows. Although they had intended to read "Demon Pond" upon reaching Yashagaike, the weather forced them to do this instead at their *ryokan*.

Mirai asked about her accommodations. After showing Mirai photos of where she'd stayed, her mother turned to Emmitt and said, "I have bad news for you."

Emmitt couldn't imagine what she was talking about. He smiled, thinking she had planned some joke. "Bad news?"

"You can stop translating *Kechō*."

His smile fell away. "What do you mean?"

"I mean that we're too late. One of our club members, who hadn't come to any of our recent meetings, went to Yashagaike with us. When we were talking on the train and I mentioned the club's plan to translate *Kechō* she interrupted me. She said it was already being translated into English. The translation was to include multiple introductions and illustrations on every page and would be published with much wider distribution than we could ever manage. I'm still not clear why I never heard about this edition before now."

"I see," Emmitt said. The news hit him harder than he thought it would. He had enjoyed working on it and it had been good practice for his Japanese. It had also brought him much closer to Kyōka's work and to the part of Kanazawa where the story was set—though that area had largely changed by now or disappeared.

"I should have inquired directly with the Izumi Kyōka Museum about what kind of translation work was being done. I'm sure they would have told me. But I imagined no one was. The city authorities that funded our last project never mentioned it. Aside from one or two academics in America, I thought we were the only ones translating Kyōka's work into English."

"I see."

"I called the museum from the train and was told that the other version of *Kechō* had already gone to print. It should be out by the beginning of autumn. I'm sorry to disappoint you."

"It's all right."

For the first time since quitting his job, he felt as if the life he had chased all this time had been illusory. The translation he'd been working on had given him an unexpected sense of purpose. Now that it was gone, he felt unmoored.

"What other translations does your literary club plan to do?" he said. "I'm ready to help however I can."

"Unfortunately, our members are clamoring to translate other Kanazawa writers. A majority of them feel we've put too much effort into translating Kyōka and want to move in a

different direction. It seems people are interested in more contemporary works."

"It sounds interesting."

"Our club won't convene this summer, so there won't be anything for you to do until at least winter. Even then, it seems likely
we'll hire a professional translator. We hope to have enough
funds to attract someone well known."

Emmitt congratulated her on the news.

"You're back to having nothing to do," Mirai said, hugging
him from behind.

But that wasn't true. Two days ago he had rediscovered an
insert from the practice translation tests he'd bought, and circled
an exam date in September. He had also called a regional test
center to ask if they offered classes in Kanazawa, and the man he
spoke with had promised to email him information. He had it in
mind to enroll in one if he could.

Now there was every reason to do it as soon as possible. If
he didn't, he would have one fewer reason to refuse to move to
Tokyo.

13

EMMITT SAW MIRAI LESS often as spring turned into summer. Her new flower arrangements, based on the magnified photographs of snow crystals, kept her occupied. She left for ikebana school earlier in the morning and returned later in the evening than ever before. Her mind had turned fecund with ideas; her sketches were strewn about her parents' house.

At the end of May a Japanese cultural center in Melbourne invited her to guest-teach ikebana for two weeks. On her final day, the center would exhibit the work she created as a visiting artist.

She would leave in two months via Tokyo, where she planned to spend several days with Asuka before departing.

Emmitt assumed the opportunity had come through her school in Kanazawa, but she told him it had come instead through the school in Tokyo that once offered her a job.

Emmitt considered joining her in Australia, but it was difficult to justify the expense now, and matching an itinerary to Mirai's exhibition schedule posed problems.

"Your ikebana has taken off recently," he said when she was packing for the trip. Two months had gone by, and his hope of accompanying her to Melbourne hadn't panned out. "It's impressive, especially because you have to stand out in a crowded field. I know it's been difficult to make your way forward."

"I don't know if it's been difficult. I've been lucky lately to have new ideas."

Her snow-crystal ikebana had led to similar arrangements based on magnifications of what she'd found on bicycle rides along the sea: sand pebbles, salt crystals, flower petals, wings of different insects. These had led in turn to arrangements on the opposite spectrum: objects in nature of great enormity—mountains, forests, even seas and oceans. She was keen to juxtapose large and small things in nature, and the results had opened up more opportunities to explore.

"Maybe I can travel to Tokyo," Emmitt said. "Not before you leave, since you'll be busy as soon as you arrive, but when you come back from Melbourne. I'd like to meet you at the airport if I can."

"That's nice of you. But it isn't necessary."

"We could stay for as long a week. We wouldn't have to stay with Asuka, either, though hopefully we could see her when she wasn't working."

She smiled while seeming to think about it. "It might be better just to stay with my parents."

Her suggestion disappointed him. More than that, he was surprised that his wanting to visit Tokyo didn't excite her. Hadn't she been after him for months to go there together?

On Friday morning he saw her off at Kanazawa Station. Unlike previous departures that took her away for more than a few days, no anguish appeared on her face, and in fact she seemed in a hurry to be off. He stood before the Shinkansen turnstile and watched her walk up the escalator to the platform.

Two days later a 7.3-magnitude earthquake struck offshore of Chiba and Ibaraki prefectures, three miles beneath the Pacific floor. It jolted Tokyo for nearly a minute, injuring several people. A tsunami warning along the Pacific Coast of Japan was issued but later canceled.

He called Mirai as soon as he heard the news.

Both she and Asuka had felt the quake—Mirai in Asuka's apartment, and Asuka at her company. One of Asuka's paintings had fallen off the wall, and an old vase had overturned and shattered. The vase had held a flower arrangement Mirai made that morning.

"But you're all right?"

"I'm just sad. Whenever Asuka came home, the vase was the first thing she saw. She called it her 'welcome home' vase because seeing it reminded her of our family greeting her when she returned from school. The vase had been in our family for years, and my parents encouraged her to take it when she moved."

She started crying softly into the receiver.

"Are you sure you're all right?"

"I'm fine. Anyway, I'm leaving tomorrow, so if there are aftershocks I'll probably be gone before they hit. Can we talk again tonight?"

"Of course." He couldn't remember them ever having Skyped twice a day when she was in Tokyo. "Is there something we need to talk about?"

"I just have a feeling it will comfort me."

He regretted their distance then, perhaps more than ever before.

She hesitated to end the call. "What are you going to do now?" she said.

"I need to make an appointment."

"An appointment for a job?"

"Not exactly."

An expectant silence hung between them, which Mirai eventually broke.

"If you don't want to tell me, I'll let you go. Let me know when we can talk again."

He wanted to tell her. But since quitting his job, he had learned not to share plans she was likely to be critical of. He would have done anything to be able to tell her.

"Be careful there," he said. "I love you."

❋

EMMITT CALLED KIMURA TO invite him out for his birthday. Kimura thanked Emmitt for thinking of him but said he would be out of town with a client until late that night.

"Is your client helping you celebrate?"

"He will if he buys the property I show him."

"Another time, then."

Before their conversation ended, Emmitt mentioned that he had visited Shiramine. "I told you about our plans to go but never followed up." He asked if Kimura, a skiing enthusiast who had surely tested the slopes in the area before they shut down, had explored Shiramine at any length.

"I never spent the night there, but I've relaxed in its *onsen* several times."

"I found it magical."

"Even so, it's hard to imagine how the town will survive. The annual events it holds don't attract many tourists. And as for jobs, there's almost nothing: a small silk factory, a bit of tofu manufacturing, and scattered forestry enterprises and lumber-yards, but the population there is too old to make a go at something new. What it has is proximity to Hakusan. For part of the year, anyway, hikers and mountaineers often pass through."

None of what Kimura had said deterred Emmitt from asking what had been on his mind since learning about the house in Tokyo Avery and Koyo wanted to buy.

"Can you look through your database for a house there you think might suit us?"

Kimura laughed. "What for? You can't possibly be thinking of moving there with Mirai."

"I have no plans to leave Kanazawa, nor her parents' house where we live—not at the moment, anyway."

"Then why do you want me to look through my database?"

"Because I want to know if there are any houses there I can afford. It's occurred to me that I might buy a second house before a first one, especially if it won't cost very much—and I've been online and found abandoned houses in other areas that cost no more than a decent suit. Mirai would never agree to live in the mountains, but a place of our own there might make her happy. I'm hoping to find something that might add to our life together."

"When did this idea come to you?"

"At the end of our trip to Shiramine."

"And if she doesn't agree?"

"If I do this, then I want to do it on my own."

"I get the feeling you haven't really thought this through."

"You're wrong about that. Anyway, the first step is talking to you about it. That's all I'm doing now, and it's perfectly harmless."

Hearing Kimura sigh, Emmitt felt bad for imposing on him.

"Don't forget, Shiramine winters are harsh. A common sight is eighty-year-old men and women climbing onto their rooftops to clear away snow. It's too much trouble for most people. But if they don't, their houses might collapse under the weight."

Emmitt recalled the sight of ladders leaning against Shiramine houses; doors leading outside from many second floors; and empty lots on various streets that were used for disposing of snow in the heavy winters. Kimura was right that winter cast a year-long shadow in the mountain town.

"But you told me before that a square meter there costs less than a one-cup bottle of sake," Emmitt said. "How can you lose on a house that costs so little?"

"There are always ways to lose."

The clicking of computer keys came over the receiver.

"Actually, two or three months ago a Hakusan City realtor emailed me specs for a Shiramine property that an elderly woman who had moved into a care home last year owned. From what I remember, it's quite big, at least by Kanazawa standards, and in the heart of town. Here, I found the email." He paused for a moment. "According to the realtor, neither the owner nor her son, who lives in another prefecture and will one day inherit it, have been ready to talk about a price, which is why it's not openly for sale. But it seems they're keen to get rid of it. The house is too much for them to deal with, and her other children don't want it, either. The realtor was sure they'd sell it for a negligible amount."

"Can I come see you about it tomorrow?"

"I should have time in the afternoon."

Emmitt thanked him. For the rest of the day he worked through different scenarios of buying a house in Shiramine, his enthusiasm vacillating over Mirai's potential reactions to it. He admitted that the odds of making her happy in this way were long. At the same time, it seemed reasonable to do. If he could acquire a house in Shiramine without spending much, he would acquiesce to Mirai's desire to stay for several years longer at her parents' house, even if they started a family then. To Emmitt, Shiramine was, like a *machiya*, a way back in time. Having a rootedness there, however slight, seemed as if it might satisfy his desire to live a particular way.

The following afternoon, when Emmitt went to Kimura's office, Kimura was on the phone with his wife. After he hung up, and he and Emmitt had exchanged the usual inquiries about one another's families, Emmitt asked him about the house in Shiramine.

"There's little incentive for the realtor in Hakusan City to show it," Kimura said, "but he promised to arrange something." He pulled a folder from his desk and handed it to Emmitt. "He emailed me photos of the exterior."

The house was nondescript, and completely different from

the Kurokawas' *machiya*, he thought with disappointment; covered in rusted aluminum siding that might once have resembled wood, its most distinctive feature was a roof that sloped
forty-five degrees from the front to the back of the house. When
Emmitt commented on it, Kimura remarked that he obviously
wasn't from a snowy region.

"It means you don't have to climb onto the roof after every
winter storm to clear the snow. Or install a heating system under
its surface, which costs a lot of money. Snow slides directly from
the roof into a creek behind the house.

"And remember," he went on, "I haven't seen this property
yet. Places like this, if abandoned a long time, might be full of
mold, or have animals living inside—or evidence of them. On
the other hand, the interior might be fine. Better than one might
think based on these photos, anyway."

According to the specs, the first floor alone was more spacious than Japanese apartments Emmitt had lived in; it was more
than three times the size of Asuka's apartment in Shibuya.

He tried to picture Mirai sitting beside him, examining the
photos. The image alternated between the awe she had cau-
tiously expressed when they stayed in Shiramine and the dis-
favor she had felt for the Kurokawas' *machiya*. It was impossible
to know how she would react.

"On the off chance that you want to buy this place, the
owner will want to sell it with as little hassle as possible," Kimura
explained.

"It would really be an off chance," Emmitt admitted.

Kimura nodded. "It's a good opportunity, but you don't want
to rush it. Remember, if I help you buy a property in Shiramine,
my commission will be so low I couldn't even buy us a decent
dinner with it."

"I suppose I should at least see it. Shouldn't I?"

"Why not? It's an excuse to drive into the mountains together."

For now, because it was only a matter of looking, he wouldn't tell Mirai what he and Kimura were doing. And if, by some stroke of luck, he found a place too good to pass up—what then, he wondered? He imagined he would either buy it and hope she warmed over time to the idea of a second home, happy at least that it had cost very little, or he would buy it and never see it again, sucking up the loss of what he'd paid for it along with an insignificant amount in annual property taxes.

"I know the owner's in no rush," Emmitt said. "But the sooner the better."

His own impetuousness worried him, yet he was excited by the plan, happy even. Happier than he'd been, in fact, for a very long time.

❋

MIRAI ARRIVED IN TOKYO two weeks later. She called Emmitt on the airport train to Nippori Station. She would transfer from there to Shibuya and stay overnight at Asuka's apartment.

"Welcome back," he said. On the other end he heard a train trundling and an automated voice announcing the next stop.

"I'm not really back. I'm only on my way to Tokyo."

"But you're back in Japan."

"Home isn't where I am right now. I'm tired, Emmitt."

What did she mean when she said that home wasn't where she was right now? "Come back to Kanazawa, then."

"I wish I could, but Asuka's expecting me. Why can't you be here?"

He hesitated before asking, "Do you miss me that much?"

She didn't answer him. At first he thought her silence meant no, but then it occurred to him that perhaps her exhibition had gone poorly, or her parents had communicated something that made her unhappy. Finally, he decided that her quietness expressed a shyness. He hadn't recognized it at first because she hadn't been that way with him in so long.

He asked how her last day in Melbourne went. The trip had ended well, she said, but she hadn't enjoyed her time there. She mentioned several disappointments with the ikebana school in Tokyo, but he could tell she wasn't eager to talk about them. Her speech trailed off as if she were falling asleep.

"I have a surprise waiting for you."

"You do?" she said. "A surprise?"

Their conversation stalled as she got up for the passenger beside her, and when they resumed talking the subject of a surprise seemed to excite her less than it had a moment before.

"Did you find another *machiya?*"

"No, but that would have been nice."

She laughed tiredly. "I'm a little sad to hear that, actually."

Her comment left him both hopeful and angry. He was taken aback by the resentment he still felt over her backing out from the Kurokawas' property. He asked what she meant.

"I don't mean a *machiya* per se. It just struck me that a house in the city would be nice. Our own house. But I know that's unrealistic right now."

"It doesn't have to be unrealistic."

"I'm too tired to think, so let's just talk tomorrow. I'm about to arrive at Nippori."

"Take care of yourself," he said. "And I mean it, Mirai. Come back early if you want. There are better reasons to return than to stay in Tokyo."

"Maybe I will if Asuka's really busy. She said she's been working late every night at the office lately but promised to be home when I get there. She said she needs to talk to me about something, and she sounded unhappy. I wonder if Shin wants her to give him another chance. If he does, I don't know that I want her to get back with him."

"It's her choice, though, not yours."

"I know. But I think I have a responsibility to advise her."

"If that's what she wants."

She was silent for a long moment. "We're pulling into Nippori now. I have to go."

As he slid his phone into his pocket, he realized how relieved he felt knowing she was back in Japan. He hoped her work wouldn't take her away again soon.

He foresaw many changes for them both, and though he'd wanted to talk about them with her just now, he had decided to wait until she was back in Kanazawa.

❋

MIRAI RETURNED FROM TOKYO three days later, following her original schedule. Emmitt picked her up at the station, as he always did, happy to be the first one she saw after descending from the bullet train platform.

"Welcome back," he said.

"Thank you. I've never been as tired as this."

He took her luggage and led her to the taxi stand.

On the way she said, "Did you get a new car?"

"What are you talking about?"

"You said you had a surprise for me."

Emmitt's heart beat wildly, and he found it difficult to speak.

"I'll tell you about it later. I want to hear more about your trip first."

They arrived home just in time for dinner. Her parents asked her about her trip, but she only answered laconically. After several minutes they stopped questioning her, and instead told her what she'd missed while she was away.

After sitting down to eat she asked if Asuka had told them her news.

"No," her mother said, looking at her with concern. "Is something wrong?"

"I guess it depends on how you look at it. She only found out yesterday at work, and I know that today she was particularly busy. That's probably why she didn't say anything yet."

"What is it, Mirai?" her mother said.

"Her company's sending her to Taiwan. She'll be there probably for two years. After that she could get transferred somewhere else."

Her mother let out a held-in breath. "I worried it was her health, or something to do with Shin."

"Didn't she say that was a possibility?" Mirai's father said.

Mirai nodded. "The worker she'll replace has been in Taipei for two years and before that spent a year in Manila. I didn't expect it to happen so soon."

"I should think she'll enjoy it when she gets used to it," Emmitt said. "Even so, it's hard to imagine her being gone for that long."

"It'll be good for her to see more of the world," her father said. "I wonder if she needs to learn Chinese."

"It certainly happened quickly," her mother said. "She's only worked there for a few months. When she mentioned that her company might transfer her, I didn't really believe it. I didn't give it any thought, actually."

"Tokyo won't be the same," Mirai said. "Going there with her gone will be an exercise in loneliness."

"Still, you have more and more opportunities there," her

mother said, "and more chances to move forward as an artist. There's no way to avoid it."

Mirai didn't say anything. "First Natsumi, and now Asuka. And that earthquake before my trip . . ."

Her father said what Emmitt had held back out of fear of angering her. "It's time to give up your idea of moving there."

She was silent again for a long moment, then stood from the table and left the room. They heard her climb the stairs and shut the door to her and Emmitt's bedroom.

"Otōsan," Emmitt's mother-in-law said reproachfully, "you're too direct sometimes. Especially with her."

"I'm her father. I can be direct with her if it's warranted. But I didn't mean to upset her. Did I say anything that wasn't true?"

Emmitt excused himself and walked up to the bedroom. Finding the door locked, he sat down in the hallway and waited.

14

OVER MIRAI'S FIRST TWO weeks back Emmitt tried to lure her away from her ikebana school. Now that she had returned, her school obligations seemed never-ending.

On her second Saturday back, lying in bed later than normal, she told him that her schedule that day was open. "Hasn't there been something you wanted us to do?"

They had awoken to thunder shaking the house, and the forecast was for rain all morning. By evening, however, it was supposed to clear.

"What are you doing tomorrow morning?" he said.

"The same as always. Going to school."

"You have class on Sunday?"

"Just my own work to get done. Why?"

"Give me the morning. Go on a drive with me."

She paused, as if thinking it over. "Why do you keep insisting that we 'go on a drive'? I'm starting to feel afraid of what it means."

"We've hardly spent any time together since you returned."

She rolled her head away, then turned back to him. "Okay. When do you want to leave?"

"No later than eight."

"In that case, I'll go to school today to get things done. That way I'll be free tomorrow. If Sunday doesn't work out, I'll be too busy to go anywhere until the following weekend."

She kicked the blanket off of her and rolled out of bed.

She left home an hour later, saying she wouldn't be back until dinnertime.

By late afternoon the rain had turned into a mist that hovered in the air like a transparent sponge, graying the city. He stood at the living room window, watching raindrops swell then fall from the branches of the pine tree in the front garden, knowing he should study the *kanji* he'd set out to learn for his translator's exam. His mind, however, was on the trip he would take tomorrow with Mirai.

His father-in-law had gone walking despite the rain. Had he been gone two hours already? The rain would have to be torrential for him to stay home.

Emmitt went back upstairs. As he sat down again at his small desk, which was covered in *kanji* cards and a sample translation test he planned to take in the coming days, he checked the weather forecast once more. He wanted to confirm that tomorrow would be fine for driving into the mountains.

The front door opened, and he heard Mirai and her mother talking in the *genkan*. Her mother had picked her up on her way back from shopping.

"Are we still on for tomorrow?" Emmitt said when she came into the bedroom to change clothes.

"As long as the weather clears. I thought we agreed on that."

"I was just making sure."

"Where are we driving? I need to plan what to bring."

Though her tone was nonchalant, Emmitt felt something pointed in her question.

"I've planned for us both. You don't have to bring anything."

"But where are we going?"

"Don't act so suspicious," he said. "Am I not allowed to surprise you?"

She smiled, but a moment later her expression made her seem displeased with him. "I've never been one for surprises. But maybe you're right. Maybe I am being suspicious."

"Of me? Why?"

As she answered him she tripped over her words. "I don't know. Over the last few months, I feel we've been more wrong about each other than right. And your surprises tend to catch me off-guard. They're usually too consequential for me to brush off."

Emmitt thought he could have said the same thing about her. "I wish you trusted me more."

"I wish I did, too."

Her words knocked his confidence over tomorrow's trip to the pit of his stomach. For a moment he nearly told her where they were going, but the confession seized up inside him. He wanted to follow his original plan.

She kissed his cheek before going downstairs to help her mother prepare dinner. Emmitt sat in his chair, staring at his study materials. The *kanji* cards spread out before him seemed like a challenge too great to overcome.

※

THEY WERE QUIET AS Emmitt drove toward the mountains east of Kanazawa. The tired-looking suburbs didn't bother him like before. The rice fields, old villages, and forested mountain slopes that now replaced them seemed impossibly beautiful. He wanted to explore them all.

After leaving the city limits, Mirai said, "Otōsan says you've been using the car a lot."

Emmitt was surprised that his father-in-law had told Mirai but never commented on this to him. "Was he angry?"

"No. Just noting it aloud, I think."

"I'm home more than I used to be. It only makes sense that I'd need the car sometimes."

Mirai covered her eyes as they passed a dead *tanuki* at the side of the road. Two crows were pecking at it; without flying away the birds watched them pass within a meter of them. Emmitt told her she could open her eyes again.

"Isn't this the way we went to Shiramine in March?"

He didn't answer her.

"Are we spending the day in Tsurugi?" she asked next.

Emmitt kept his eyes on the road, which had brought them to the first in a series of tunnels, still not answering her.

"In Tsurugi," she continued, "there's a stone lion museum, and between there and Shiramine there's a dinosaur museum, but there's no point being secretive about either one. Ah, there's a gondola ride nearby, and a paragliding station on the mountain. You're not taking me paragliding, I hope."

The road grew steeper as raindrops began spattering the windshield. They soon saw mist covering parts of the mountains to each side, and rain, falling heavier now, curtained off what they could see for the next few miles.

"So much for good weather," Emmitt said.

"It's not supposed to last."

When he exited the mountain road and climbed the short hill leading into Shiramine, the rain stopped. The mists began to lift off the mountains and burn away.

Mirai stared at him as they drove past the central square and *onsen*.

He turned at a corner where a shrine stood, then made a sharp right. The road narrowed as they passed several houses and a Buddhist temple with a large bell mounted before it. An empty gravel lot appeared on their left.

Emmitt pulled into a driveway, at the head of which stood a freestanding garage and a vegetable garden, and turned off the engine.

As he opened his door, he recognized the familiar sound of

flowing water. It had nearly overwhelmed him when Kimura had taken him here and he'd stood in the driveway, the house and its surroundings so perfect they were nearly unreal to him. He didn't hear Kimura when he asked Emmitt what he thought. He heard him the second time, when Kimura had walked up beside him, and Emmitt could only smile and shake his head. He replied, laughing in disbelief, "The photos you showed me did no justice to this place. Of course, I haven't been inside, but already it's one hundred times nicer than I expected." His appreciation only swelled after Kimura led him inside and they'd explored its three floors together.

Leaving the car, a hot summer breeze wrapped Emmitt with the smell of the forest. He was already sweating as he stepped onto the driveway. He knew that if he had made a mistake in buying the house, he would find out in the next few moments.

Mirai hadn't unbuckled her seatbelt by the time he reached her side of the car, and she got out with what seemed deliberate slowness. He walked with her down the short driveway and thought that during their visit in March they'd never come along this road, which meant this was the first time she'd seen the house. They paused at the front door. Emmitt took out two sets of keys and handed her one.

Tears rolled down her cheeks.

"So . . ." She turned around, then stepped to the side of the house where they could see land sloping behind it to a stream. "This is ours now, is it?"

He worried that she'd consider what he'd done unforgivably selfish—a calculated move to prevent them from moving to Tokyo. And yet inside himself he felt surge a sense of pride, and an eagerness to share this with her.

"All the signs point to that, do they?"

"More so when you don't deny it," she said softly.

He thought he detected disappointment in her voice, but her

curiosity about the house and the surroundings made him ten-
tatively reconsider this. He unlocked the front door and held it
open. Glancing inside, he knew he had done all he could to prepare for this moment. He worried she would refuse to enter, but
then she moved through the door and to the *genkan*. He followed
her inside, noting her every reaction.

The last time he left he had turned off the breaker switches
to everything but the refrigerator, and as he flipped them on
again the old fans he'd plugged in started up. The rooms here
were stifling.

He returned to Mirai, then trailed behind her as she explored
the connected rooms, opening their sliding doors and pausing
before stepping onto their tatami floors. The entire first floor was
in the traditional Japanese style—only the kitchen, toilet, and
bathroom were of modern design—which had been for Emmitt
another reason to buy the house.

The previous owner had left cheap, mismatched furniture
behind, along with old wooden toys, electric appliances, and
scattered clothes, all of which he'd consolidated in a small room
to one side. He assured her that he would throw most of it away,
but she didn't reply to this.

She passed slowly through the kitchen, then a bedroom
without windows, and into the middle of a large central room,
where she leaned her back against a white plaster wall, looking
at him obliquely. She shook her head back and forth with tear-
filled eyes.

Still shaking her head, she continued into a connecting sunroom. Pushing aside a *shōji* panel before the window, she looked
out toward the stream and the forested hillside. To Emmitt, the
view had not lost one bit of its magic.

"What made you do it?" she said. Her voice was raspy, as it
often was when she'd been crying.

"It was free. How could I not do it?"

"And that's a good reason, you think, to get a house?"

He didn't know how to answer her.

She turned away to climb to the second floor and he followed her, but at a greater distance now.

The space upstairs, having fewer walls, was more open than the floor below, its design not traditional but filled with dark wood and paneling. Light streamed inside through windows that gave a view of the houses along the street and the forested slopes on the opposite side of Shiramine.

When she climbed to the third floor—a small, unfinished space through whose front windows the mountains seemed bigger, closer, and even denser with trees—he returned downstairs. Waiting for her in the kitchen, he listened to her hesitant footsteps, picturing her as she explored. He heard her walk back and forth, and then the sound stopped.

Several minutes passed before she descended. She entered the kitchen and stood across from him. She didn't seem angry so much as perplexed, as if she couldn't understand what they were doing in this strange house.

"I don't intend for us to live here," he said. "It's where I want to be when I can get away from the city. I hope you'll feel the same one day if you don't like it now."

"The previous owner wanted nothing for this place? What was the catch?"

"There was no catch. The average square meter in town sells for next to nothing. When Kimura explained to the owner that I would free her from having to pay for its demolition, because I planned to renovate it rather than rebuild, and because I was willing to receive it 'as is,' which meant she wouldn't also have to pay to remove the years of accumulated things it contained, she admitted it was a better idea than she first thought."

She had been looking through the far door of the kitchen

into the sunroom, but she glanced at him sharply now. "Kimura helped you?"

Emmitt nodded. "He reminded her that the house, being older than twenty-four years, was by law valued at nothing, and the land was worth much less than the estimate. The owner saw that Kimura's suggestion would save her a great deal of money. He calculated her savings at two-and-a-half million yen."

"I'm relieved you paid nothing for it," she said. "But Emmitt, it's a big commitment for a house so far away."

"I'm not planning to die soon. Even if we let it sit for a few years, it will still be here waiting for us. Do you realize what a place like this would cost in America?"

"I don't care what it would cost in America," she cried. "To be honest with you, I care nothing at all about it."

"What does that mean? I can see you're disappointed, but—"

"I'm not disappointed, Emmitt." She sighed and walked to the end of the kitchen, then turned around to face him again. "I feel confused. Completely at a loss." She thought for a moment and said, "What are your plans for this place?"

"Only to make it ours by renovating it where I can. It won't ever be as nice as your parents' house, but it doesn't need to be, does it?"

She appeared resigned but not angry, and he realized that was the starting point he'd hoped she'd give him.

"It's funny this happened when it did," she went on. "I don't think I want to live in Tokyo."

Her words stunned him. "Why not?"

"I've seen how difficult it's been for people I know there, and it's become a distressing place for me recently. Also, with Asuka moving to Taipei that leaves only me to care for my parents as they get older. And then there's us."

"What about us?"

"We have a lot here already. A good life. Why risk all that?"

"But that's not how you felt before."

"That's not true. I did feel that way before." She looked at the ceiling as if thinking how to explain herself. "I know I've accused you of having your priorities out of order. But if I can accuse you of that, I realize now that you can accuse me of the same thing. What we had before made me happy, but at the same time I could see your work was making you miserable. And when you quit your job, I was afraid of how it would affect us. I didn't know what to do for you. Then I started to think I was to blame for your unhappiness, too." She stopped Emmitt from interrupting her. "If so, wouldn't it be natural for you to withdraw from me after quitting the university? I don't know if I tried to overwhelm your plans with my own; whatever I did, I wanted to protect you. I was trying to protect us."

Emmitt had walked up to her as she'd been talking, and he wrapped his arms around her now. They stayed like that, not speaking, in the house's silence.

"It smells funny in here," Mirai said, pushing her face into his chest.

"I've cleaned the kitchen twice already. I could use your help cleaning it again."

She went to open the windows, and a warm breeze blew inside. "That should help for the time being, anyway."

"You're not angry about the house?"

"I am, a little. Conflicted, really. But I'm more tired than anything." She paused and added, "I hope this will settle you."

What she wished for him would not come from having this house, but from understanding what had happened between them, and from her telling him those things she had kept to herself. He felt more relief at her openness than at anything she'd said.

"I'm hungry," she said. "Do you know where we can get something to eat?"

They walked into town to buy bento lunches.

"The house needs fixing," Emmitt said as they ate. "But there are no holes in the walls and the floors aren't collapsing. A thorough cleaning would make it livable until wintertime."

After lunch they walked behind the house. Together they looked down an embankment at a tree-lined stream. The greenness around them was both deep and bright in the sunshine.

Emmitt suggested they return to Kanazawa.

"What were all the boxes in the *genkan?*" she said.

"Things I brought from home."

"Why don't we unpack them before going back? And maybe clean one or two rooms."

Emmitt welcomed the idea. He wanted to make the house inviting so she would want to spend time together here.

For the next two hours they cleaned, hung pictures on the walls, unpacked a new coffeemaker, and stocked the bathroom with toiletries and clean towels.

On the way home, Mirai suggested introducing themselves to their neighbors. "We'll need gifts, of course. Maybe next weekend I'll make small flower arrangements."

Her mood had transformed, Emmitt thought. He was grateful for this, but how long would it last?

They returned to Kanazawa in the late afternoon. Mirai couldn't believe Emmitt hadn't told her parents about the house, and she wanted to do so now.

"They'll want to see it," she said. "But I'd like to make it more presentable before they do."

Halfway home her head fell back against the seat. When he glanced at her he saw her smiling, staring toward the mountains that trailed off to the side of the highway.

❋

IN THE SMALL, WALLED garden in front of the house, her father stood atop a short ladder trimming their old pine tree while her mother knelt at the end of the stone walkway, sweeping up fallen pine needles, weeds she'd pulled, and the shed skins of cicadas she'd plucked from the wall and tree. As her parents looked up at them, Mirai dangled in front of her the keys to the new house.

"What are you doing?" her mother said. "What are those?"

"Emmitt has something to tell you," Mirai said. She gestured for him to share their news.

This wasn't how Emmitt envisioned announcing the house to them, but he decided it would be better to get it out of the way. "I bought a house in Shiramine."

His father-in-law grabbed a branch to steady himself. "What did he say?" After he stepped to the ground, he and his wife looked from Emmitt to Mirai and gaped at her.

"He bought a house in Shiramine?" his mother-in-law stammered.

"The house was free," Emmitt explained, as if discussing money might be some kind of relief to them. "It's in good condition, but I still plan to renovate it."

"You're moving to Shiramine?" Mirai's father asked her.

"Of course not. I guess you'd call it a second home."

"Do you have a first home you haven't told us about either?"

"I'm pretty sure this one is enough for now," Emmitt said.

"Why would you do such a thing?" his mother-in-law said. "And when did this happen—while Mirai was away?" When Emmitt nodded she said, "Why didn't you tell us what you were doing?"

"I wanted it to be a surprise."

Mirai's parents laughed in disbelief.

"Well, you accomplished that," his mother-in-law said. "I need to sit down." She lowered herself onto a rung of the ladder her husband had stepped off of.

Mirai's father was watching Mirai with a slight grin. "You look more pleased than I would have imagined."

"It's not a bad place, Otōsan. It's not bad at all."

"Well, what are we doing just standing here?" his father-in-law said. "This calls for a celebration."

Mirai's mother looked unconvinced, but she got to her feet and followed her husband inside.

"In the spirit of not spending much," Mirai said as Emmitt slid the front door shut, "let's go have *yakitori* and beer."

"It should be up to Emmitt. Why don't we let him decide?"

"I'm fine with that," Emmitt said.

He thought her parents would have reacted differently to his having bought a house in the mountains. He had expected them to be disappointed—and perhaps they were. He remembered how differently they had acted when he was planning to lease the Kurokawas' *machiya*. Back then, it seemed that nothing he did could please them.

15

SEVERAL DAYS LATER MIRAI had to fill in for a school chaperone to a student ikebana exhibition in Toyama City. She'd not been given advance notice, but after many absences from school over the last half-year her position had become tenuous. "I have no choice," she told Emmitt. He drove her early to the school on the day of the exhibition and waited for her to board the chartered bus.

That afternoon, after several hours of studying, Emmitt went to jog along the Sai. On his way, a police car passed him. As it drove by, he spotted someone in the back seat but thought nothing of it. So little crime existed in Kanazawa that the sight barely registered with him. The police car turned at the corner from which Emmitt had come.

The early September coolness invigorated him and he doubled his normal run. An hour later, resting on the opposite riverbank, he went to soak in a public bath a short walk away. He called his mother-in-law's phone, and when she didn't answer he left a message saying he wouldn't eat at home that evening. He didn't return until 8 p.m. By then, the drama that had played out in his absence was over.

"I'm home," he said as he came inside. When no one replied, he repeated himself.

His father-in-law sat before the TV drinking sake while his mother-in-law ironed clothes in the narrow space behind the sofa. Someone had muted the TV, and the only sound was the steam iron's hissing.

"Did I interrupt something?" he asked. When no one

answered, he said, "Did you get my message? I headed to the baths at Manten-no-Yū after running." He laughed and added, "I had to change back into my running clothes, so I need another shower now."

When still no one replied, he wondered if he had angered them. Had he overlooked a special day, or done something to ruin their dinner? "What's wrong?" he said.

"You're going to wish you were in your mountain house," his mother-in-law said. "Or that you'd married into a different family."

"Why's that?"

"Ask Otōsan," she answered with false cheer.

Expressionless, Emmitt's father-in-law unmuted the TV. Loud chatter filled the room, and he reduced the volume to a level they could talk over.

Emmitt sat catty-corner to his father-in-law. Arrayed on the coffee table were pamphlets about the police and hospital services in Kanazawa. A filled-out form lay beside them. Behind him, his mother-in-law cleared her throat as he pulled it closer.

It was a police report; his father-in-law's name was written across the top. Emmitt glanced at his mother-in-law, but she wouldn't lift her eyes from her ironing.

"Did something happen when I was out?" He turned to his father-in-law. "Did you get in some kind of fight?"

His father-in-law calmly chewed the inside of his mouth, his eyes glued to the TV.

"He's sixty-six years old," his mother-in-law answered, "and he got into a fight. According to the police, he attacked a visiting baseball team from Kyushu." She laughed, as if at the absurdity of it. "He claims they provoked him."

Struggling to process this, Emmitt said, "Where?"

"In front of a statue on Eki-Mae Street, between the station and Ōmichō Market."

His father-in-law finally spoke. "I did the right thing confronting those boys. The police thought so, too. That's why they only gave me a warning."

"I wish you'd stop drawing these statues once and for all. You'll make people think you're perverted."

"I should be so lucky it were true," he growled. "Perversion drives every artist who's worth a damn."

As they argued, Emmitt pieced together more or less what had happened that afternoon.

At an intersection half a block behind the M'za department store, where his father-in-law had been visiting the statue of a nude titled *Promontory*, a group of young men in team jackets were walking together when they came upon him sketching. The traffic light there had turned red, forcing them to wait at the crosswalk. Immediately they spotted the statue and began gawking at its nudity. Several boys photographed it, and soon all of them crowded around it, posing and laughing, one even reaching up as if to touch the statue's crotch. When the light turned green they were too busy acting lewdly to notice they could cross. When it again turned red, stranding them a second time, Emmitt's father-in-law grew enraged.

It would have been suicidal to fight even one of these baseball players, much less their whole team, yet that didn't stop him from approaching a young man who'd been caressing the statue's leg and slapping him. The young man reeled back. Emmitt's father-in-law lunged forward and grabbed his throat with both hands. His teammates yanked Emmitt's father-in-law off and threw him to the ground. Two of them kicked him, but others intervened and stood looking down at their assailant, some yelling at him, some videoing him, some finally checking to see if he was hurt.

A small police station sat across the street. Almost immediately two officers ran through the oncoming traffic to where the fracas had occurred. Although a few baseball players had videoed the assault, their recordings had also captured their teammates in unflattering circumstances. Still, they showed Emmitt's father-in-law attacking the young man.

The police questioned him for an hour. Rather than arrest him, they issued him a verbal warning and, after finding on his phone dozens of photos of the statue, and a sketchbook with drawings of it, suggested he stay clear of the intersection from now on.

When they took him home, Emmitt's mother-in-law was waiting for him. The police had phoned her about the assault. She showed them more pictures her husband had drawn. As they flipped through them, she berated her husband for his unhealthy interest in the city's statues. The police remarked that none of the drawings seemed lewd, and when she asked if they looked like her, they paused and said in some embarrassment that they did. The drawings persuaded them that Emmitt's father-in-law had artistic talent, and that his behavior wasn't a matter of perversion or mental illness. They respected his claim that he'd been defending a subject of his work from the poor behavior of the young man he'd attacked. "I was protecting on my own the dignity that a treasure of the city deserves. Am I to be punished for that? Would you not have tried to stop them yourselves had you witnessed the same? Your station sits across the street, and not one of you came by in all that time to intervene." Unsure how to respond to the tables being turned on them, they bowed in confused apology. When they left, they weren't sure whether to thank him or issue a final reprimand. In the end, they awkwardly tried to do both. Emmitt's father-in-law felt his conduct had been vindicated, but his wife remained furious with him.

Emmitt listened to all of this as if from some distance, never once joining the conversation, never attempting to take sides. When his mother-in-law stopped talking, Emmitt said, "Why did you ask the police if the statues looked like you?"

A residual anger over what had happened shone in her eyes. "I was trying to show the police that he had artistic aims, that he wasn't merely drawing the nudes out of perversity."

"But why do his drawings always have some connection to you?"

"He's cruel, that's why."

His father-in-law had been studiously ignoring them until now, but at hearing this he looked up at her and shook his head.

"Mirai told me you were once a sculptors' model."

"I thought you knew that," she said. "Anyway, I wasn't the model for the statue he drew today. And I wasn't the model for any of those he drew before that."

"I don't understand."

"There's nothing to understand, Emmitt. It was a long time ago."

Turning again to his father-in-law, Emmitt saw he had no intention of adding to the conversation. Emmitt asked if Mirai and Asuka knew what happened.

"Not yet. It's better for me to tell them."

Her husband still said nothing. He accepted no blame for his behavior, and thus had no feeling one way or the other what anyone did.

"Please do it soon," Emmitt said. "I don't want Mirai thinking I kept something like this from her."

His mother-in-law nodded distractedly.

"Your iron's smoking. I think it's burning Otōsan's shirt."

She pulled the shirt off the ironing board and tossed it atop a pile of clothes on the sofa.

Emmitt left his parents-in-law alone to work things out. He wanted to talk to his father-in-law more, to ask him privately about the drawings, but it would be better to let the air clear first. It felt like an excuse, however, not to do something he felt he should.

※

EARLY THE NEXT MORNING, a trash removal service appeared on the street beneath Emmitt's window. The doorbell rang and he heard his father-in-law open the door. Emmitt had gone to bed before Mirai's parents, so he didn't know that last night his father-in-law had dragged the boxes containing his artwork to the *genkan*, where the workers could easily remove them today.

At first Emmitt thought the workers were taking away old clothes to a donation facility, but when he realized what the boxes were he protested.

"Why are you doing this? They'll destroy them—put them in an incinerator so there will be no trace of them afterward." When he saw his words had no effect he added, "These aren't just pictures you've made; they're part of your past."

"That's why I'm letting them go. It seems I've been trying without success to return to the past through them. But they became a part of me many years ago, when I created them. Those memories will ruin me if I let them."

"How can the past ruin you? You're not a criminal. You've done nothing wrong."

His father-in-law shook his head, refusing to answer.

When Emmitt turned his protest to his mother-in-law, she told him it was her husband's decision.

"Understand, Emmitt, I would never ask him to destroy

them. From the beginning, I only wanted him to stop conflating those statues with me."

"But he's throwing away all his work, not just what he did the last few months."

"Perhaps this will free him to do something better with his time. He needs to find new meaning in his life."

"But didn't drawing allow him to do that?"

"Of course. But he can always draw something else. I've suggested still lifes and images from nature. Also, there are an unlimited number of hobbies he could get involved in . . ."

The workers finished quickly, lingering only for Emmitt's mother-in-law to sign a form.

✳

EMMITT'S FATHER-IN-LAW STOPPED DRAWING. He continued his daily walks, even extending them at times, but he no longer brought his sketchpad and drawing pencils with him and Emmitt never saw again the easel and paints he occasionally took on clement days. It was as if the incident with the baseball players had drained him of his vitality.

Mirai had been upset to learn of her father's fight and seemed to think it was better to let him work things out on his own. If he needed anything, wouldn't he say so?

A week later Emmitt asked Mirai to help him buy online what her father would need to draw and paint again.

"Let him come back to it on his own," she said. "It will backfire if you force it on him."

"But he was forced to give it up."

"No, he wasn't. When he realized he was hurting Okāsan, he quit."

"Having a creative outlet was good for him. Look at him now.

He feels he has nothing. Even less than he had before resuming his art a few months ago."

"But he doesn't have nothing. He has what any other person has. He just needs to find his way to something new."

"The least we could do is encourage him. Doesn't it seem like he's simply thrown in the towel?"

"What's the point of encouraging him if he'll only behave the same way? In any case, it's his choice."

Emmitt raised the issue again two days later, this time with Mirai and her mother. His mother-in-law agreed with him but said that encouraging him wouldn't do any good.

"I bring it up with him every night before we sleep. I tell him, 'Why can't you select a different subject? Why does it have to be those statues in the city? Or your remembrances of me from when we were young?'"

He imagined them talking to each other from separate beds, and how much harder that distance made it to reach each other. He asked why he didn't draw her as she was now.

"I won't sit for him, that's why. Once we had Mirai, I stopped modeling for him. I've told him to find different models, nude ones even, and I don't mind him paying a fee for their time. But he's stubborn. I can't be bothered with such foolishness, frankly. I really do want him to continue painting. He has rare talent that could have taken him places when he was younger and might still take him places now. And he also has a vision, disagreeable though it is."

That night Emmitt entered the kitchen to refill a glass of water. It was after midnight, an hour since his parents-in-law went to bed. As he stood at the sink, he saw someone in the living room, sitting on the sofa in the dark. He knew it wasn't Mirai, because she was upstairs lying in bed.

"Otōsan?" he said.

"He's asleep."

Now that his mother-in-law had spoken, he could see the shape of the body before him was hers. "What are you doing here?"

"I'm not tired." Her voice was just above a whisper.

Emmitt washed and dried his glass, then joined her. He sat in the chair beside the sofa. Almost without thinking, he voiced what had been on his mind for many days.

"Why did Otōsan become so obsessed with the statues?"

He knew that his parents-in-law were keeping something from him and Mirai, and until now he thought he shouldn't persist about issues he wasn't welcome to know about. But things had changed, and he no longer cared about being polite. He was perplexed that no one else seemed worried about his father-in-law.

He waited in the darkness for her answer. He was thinking of how to rephrase his question when she replied.

"You know already that I used to model when I was young."

"Yes, but I know nothing more than the fact itself."

"I see. Well, I suppose that Mirai doesn't know more, either. If she did, I'm sure you would have asked her already."

"I've asked her many times. Asuka, too. Is there a reason they know nothing about it, and aren't even curious? Is there something you want no one to know about?"

"That seems to be Otōsan's feeling—that I'm hiding something. Neither Mirai nor Asuka is interested, apparently."

"What do you mean that it seems to be Otōsan's feeling?"

"He's convinced I'm keeping something from him." She took a deep breath and shook her head, as if in exasperation. "The truth is that I used to want to be an artist myself. I had a certain amount of talent, I suppose, but growing up no one ever encouraged me to develop it. I don't think I had what was necessary to succeed, not like Asuka and Mirai, and not like Otōsan, who gave up on his talents for a normal career—for a conventional life to provide for us. Though in the beginning I tried to support him, giving him half of my own meager salary and secreting to him supplies that my artist friends didn't need or had thrown away. I offered to support his widowed mother for a time, too, even though I could hardly offer her anything, but he was too ashamed to let me." She paused and said, "I grew up poor and moved around more than most people my age. And my parents were always fighting, always getting into some kind of trouble. So when I was old enough to take charge of my life, a conventional life was what I wanted.

"I started modeling in high school. I was seventeen. And I guess I modeled until I no longer needed the money; I think I was twenty-five then. You've probably connected the dots and realize Otōsan's interest in the nudes around the city has something to do with my modeling."

She looked toward the hallway, as if someone might be there eavesdropping. But aside from the refrigerator humming and the occasional car passing by, the house was silent. She continued, her voice even quieter than before. "My modeling was rather scandalous back then, which is why I agreed to do it only if the artists protected my identity. When they asked me how, I told them to give me a different face. And they did, but not always to the extent I expected.

"Otōsan's convinced that I modeled for one or two of the statues in the city, the ones he's been drawing. He found no fewer than fifteen on his walks, but he only sketched a handful— the ones he thought were most likely me. In the beginning he used to show them to me and ask if I knew the artist. More often than not, if the artist was from Kanazawa and worked during the time I modeled, I did. But the years the sculptures were created

almost never matched the years I modeled. Undeterred, he suggested the artists could have finished the sculptures several years
after starting them. He said plenty of artists also work from memory, or try to improve on works they made earlier. He refused to
believe that I couldn't have modeled for perhaps half the city's
statues. How can you argue with that? So, as much as possible, I
ignored his efforts to draw. Just like I did when we first married
and he wanted me to sit for him."

"But why did it have to be you?"

This time she paused for half a minute. Emmitt saw he had
touched on something she wasn't ready to open up to him about.
At the height of his discomfort, though, she answered.

"I had a relationship with an artist before I met Otōsan. He
was young and creative, brimming with the vital forces of life.
He was a close friend of Otōsan, too, even though their person-
alities were polar opposites. I knew from the outset that Otōsan
was reliable—it was his most attractive feature, enough to lure
me into a relationship with him instead—but I never felt that
way with . . ." She paused again, twisting in her seat. "But there's
no point in dwelling on that. He died shortly after Otōsan and
I married. My perception is that Otōsan's obsession with the
statues has more to do with him than with me, which is one reason I find his work so disagreeable. I've never quite understood
it."

Mirai opened the bedroom door upstairs, startling them
both. They listened to her climb downstairs.

"Do you have any plans to translate Kyōka now?" his mother-
in-law said to Emmitt as Mirai shuffled into the room and sat
beside her. Emmitt's hesitation allowed Mirai to ask what she
was still doing up.

"Otōsan was snoring louder than usual."

"I thought you were sleeping," Emmitt said to Mirai.

"I lay down, thinking you'd come back soon. But when you didn't, I went looking for you. What are you two talking about?"

Emmitt and his mother-in-law looked at each other. Emmitt wasn't sure what to say.

"This and that," her mother said. "We don't get many chances to talk, do we, Emmitt?"

"I suppose not."

She lifted her hands and let them fall back into her lap. "Well, why don't you two go to bed. I'm afraid I'll fall asleep here if I don't go back now."

"You should," Mirai said. "You're going to be exhausted tomorrow if you don't."

"You're right. Thank you."

Her mother bid them goodnight again and left the room. They heard her bedroom door open and click shut.

Mirai tugged Emmitt to his feet and hugged him for a long time. "Let's go. You can tell me what you and Okāsan talked about in the morning."

He followed her upstairs. As he brushed his teeth, Emmitt thought about his conversation with his mother-in-law. Perhaps it wasn't that strange that Mirai and Asuka knew so little about her modeling. Even after hearing what he had tonight, he knew much had been left out. He didn't feel it was his business to know more than what he'd already learned, but it seemed the only way to understand what motivated his father-in-law's behavior. It also seemed important to know their past so that he and Mirai, despite having different lives than her parents, didn't repeat it.

By the time he'd finished brushing his teeth, Mirai was sound asleep.

He left the room as quietly as possible and returned to the living room. He sat on the sofa, wide awake. After five minutes the door opened down the hallway and Mirai's mother came and stood across from him.

"We didn't finish talking. You have another question, don't you?"

Emmitt stared at the figure of his mother-in-law. In the dim light filtering in from outside, her nightgown was transparent, revealing the outline of a half-naked body beneath it. "Where is the statue Otōsan's looking for?"

"Why should I say? Assuming that I even know."

"I won't tell anyone."

She was quiet for a moment. He saw her turn toward her bedroom, then to the stairs where Mirai was sleeping. "It's in a small park on Mt. Utatsu, between Tenjin Bridge and Renshōji. At one time you could see Hakusan from where it stood. The park became overgrown, and the city decided to redo it and took the statue down. Otōsan knows nothing about it, and I've never told him." When Emmitt didn't say anything, she went on. "For maybe a year I used to go there every day to take care of it, but I stopped when I realized how meaningless it was. Although I was suffering, I realized that one can't bring people back. And I had someone who loved me, who was still very much alive, who had no idea what I did while he was at work. I guess I turned from death to life, from fantasy to the reality of all I actually had."

"And that's why you won't model for Otōsan any more . . ."

"What I've let go, he's kept inside himself all these years."

She stifled a yawn that shook her entire body. Without another word she turned back to the hallway and walked to her room. Emmitt sat there for a long time, trying to fit together the pieces of what his mother-in-law had told him.

※

THE FOLLOWING EVENING EMMITT was filling boxes with more things to bring to Shiramine when his father-in-law knocked on his door, which was open already. Emmitt sat up and looked at him.

"You're planning to take a lot there, I see."

"Just some cleaning supplies, study materials for my translation test next week, and most of the Kyōka books Okāsan gave me."

"You're still planning to read them?"

"I've come back to the idea of translating something that's not yet in English. His stories are worth the struggle."

His father-in-law glanced around the room. "Are you heading up there soon?"

"A public bus leaves from Korinbō in the morning."

"You can't possibly take all that on a bus. Use the car if you want. Okāsan and I won't need it."

"I'll be there all weekend."

"You can still use it. But under one condition. You have to take me with you."

Emmitt didn't mind his father-in-law accompanying him. Even if he didn't want to help Emmitt work on the house, there was plenty in town to occupy him, especially the hot spring baths and the vending machines around town that sold beer, sake, and whiskey. He could also walk to his heart's content.

"Of course," Emmitt said. "I have a bottle of local sake there that I've been waiting for a special occasion to open. I hope you don't mind drinking it out of coffee mugs."

His father-in-law chuckled. "I'll bring proper sake cups to use."

"Can you be ready before seven?"

His father-in-law nodded, lingering in the doorway. Emmitt was aware of him watching him pack.

"Where are your climbing things?"

"My climbing things?"

"I thought you wanted to climb Hakusan this year."

"I've been too busy lately to give it much thought."

"You're not very busy. In your day-to-day life, I mean."

Emmitt looked through the door beside his father-in-law and considered what he had said. "I don't think it's a good idea to climb it together. You know everyone opposes it."

"They oppose most things I try to do." He smiled when he said this, but Emmitt sensed a bitterness behind the words.

"Maybe so, but in this case they have a point. If you want to climb Hakusan, wouldn't it be better to go with a group? It would be safer that way, too. Neither of us has much experience."

"The way everyone reacts when I talk about the mountain, you'd think I was a child."

"I'm sorry, Otōsan."

His father-in-law waved away the apology. "I understand. I've been a nuisance, I suppose, as usual."

"That's not what I meant."

He nodded and gave a last look around the room. "I'll see you in the morning, then. Good night."

"Good night."

After he'd finished packing, Emmitt showered and went downstairs. "I'm going to bed," he told Mirai.

"I'll be there soon."

She and her mother were looking over Mirai's ikebana sketchbook and talking. "Okāsan and I want to visit an event at Shirayama-hime Shrine tomorrow," Mirai said. "A special shuttle runs there from the station in the afternoon."

Emmitt had heard on a TV news story that the shrine, halfway between Kanazawa and Shiramine, would hold a large festival to celebrate the 1,300th anniversary of the first pilgrimage to Haku-san. When he'd asked his mother-in-law about it, she told him that 1,300 years ago a female deity claiming to be the embodi-ment of the mountain visited the monk Taichō in a dream. If he wished to meet her, she instructed him, he had to ascend Haku-san, and at its peak he would find her. As promised, he climbed the mountain and met the goddess Shirayama-hime at the top. She is enshrined there now with Izanami and Izanagi—the orig-inal spirit-gods of Japan, of the Japanese people, and, according to Shinto doctrine, of heaven and the universe itself. Hakusan is sacred because it's said to be where the original gods dwell.

Mirai explained that there had been celebrations of this throughout the year, but tomorrow's would be the biggest of all.

"You and Otōsan could join us there after spending the morning in Shiramine."

"He told you our plans, did he?"

"He's excited about the trip," Mirai's mother said.

"Afterward," Mirai said, "you could drive all of us to Shira-mine to spend the night. Then on Sunday we can clean the house with you and return to Kanazawa whenever you're ready."

"I wasn't expecting everyone to join me. But it'd be nice to go up together."

But what he expected least of all was what she had offered him. She had said no only six weeks ago when he'd suggested finally meeting her in Tokyo, and now she was organizing a fam-ily trip to the house he'd bought in Shiramine.

He would have liked to make improvements on it before his in-laws visited, but their enthusiasm to see it right away was sat-isfying. He told himself that as they came up again and again they would remember what he'd started with and how much more liv-able he had made it.

He envisioned going to Shiramine often now and hoped that Mirai and her family would treat the work he did there no differently than his former work at the university.

It occurred to him that if Mirai started doing ikebana in town, he might be willing to teach English there. The next time he went up, he would need to look for a local English-language school.

16

A REGIONAL SUMO TOURNAMENT, held annually at Yasaka Shrine in Shiramine for more than a century, was scheduled for the weekend Mirai's family planned to visit. Emmitt first learned about it from his father-in-law on the drive there.

"The participants will be amateurs," he added, "but it's better that way. It's a purer version of sumo. Except for the rituals, I imagine it will be closer to what sumo was like two thousand years ago when it originated."

His father-in-law slept most of the way to Shiramine. When they came upon the town, Emmitt exited at a small bridge near his house. At the second street they approached he slowed down to see the sumo ring. Before Yasaka Shrine, four wooden pillars rose from each corner of the earthen square where the organizers had built the ring. It was outlined with hand-braided bales of straw; purple fabric descended a meter from its top beams. To the side was a long, open tent for seating, and behind the ring, scaffolding from which hand-painted sponsor advertisements hung. The backdrop was of the shrine and a forest climbing a hill. His father-in-law nodded as if to approve of what he saw.

Emmitt turned and in a few hundred meters stopped before his driveway. The morning sunlight covered the house like a fresh coat of paint, its brightness making the rusted siding less conspicuous. The house was larger than his father-in-law's, and the background of forest like a painting. The more accustomed he got to the idea that the house was his and Mirai's, the more he appreciated it, blemishes and all.

"Here we are."

His father-in-law leaned to the side and looked up. "It's more of a house than I expected, considering it cost you nothing. But it may be hard to sell in the future. You may be stuck with it for the rest of your life."

Emmitt had considered this before buying it, and it had felt like an incentive to proceed. He'd wanted to complete the transfer of property to his name before anyone could question what he was doing.

As soon as they entered the house, his father-in-law said, "Maybe you should give me a tour of the place."

Emmitt walked him through the first floor before taking him upstairs. His father-in-law asked no questions as they passed from room to room, though he looked at everything carefully, as if seeking some flaw Emmitt hadn't yet seen. His reticence could mean anything, Emmitt thought.

The wooden steps to the third floor were unstable, but Emmitt and his father-in-law could see most of it from the floor below. When they came back to the first floor his father-in-law chose a bedroom to sleep in.

"It's better that Okāsan and I be close to the exit in case this place collapses during the night."

"You can sleep at an inn if you're afraid."

He waved away Emmitt's suggestion.

Emmitt brought his father-in-law's small suitcase into the room he'd chosen and asked if he wanted a tour of the outside, too.

"I'll look around later. I feel like walking through Shiramine now. I'm curious to see how it's changed."

"People are friendly here. I'm sure you can start a conversation with whoever you run into."

"Don't worry if I don't come back immediately. If I find a nice spot I may sit and read for a while." He pulled a small book from his jacket pocket.

"Did you find that here?"

"I brought it from home. It's a collection of Noh plays."

Upon hearing this, Emmitt recognized the book his father-in-law often read.

"I'll get out of your way now. If I can help with anything, let me know."

"How are you going to help if you leave?"

"I always thought that leaving was a kind of help." He headed for the front door and stepped outside.

Emmitt went to find the futon sets he'd found in the house and had dry-cleaned in Kanazawa. He then began to arrange for himself a small study in the corner of the second floor. The previous owner had left behind a desk and bookshelves, which Emmitt pushed before a window.

As he stood there looking outside, a figure emerged in the distance, walking along a street. Dwarfed by the mountains, and even the town's main temple he passed in front of, he was reading as he walked. Emmitt felt like shouting to his father-in-law, to have him turn and see him in his own house, but the peacefulness of the morning was too perfect to disturb.

❈

AT NOON, EMMITT'S FATHER-IN-LAW came home and said he was hungry. Emmitt led him to a small restaurant in the town center. Inside, they sat around a wooden hearth, the border of which served as a countertop.

They ordered set meals of fried river fish and mountain

vegetables. As Emmitt got up to pour tea from a thermos, his father-in-law asked the old woman who'd taken their orders for beer and sake.

A minute later she brought over a porcelain sake carafe and cup. "You want beer, too, don't you? A large or small bottle?"

"May as well make it big."

A young man brought their meals out. The old woman followed, holding a beer and small glass. Emmitt poured for his father-in-law.

His father-in-law lifted his cup: "To your life in the mountains."

They fell into a comfortable silence as they ate and drank, and Emmitt realized that he felt accepted by his father-in-law in a different way here. Having a home of his own, and having acquired it without anyone's help—not even Mirai's—seemed to have put them on an equal footing. He also sensed that his father-in-law admired him for what he'd done.

Emmitt glanced at him as he raised his head and gazed out the window. He did this several times during their meal.

"You keep looking toward the mountains," Emmitt remarked, "as if they're distracting you."

"They remind me of a story in that book I took on my walk." His father-in-law leaned back to survey their half-eaten meals. "Do you know the Noh play *Yamanba*?"

Emmitt knew it because Mirai's parents had seen it two or three times since he'd married Mirai and moved into their house. "I've heard of it but don't know the story."

"Zeami wrote it. Perhaps you've heard of him?"

This time Emmitt nodded. "He was a famous playwright five or six hundred years ago."

"In my opinion, *Yamanba* is one of his most important plays. And maybe one of the least understood."

He explained that in the play a group of itinerant dancers meet an old mountain woman—the *yamanba*—on their way to a temple in Etchū province. After learning that the travelers are entertainers, the mountain crone asks a young lady in the group to sing a song about a woman such as herself. It's only when this traveler begins singing that it becomes clear the song's subject is the very *yamanba* before them.

"But the old woman isn't just any mountain crone. She herself isn't real, not in a human sense. She embodies the human condition, but also nature itself—all of the universe, in fact. She leads her life according to nature and its rhythms. She exists, she says, because the Buddha exists. When she speaks of Buddha's law, we're compelled to care about what she says."

He removed the book from his jacket pocket and pushed it toward Emmitt. "Rather than ask me what it means, it's better if you read it sometime."

"I'm not likely to understand it well."

"You will if you put the effort into it. But don't shrug it off like Mirai and Asuka. They think it's a simple story from feudal times, boring and irrelevant to their lives. But you can be sure that the *yamanba* exists. She is stuck forever in the mountains, her transmigration incomplete, contemplating Buddha's Law. That's her fate, to have a destination without end. Some literary scholars say she's the most sympathetic figure in the Noh canon, even though she's not human. When you understand the play's deeper meaning, you can't help but be moved."

His father-in-law filled an empty water glass with sake, which held more than twice what his sake cup did. Between generous sips from it he said, "It's not easy to follow, but Okāsan and I both like it. Maybe it's because we're getting old and have come to care about these things."

"Mirai won't see it?"

His father-in-law laughed. "We invited her once. That was enough for us to decide never to do so again. But it would be good for you to see it. And Mirai, too. Although you're a foreigner, you have a better appreciation for Kanazawa culture than her. She could learn from you."

After lunch, his father-in-law said he wanted to go for a long walk and then visit the *onsen* in town. Emmitt reminded him that they would leave for Shirayama-hime Shrine at five o'clock to meet Mirai and her mother.

His father-in-law nodded and turned in the opposite direction of town. Emmitt was about to call out that there was nothing of interest that way, but then thought he might want exactly that.

※

AT FIVE O'CLOCK, EMMITT'S father-in-law still wasn't home, so Emmitt left the house with the door unlocked and drove to Shirayama-hime Shrine.

He found the shrine and parking lot teeming with people, and it took several minutes to approach the large *torii* at the entrance where Mirai had told him to come. She and her mother were standing among hundreds of visitors, behind a policeman attempting to direct traffic. Emmitt managed to pull in front of them, nearly hitting several people hurrying from the shrine grounds.

Mirai and her mother climbed into the back seat.

"I never imagined so many people would come," Mirai said. "But it was worth the crowds, wasn't it?"

Her mother nodded, then turned to Emmitt. "I'm sorry you had to take care of Otōsan all this time. Where is he now?"

"He didn't get back before I left. I assume he's at the hot spring."

Emmitt proceeded toward the exit and was soon back on the road to Shiramine. Mirai and her mother described what they'd seen at the shrine. Mirai's mood was more positive than at either time they'd come up before, and better in general than in the last several weeks. Was she proud of hosting her parents? Was she proud of him?

At night, aside from the main square where the visitor center, two inns, and Shiramine Onsen were, streetlights were sparse and barely lit the town. He drove slowly to the sumo ring, and as he turned there he put his foot on the brakes.

Mirai gasped. "It's that man again."

In the middle of the street, illumined by the car's headlights, the blind masseur they had seen at the *ryokan* in April was walking toward them, tapping his cane from side to side.

Emmitt flickered his headlights, but when the man didn't react Emmitt revved his engine. "He must be completely blind." The masseur turned finally and made his way to the side of the road.

Emmitt waited for him to pass before continuing toward the house.

As they stepped out of the car, the masseur's whistle pierced the air.

Emmitt's father-in-law was sitting on the step before the entrance to the house. All around swirled the droning of cicadas and the deep chirruping of frogs. Without moving from where he sat, he welcomed them back.

Mirai asked him if he'd seen the blind masseur.

"He just finished giving me a massage. I suppose you saw him walking up the road."

"You let him give you a massage?"

"Why not? I heard him playing a Noh libretto on a pair of hand drums as he walked past the house. I asked him what play the libretto was from, and we started talking about Noh. For

someone who can't watch a performance, he was more knowl-
edgeable than I'd expected."

Mirai lifted her hands to her face, as if to hide from what he'd
told her.

"Emmitt said you spent all afternoon at the *onsen*," his wife
said.

"Not all afternoon. I talked to people here and there—resi-
dents, parents of the kids in the sumo tournament tomorrow, a
few mountain climbers. Why didn't we come to Shiramine more
often before?"

To Emmitt he said, "Join me in town when you get a chance."
He stood up and with a bottle of sake Emmitt hadn't seen started
walking into town.

"We just got back and you're leaving?" Mirai said.

"Have you eaten yet, Otōsan? I brought homemade bento,
you know."

"I ate some dried squid earlier. I'm not hungry now."

They watched him walk away, the sound of his wooden *geta*
ringing in the street.

"Where did he get those wooden sandals?" Mirai said.

"He found them inside."

"But someone else wore them first. It's unseemly, isn't it?"

"Let him be," Mirai's mother told her. "I'll buy him a pair
tomorrow if we can find some."

As they entered the house, she looked around and exclaimed
in wonder.

"You paid nothing for all this?"

"There were transaction fees, and registering the property
wasn't free, but the sale itself cost me nothing."

Mirai told Emmitt he could go drinking with her father if he
wanted to. "But eat one of the bento before you go. Okāsan will
be upset if two go uneaten."

"Shouldn't I give Okāsan a tour of the house?"

"I can do it. Wouldn't you rather be out drinking? With the sumo tournament tomorrow, you and Otōsan probably won't be the only ones."

He apologized to his mother-in-law for leaving as soon as she'd arrived, but she told him not to worry.

He wolfed down half his dinner as Mirai and her mother slowly made their way around the first-floor rooms.

"I'll eat the other half when I'm back," he called to them.

For some reason, he didn't want to leave his father-in-law to drink alone in Shiramine.

As soon as he left the house, he turned around to look at it again. He could hardly believe that Mirai and her parents were here to spend the night. He realized that he would have felt disappointed if they'd shown their disapproval, but that they'd not been critical of the house, nor of him, was almost unexpected.

He hurried toward the center of town, elated.

17

AT 5:30 A.M. A golden light spread over the peaks encircling Shiramine. Sunshine poured through the second-floor windows, and birds fluttered noisily in the trees. Lying on the futon beside Mirai, who had pulled the cover over her head, Emmitt wrapped himself around her. He felt torn between getting up and spending the whole morning like this beside her, stretched out in the warm sunlight. He felt he'd never known peace or bliss like this.

He heard sounds from the kitchen, and soon the smell of coffee wafted into the room. Reluctantly, he dressed and went downstairs.

His parents-in-law were eating breakfast before the alcove in the largest Japanese-style room in the house. Here, too, sunshine cascaded through the long windows, one of which they had slid open.

"We helped ourselves to coffee and bread," his mother-in-law said as he stood in the doorway. "I hope you don't mind."

"Why would I? I've been helping myself to your food for years. Were you comfortable last night?"

"More than if we stayed at an expensive inn. I felt at home. Did you hear Otōsan in the middle of the night?"

"No." Emmitt assumed she meant he had snored. "I slept deeply."

"He got up at four o'clock. I told him not to walk through town, but he went out anyway. Thanks to his restlessness, I hardly slept."

"You went out at four?" Emmitt said, turning to his father-in-law.

"I was wide awake."

He knew his father-in-law sometimes had trouble sleeping, but even so, he didn't know what to say. "Did you see anything?"

"I heard monks chanting at the door of a temple. But then the mountain cold hit me and I kept walking."

Sounds of viewing tents and food booths being assembled up the street trickled through the window. Eventually Mirai came downstairs. She hadn't heard her father during the night, either.

At eight o'clock Emmitt gathered his study materials and went behind the house, where he'd set up a small bench at the edge of his property. The trees rising from beside the stream shaded him, and he studied there for over an hour as Mirai and her mother swept, vacuumed, and beat the futons in the windows upstairs.

Mirai called to him to say that the sumo event would be starting soon.

As he came back inside he spotted his father-in-law in front of the house. He was facing the shrine up the road, where people's voices loudly buzzed.

"Setting out now?" Emmitt asked him.

"I've been coming and going for a while. But I think I'll go back to stay and watch."

"I'll join you there soon."

Emmitt went inside to change his clothes.

Mirai was cleaning the first floor while her mother was already preparing lunch. She complained that he didn't have everything she needed in the kitchen but said she would try to make do with what was there.

"You don't have to cook," he said. "There are restaurants in town, and you'll be lucky if Otōsan doesn't fill up at the food stands."

"I want to introduce the smells of a home-cooked meal here. Why don't you go to the sumo event and keep Otōsan company? We'll call you back when lunch is ready."

Even before he reached the top of the street he saw three young men on a wooden scaffold, attaching more signs bought by local sponsors. The signs extended between the main shrine and a bronze horse atop a pedestal.

Emmitt walked beneath the *torii* in front. All down the long stone path of the shrine, food stalls had been set up. Gathered closer to the ring were parents of the small children now wrestling, and a large tent beneath which local politicians and company sponsors sat on cushions drinking sake. On opposite sides of the ring, two groups of children faced each other, fidgeting with their loincloths while waiting for the ring announcer to call their names. Emmitt felt this could be Shiramine fifty or one hundred years ago.

He approached his father-in-law behind a low stone wall of the temple next door, where he was watching the sumo bouts from the side.

"There's plenty of space closer to the ring," Emmitt said.

"I'm fine here. It's only children banging into each other, anyway. After lunch, when the men wrestle, I'll get a better seat."

Emmitt hoisted himself onto the wall and sat there watching the young boys wrestle. After each bout the onlookers laughed and applauded. Most children looked as if they couldn't understand why they were there, but once in the ring they did their best to push their opponent out of the circle. Whenever a particularly small wrestler defeated a much larger opponent, the crowd erupted in cheers and laughter, with some men calling out jokes and encouragement in the local dialect.

When each child had wrestled several times, two groups of high school boys faced off. They were strong and fast, and when they came together to throw each other to the ground or out of the ring, their bodies collided hard and the audience gasped and clapped their hands. Emmitt's father-in-law stepped closer to the wall, muttering his encouragement.

"They're not half bad," Emmitt said after an evenly matched pair of students wrestled for over a minute before someone won.

"They're better than I expected for such a small mountain town."

The high school matches lasted an hour. As before, they were followed by a trophy ceremony and speeches.

When Emmitt turned around he was surprised his father-in-law wasn't there. Unable to see him in the crowd either, he imagined he had left to find a bathroom or was back in line to buy more beer. Already it was noon, however, and Mirai and her mother expected them home soon. He let himself down from the wall.

On his way past the ring he saw Mirai approaching the shrine. He wound his way through the crowd to her.

"Did you see Otōsan?" he said as he came up to her.

"No. Are the sumo matches over?"

"They're just taking a break. The adults wrestle next."

"Where'd you say Otōsan went?"

Emmitt shrugged. "We were watching the matches together and when I looked back to him he was gone. I'm sure he's here somewhere. He seemed to enjoy the high school matches quite a bit."

"I came here to round you two up for lunch. I guess we should wait."

Mirai bought another beer for her father to have with the lunch her mother was making. The line was long, however, and it took her fifteen minutes to get it.

"I called Okāsan from the line. She said Otōsan wasn't home yet."

They looked for him again around the shrine, then returned through the center of town. When they didn't find him at the tourist center, they continued, cutting through the narrow walkways between houses.

Mirai announced their return as she stepped through the front door. Her mother had set a small table with paper plates and wooden chopsticks. She was pouring bottled tea when they entered.

"Is Otōsan back?" Mirai said.

"No, it's just been me here since you left."

"Knowing him, he went for a walk," Mirai said. "But where would he have walked to?"

"He left his phone on the table," her mother said, shaking her head.

"Can you run back to the shrine and see if he's there now?" Mirai asked Emmitt. "If not, we'll eat without him. We'll keep the food warm and he can eat whenever he feels like it."

Emmitt jogged back up the road. The shrine was more crowded now, and men ranging from what looked like twenty years of age to sixty filled the area in front of and behind the sumo ring. The VIPs under the tent had become rowdier; empty sake bottles that hadn't been there before littered the ground.

He wandered through the temple buildings next door, but there was no sign of his father-in-law anywhere. Shiramine was built for walking and he could have headed off in any direction, Emmitt thought. As he stood by the sumo wrestlers' changing area beside the shrine, he saw a sign for a hiking trail. But Emmitt didn't think that would be enough to attract him.

For someone who loved sumo as much as his father-in-law did, it was odd he wouldn't watch the more competitive matches.

The phone in his pocket buzzed.

"You've been gone twenty minutes," Mirai said. "If he's not

there, come back and the three of us will eat. We can look for him again later."

Emmitt made his way around the front of the shrine again, passing the children who had wrestled that morning, along with their teachers and parents. Two taxis drove by the entrance, and Emmitt waited for them to pass before continuing to his house.

"I have no idea where he went," Emmitt said when he got home.

"It's not the first time he's done this," his mother-in-law said, "but he's usually not so inconsiderate. Do you think he got lost?"

"I don't see how. Even if he walked along the prefectural road he could see Shiramine for some distance."

By the time they'd finished lunch, however, Emmitt had developed a sense of foreboding. Remembering the taxis he'd seen, and thinking of the perfect weather forecast for today and tomorrow, it occurred to him that he might have left Shiramine without telling anyone. "What was Otōsan wearing this morning?"

"I thought you saw him."

"I wasn't paying attention to his clothes."

"A pair of dark blue sweatpants," his mother-in-law said, "and a long-sleeved white shirt and green windbreaker."

Emmitt turned toward the *genkan* and spotted the *geta* his father-in-law had worn earlier. "And his shoes?"

"You're going to find him by looking at people's shoes?" Mirai said.

"He's not wearing his *geta*."

"He gave up on those," his mother-in-law said. "He had on an old pair of hiking boots, if I remember right."

Mirai looked at Emmitt. "You think he might have gone hiking?"

"I don't think anything right now. But if in an hour we still can't find him, I might drive up to the base station at Bettō Deai and ask around."

"How would he have gotten there? By walking? It's a forty-minute drive from here."

"There are buses, aren't there?" his mother-in-law said.

"Only one or two a day. But I've seen taxis in town. Of course he's probably just in a café we haven't discovered. Or watching sumo from some place he thinks we'll never find."

"Why does he behave that way?" Mirai said.

"He's always been like that. It doesn't necessarily mean anything."

Emmitt stood up. "I'll go back to the shrine. If I find him, I'll let you know."

He hadn't made it to the street in front of his house when he heard the door shut and saw Mirai hurrying toward him. "I'm coming, too. Okāsan will stay here in case he returns. It's now twelve-thirty. If we don't find him by one, she says we should drive to Bettō Deai."

"Hakusan's a three-thousand-meter climb. If he's there, every minute we fall behind him will be a serious disadvantage." Emmitt thought to himself: Who's to say he'd even stay on the designated trails?

She told him she would check the sumo area and, if he wasn't there, search around both rivers. She asked Emmitt to try the *onsen*, folk house museum, and silk factory and meet her back at the shrine.

Emmitt paid the entrance fee to the *onsen* but found no sign of his father-in-law. He left and started to jog toward the highway. The road behind it stretched for half a kilometer, passing a graveyard darkened by the shadows of tall cypresses, before ending at the folk house museum, where another tourist bus idled.

He asked the woman at the ticket booth inside if an older Japanese man had visited on his own within the last hour. Looking at the photo he showed her of him on his phone, she said she'd only sold tickets that day to a few small tourist groups and didn't remember an old man coming by himself.

Emmitt bought a ticket anyway and hurried through the folk houses on display. Upon reaching the final house on the map he'd been given, he asked a tourist group there if they had seen an older Japanese man visiting on his own. No one had, however, so Emmitt turned around and left.

When he arrived at the silk factory he ducked beneath the *noren* at the entrance and inquired about his father-in-law with the ticket seller inside. Although she, too, hadn't seen an older Japanese man enter alone, she told him he could step inside to look for him. She shook her head when he showed her his photo.

The first floor was empty of visitors, but on the second floor several tourists were watching women make kimono cloth on wooden looms. Off to their side, an elderly man gazed out the window at the near forest. He wore a hat like his father-in-law had—Emmitt couldn't remember if he'd seen him with one that morning—and a sweater and jacket that were similar, too. Emmitt jumped toward him only to see that the man bore no resemblance to his father-in-law.

The man stared at Emmitt, who apologized for having startled him.

A minute later Emmitt had circled back to where he'd entered the building, stepped outside, and called Mirai. He told her he'd seen no sign of him, then asked if she'd had any luck.

"No. I couldn't find him, and the people I asked were no help."

"Have you called Okāsan?"

"A minute ago. He's not with her, either."

They agreed to meet at the house and plan what to do next from there.

✳

THERE WAS NOTHING TO lose by driving to Bettō Deai. If his father-in-law turned up in Shiramine, Mirai would call to let him know, then he could drive back having wasted nothing but time. And if his father-in-law had somehow made it to Bettō Deai intending to climb Hakusan, Emmitt would only be a short distance behind him.

Although he would have set off more than an hour later than his father-in-law, he imagined he'd have an easier time hiking and could catch up to him fairly quickly. The greater worry was that his father-in-law would injure himself, and Emmitt would be stuck on the trail unable to help him.

He backed out of the driveway but had to wait between there and the highway for people watching the sumo matches to clear out of his way. He kept his eyes peeled for his father-in-law alongside the highway and on the roads that occasionally led into the forest. As he drove, he grew convinced that his father-in-law had taken one of the taxis Emmitt saw at the shrine, or had even caught a ride with climbers he'd met in town.

After fifteen minutes he came upon construction crews working on the tunnels along the road, readying them for the long winter ahead. What should have taken them a few minutes each time they made him stop ended up taking much longer, and Emmitt had the sickening feeling that the delays had started with him, not with traffic that had passed here earlier.

On the second delay he called Mirai, but she had found nothing indicating her father was still in town. "Please be patient," she said, "and do your best to find him." When she suggested taking a taxi to Bettō Deai, Emmitt discouraged her. "The last thing we need is three of us on the mountain in different places. If I need you, I'll let you know."

"What will you do about coming back?"

Did she not realize that he would almost certainly end up stuck on the mountain with darkness falling? Or that he might have to turn back without having found her father? He didn't want to consider either scenario.

"I don't know. I'll deal with the situation when it comes."

He glanced at the battery level of his phone and was sickened to find it less than half-charged. He told her this and said he'd better go.

When he arrived at Bettō Deai he parked his car and ran across the lot to the visitor center. Inside he showed the staff there, one older man with glasses who looked remarkably fit, his father-in-law's photo and asked if he had seen him. The man said no and asked him why.

"I think he might be climbing the mountain, and I've come to bring him home." When the man looked at him oddly Emmitt added, "He didn't tell anyone he was coming here. And I'm worried he'll injure himself."

He asked the man if he could call any trail patrol on-duty. But the man said there were only hikers between here and the lodge near the summit.

"If you suspect he's climbing the mountain, you'll have to find him yourself. If it's true he started two hours ago, he could be two kilometers along the trail already. But if he's in poor physical condition he might not have gotten far."

"He's been walking twenty kilometers a day for several months. But he's not young, and his leg sometimes gives him trouble."

"Dusk falls quickly in the mountains, and you don't want to

risk climbing down in the dark. There are deaths in this range every year, I assure you. It's possible to find yourself in serious trouble without warning."

"How far up is the lodge?"

"You'll never make it before it closes its doors at 4:30. That's how important it is to get off the trails before dusk."

Emmitt felt a sinking in his stomach. It was nearly 2 p.m. "Thank you. I'll try to be back quickly."

"Don't waste your time with me. The last bus of the day leaves from over there and I can hear the driver approaching."

Emmitt hurried outside, thanking the man over his shoulder.

The bus driver, too, didn't recognize Emmitt's father-in-law in the photo he was shown. Emmitt dumped himself in the front seat of the bus. Drumming his fingers on his armrest, he repeated under his breath, "Why aren't we leaving? Let's go. Let's go. Let's go."

Turning around, he saw he was the only person on board.

18

THE BUS ADVANCED SLIGHTLY up the mountain to another parking area. After jumping off, Emmitt asked the driver where the hiking trail started, then hurried in that direction.

He soon came upon a building with bathrooms, vending machines, and hiking route information. A handful of climbers were here, all of them tired-looking, as if having recently returned from a difficult climb. Past the building he saw a long, narrow bridge, wide enough only for hikers to walk two abreast, its sides nothing but wire cords, and one more hiker crossing it to leave the mountain.

He asked the hikers if they had seen his father-in-law, once more pulling out his phone to show his photo. Not a single person recollected having seen him.

By the time Emmitt crossed the bridge to the other side, his heart was racing—heights were not his forte. He hurried up the mountain path, which at its start was a mostly level walkway of gravel and rocks that served as steps.

The path soon rose, its steps becoming irregular and steep. Without hiking shoes, it was difficult finding traction. Training his eyes downward, he tried whenever possible to walk on hard dirt, wood purposely laid down, and even exposed tree roots. He went as fast as he could.

After only fifteen minutes he found himself short of breath, his legs already burning. Such conditions couldn't be easy for his father-in-law, but Emmitt had to concede that the old man was probably in better shape than he was.

He arrived at a break in the trees along the path. From here he could see a smaller mountain opposite him, its entire slope forested, with water cascading down manmade channels. Cranes and bulldozers stood on a road under the sun, ready to continue repair work that appeared at most half-finished.

A young man appeared above him where the path grew rockier and steeper; as he ran down, Emmitt was forced to step off the trail to let him pass. He dashed by as Emmitt tried to ask if he'd seen his father-in-law farther up.

Emmitt stepped back onto the trail, catching his breath still and rubbing his legs. He glanced at his watch and kept climbing.

The sky had deepened in color since he'd arrived at Bettō Deai, hinting that the sun would soon slide below the mountains to the west. With the high peaks towering above him, he guessed it would pass out of sight an hour before setting over the ocean.

After ascending another two hundred meters, he came across a rest area. Despite the temptation to sit on the large, shorn rocks, or on a wooden bench before an overlook, he headed for the lone building here, which had a tap before it with potable water from which he drank. Inside the building were two bathrooms. He peeked inside each one only to find them empty, then approached two groups of climbers who happened to be there.

When he told the first group that he was looking for his father-in-law, the second group came over. Both had passed an old man hiking alone up the mountain.

"How long ago was that? And where?"

Neither group could remember where, but each said they'd seen him around an hour ago. Emmitt showed them his photo. As he did, he noticed the power in his phone had drained further, and here in the mountains he had no service. He would have to contact Mirai from the lodge, assuming he made it there.

"It could have been him. But I'm not certain."

"Normally we greet whoever we pass. But he didn't meet our eyes."

"I remember the same thing. He seemed very focused on what he was doing. I guessed that he wasn't used to climbing."

"He might have had a bottle of water, but I noticed he wasn't carrying a backpack."

"Was he struggling?" Emmitt asked.

But everyone said he was climbing at a normal pace: slow but steady. He had struck them all as incredibly determined.

After a moment someone said, "He might have been limping a little."

Emmitt thanked them and resumed climbing with renewed energy.

An hour or an hour and a half wasn't an insuperable gap to close, but he knew that if he caught up to his father-in-law it would be in darkness. Emmitt's only hope to meet him before that was if Mirai's father gave up on reaching the lodge and came back down the mountain.

The light was fading further by the time he reached a wooden marker that read "Bettōnozoki. Alt. 1,750 m." He had been climbing as fast as he could for the last forty minutes, but the path, somehow turning steeper, now forced him to stop again to catch his breath and massage his legs. Although he was sweating, the air was already cool; he assumed it had more to do with the sun's position than the altitude he had reached. Without his noticing, the sun had fallen behind a tall, curving plateau. To the left of this were rows of smaller mountains whose slopes appeared dull with the distance and darkening light.

He peered up the trail only to see that it disappeared, but it came back farther up. It would take at least twenty minutes to reach that point, Emmitt thought. There was no sign of anyone there.

As he continued climbing, he realized that if it were to turn dark suddenly he would be lucky to have enough battery power in his phone to use its flashlight to return to the base station.

But there was almost no chance of returning without the benefit of any light source, and even if he reached the bridge he would have a hard time crossing it at night. Since turning around would mean giving up on finding his father-in-law, he tried to stop thinking about it.

The prospect of spending the night on the trail was unpleasant. In only a jacket, and despite or perhaps because of his sweating, he already felt the alpine chill. He regretted not buying water at the building before the bridge. And having not eaten much for lunch, he was hungry. Although he'd been told that the lodge near the summit rejected hikers after four-thirty, he thought they would surely make an exception considering his circumstances.

He stopped for a moment to stretch—his legs burned and his back had stiffened from sustained exertion he wasn't used to. Willing himself on, he tried to increase his pace, hoping to spot his father-in-law somewhere up the trail soon.

By the time he'd gone almost a kilometer farther and reached a marker for the Jinnosuke Shelter Hut, the shadows of trees along the path had lengthened, and the air was becoming increasingly dark and cool. According to the marker, the lodge was 3.4 km away. He bent over, puffing heavily, his throat scorched by a need for water. The pain in his legs now extended from his thighs to the ends of his toes, and he wondered how he could do this when he'd never been able to climb the stairs to his old university office without getting winded.

The path became easier where the ascent continued along wooden tracks. But they ended quickly, and again the path grew steep and rocky.

Another marker appeared saying he was three hundred meters from Jinnosuke Shelter Hut. He stopped walking and glanced up. Streaks of magenta and indigo colored the sky where the sun had fallen below the mountain peaks, but on the opposite side it was dark like a bruise—not yet the dark of night, but the dark of night's final warning. He knew he would reach the shelter hut with enough light to see by, but if he kept going, with the lodge at the summit still far away, he would risk perhaps two and a half more hours on a difficult trail in darkness. He hoped it, too, would have potable water.

The shelter hut appeared as he ascended another rise. He climbed the short stairs to it and paused. It was unexpectedly large—a wooden cabin that resembled a traditional Japanese farmhouse. There were toilets inside, and a long basin beside the door with spigots that ran fresh water. He immediately drank from one, then walked to the overlook and looked down from where he'd come, then back up the mountain—a steeply ascending wall he still had to climb. For a moment the summit looked closer than he realized, and this lifted his spirits so much he thought he might reach it with little problem. But a moment later he decided that the peak visible to him was not the summit after all. It lay farther back, and after he scaled this peak at least one more would still await him. His spirits plummeted.

He trudged back to the shelter and stepped inside. He looked around for lights, then a lamp, then a heater, but the shelter seemed to lack electricity. His father-in-law wasn't here, either. If he had stopped here, there was no indication.

Outside, he listened for other climbers, perhaps those returning later than they had planned. But he only heard the rustle of tree branches and the wind pushing over the mountainside. He cupped his hands around his mouth and shouted up the trail, "Otōsan!" He turned squarely toward the imposing peak before him and did it again. The only reply was the echo of his own voice.

The darkness and the cold seeped further into the air around him, like a droplet of ink injected behind his eyes.

Goosebumps covered his arms and he wondered if it might be better to stay inside the hut, where it would at least be warmer, and keep a vigil for his father-in-law. But perhaps there were other shelters on the way to the top, he thought, and headed back to the trail.

He soon came across a marker with "Zinnosuke Shelter" written on it, and then several picnic tables and a posted trail map unreadable in the failing light. He could see down into the valley from which he'd climbed. It seemed impossibly far away. Knowing he'd climbed just over halfway to the lodge struck him with disbelief.

Half an hour later he reached another trail marker. Again he turned to gaze into the valley below, and from here he could see the roof of the shelter hut where he had stopped. He knew that in another fifteen minutes, if he looked back down, he would see nothing at all.

He forced himself to keep climbing, calculating that at his present pace he would reach the lodge in two more hours. If his father-in-law were on the same trail, he couldn't help but be impressed by the old man's stamina and determination.

If he had light to see by, he would have been able to look farther up the mountain. As it was, he could only see a hundred meters in front of him, and because the trail continually turned, it was often less.

He felt the cascade before he heard or saw it. As his feet left the hard-packed dirt and made contact with the flat stones on this section of trail, he slipped and fell, half onto his back and half onto one side. Cold water seeped through his clothing before he could get to his knees and check himself for injury. The darkness was so complete now that he could barely see his own hands before his face. He sat awkwardly with his legs beneath him, struggling to catch his breath.

"Did you hurt yourself?"

Emmitt jumped at hearing the voice. It had come from a short way up the trail, where more water ran down the mountain. For a moment he thought he had only imagined that someone had spoken to him.

"I said, 'Did you hurt yourself when you fell?'"

Emmitt recognized the voice the second time he heard it. Though relieved to have found his father-in-law finally, he couldn't help but wonder what he was doing here of all places. Had he merely caught up to him? He had long lost hope he would bridge the gap between them.

"I'm fine," Emmitt said. "Have you decided to camp here or are you on the way down?"

"Come closer," his father-in-law said. "There's a tap here with drinking water from the mountain. You can't see the sign now, but it says that drinking it will make you live longer."

"Considering our situation, that doesn't sound like a bad idea. Are you all right?"

"I also fell where the water runs over the stone path. But I fell here, not where you did."

Emmitt made his way to his father-in-law. He was sitting with his back against a rock that was covered with tiny ferns, and his legs jutted out before him as if he might only be stretching them. His hair was disheveled, stubble speckled his jaw, and his cheeks were red from the cold.

"How long ago did you fall?" Emmitt said, finding the tap in the wall of rock and replenishing himself from it.

"Half an hour ago, maybe. Maybe longer."

The news alarmed Emmitt. "You must have hurt yourself if you've been here all that time."

"It's just my old injury. Nothing serious. I'm waiting for the pain to go away."

"And if it doesn't, what then? There's a shelter less than a kilometer below us. We could get back there in half an hour."

"I haven't come this far to stay in a shelter halfway up Hakusan."

"You intend to climb to the top?"

"I've already come this far . . ."

Emmitt held back from criticizing his father-in-law's stubbornness. He leaned toward him and asked how bad his leg was.

"I twisted my knee and landed on my hip. I've scraped my hands, too, but I managed to wash them off."

"It would be a lot easier going down."

"Then go down if you want." He took a large stick Emmitt hadn't seen and pushed himself to his feet. He rose shakily, struggling to maintain his balance.

He watched his father-in-law look up the trail, squinting into the distance.

"You missed the day's best sumo matches. Things were just getting exciting when you disappeared."

"Do you have any food?"

At the mention of food, Emmitt felt again the knot of hunger twisting in his stomach. "Do you think I took time to pack a meal before coming to find you?"

His father-in-law spoke again before Emmitt had finished. "It will be difficult getting to the top without food."

The light from the sky shifted and Emmitt saw the scratches on his father-in-law's face and hands and the rips in his jacket and pants. There was a large bloodstain on his knee. Emmitt approached to take his pulse. His father-in-law pulled his wrist away, but Emmitt grabbed it and counted his heartbeats. Satisfied, he let it go.

"Do you suppose anyone else might be on the trail?" he said.

"We're not the only ones."

"What are you talking about? Who else is here?"

"There's an old woman ahead of us. She hasn't crested this section yet. She's waiting for me to go on."

Emmitt looked up the trail. In the darkness the mountain was a solid wall before them, jagged along its topmost edges and darker than the night-filled sky. He could no longer see where the path turned and climbed.

"I don't see anyone. Who is this woman, anyway?"

"I've been following her all this time. When I passed the last hiker I saw, she appeared ahead of me. She's older than me, with long white hair. She doesn't seem to be carrying anything aside from a headlamp or lighter she uses to guide her."

"You're saying there's an old woman on the trail ahead of us who's waiting for you to push on?"

"I've called to her several times, but she must be beyond range of my voice. She only stops when I do, and refuses to approach me even when I wave to her."

Emmitt scanned the dark wall before them but again saw nothing. As he turned back to his father-in-law, he thought he noticed, at the corner of his vision, a light flicker. He looked back. Had he only imagined what his father-in-law suggested? Although there were still fireflies in wooded areas of Kanazawa, surely they didn't live this high up. If an old woman really was ahead of them, the last thing he needed was to be in charge of two elderly hikers caught on the mountain after dark.

His father-in-law removed a cigarette lighter from his jacket, lit it, and waved it overhead.

"Where did you get that?" Emmitt said.

"Someone left it at a rest area. Look, over there."

Emmitt turned once more and saw what appeared to be a flame dancing in the distance. He tried to gauge how far ahead it was, but it was too dark to guess with certainty. Was his father-in-law actually communicating with someone using the lighter he had found?

A gale arose and blew over them for half a minute. It rattled the sign where the spring water flowed, and the sound of the wind and water was like the keys played on the higher end of a piano, barely audible. Emmitt saw his father-in-law was mesmerized by it, too. When the wind passed, the music died away.

As they set out together up the path, torturously slow in the darkness, Emmitt said, "Why did you do this? What on earth made you run off to the mountains without a word to anyone? Surely you knew what it would do to us when we realized you were gone."

"It was my only choice. If you thought about it for even a moment, you would understand."

Emmitt considered what he said. But there had to be other ways. If he'd pressed Emmitt a little more, they might have come here together. But he knew, in the face of complaints from Mirai and her mother, that they wouldn't have. He supposed his father-in-law was right, but that didn't make his decision to come here less of a mistake.

"You could have chosen not to go."

"I told you I had to climb Hakusan once more before I died."

"Why must you always be so morbid? You're not about to die."

"Maybe not. But climbing Hakusan doesn't get any easier when you're my age."

They passed between a group of boulders, which appeared as black smudges against the sky. A sliver of moonbeam fell on a signpost leaning forward thirty degrees, but they didn't use their lighter to check the elevation or how much farther it was to the lodge.

A minute later, however, his father-in-law flicked his lighter on and off.

"What do you think that light is up there?" Emmitt said. "Or is it just an optical illusion?"

"It's the *yamanba.*"

Emmitt tried but failed to see his father-in-law's face. Surely he was joking.

"But she's not real."

"Of course she isn't. But what does that matter? In Zeami's play she admits she's not human, that she has no known origins, that her life's path is determined by the clouds and rain. What matters is that Zeami set *Yamanba* in the mountains bordering here, and the mountains here are sacred."

"But you're being illogical."

"It's a Buddhist play. The most Buddhist of all Zeami's plays, in fact. Perhaps it doesn't resonate with anyone these days. I can see you don't get it."

"Then help me get it."

His father-in-law started to give examples of the mountain crone expounding on Buddha's Law—that she exists because living forms on earth exist, and that they exist because the Buddha exists, and that enlightenment is possible only when evil, too, can take its hold in the universe—but Emmitt couldn't understand the points he was making and interrupted him.

"Let me ask a simpler question. What did you expect to accomplish by climbing this mountain?"

"This accumulation of mud and dust?"

Emmitt stopped walking, exasperated.

"I only hoped to visit again the place where an old friend died." His father-in-law paused now, too, slightly ahead of him.

"You would risk your life to do that?"

His father-in-law chuckled as if, even now, he thought Emmitt was exaggerating the danger. "Okāsan never came here. Even after all these years, she never bothered."

"Why would she? Because she knew him, too?"

Emmitt could hear his father-in-law breathing—more laboriously than before. "That 'him' you so casually refer to wasn't some mere acquaintance of ours. He and Okāsan dated for a year before I came along."

He stopped speaking, but Emmitt needed to hear more. "Go on."

His father-in-law hesitated, then said, "When his parents found out, they forbid the relationship to continue. She was from a poor family, as you know, whereas he came from money and power. Over time his parents became worried about his marriage prospects, but he rejected every effort they made to arrange this for him. My parents had been close to hers, and though her family was down on its luck, my father, before he died, had been a respected member of the art university in town and had a good reputation as a painter. Her mother and mine had also studied the tea ceremony together for many years. I was thirty-two then and my mother, too, was worried about my future. They wanted us to marry.

"For whatever reason, Okāsan agreed to this, which meant breaking things off with him. She resisted doing this for several months, until finally he said it would do her no good to cling to him any longer. Shortly after that, perhaps to make up for the anguish she'd caused her parents, she went along with efforts to match us. By that point I wasn't holding out much hope, but to my surprise things moved forward quickly. Two months later we got married.

"I didn't know it then, but Okāsan and her former boyfriend continued to see each other when they could. They saw each other even after we married, but only for half a year."

"What happened?" Emmitt said, as his father-in-law continued climbing. He followed behind him, taking each step slowly and carefully.

"He invited me to climb Hakusan. We planned to spend four or five days in the mountains, starting in Shiramine and making our way by foot to Bettō Deai, from which we'd climb to the top. He wanted to talk to me about Okāsan, and I was eager to learn how I could put a stop to their continued rendezvous. At first I was understanding, for I, too, had once lost someone I'd loved deeply to another, and I knew the difficulty of ending things. Also, my feelings for Okāsan had quickly become so strong that I was ready to forgive her anything. And it was easier for me to forgive something that had existed before I came along. I had only been waiting for the natural death of the relationship to occur. I felt it would sooner or later. But at some point I realized that was naïve. There was an equal likelihood that she would leave me. But like I said, I loved her deeply by then and wanted to see how we might resolve things. And there *was* a natural death. But I never dreamed their love would end how it did. He was only twenty-eight when he died." He paused before adding, "I think it was fear that kept me from agreeing to climb Hakusan with him when he asked."

Emmitt listened to this story in fascination, shocked by what he was hearing. But even after his father-in-law told him this, he didn't feel it explained why he had come here like he did. Before Emmitt could ask, however, his father-in-law cleared his throat and went on, his voice quivering.

"Okāsan was pregnant at the time. I didn't know this, though. I only found out because the news of his death nearly made her miscarry. She collapsed in pain the night she heard about it. She was in the hospital for more than a week, but the doctors helped save her pregnancy. That was lucky for you, because later she gave birth to Mirai."

Emmitt stopped walking. After a few more steps his father-in-law stopped, too.

"I know what you're wondering. Anyone would after learning what I just told you. The fact is, we never tested to find out. Okāsan suggested several times that we do so, but I always resisted. What was the point? I loved Okāsan more than anything, and by the time Mirai came into the world I knew she loved me, too. Perhaps not yet as much as she loved the man who died, but I felt it would happen one day. I felt that Mirai, whoever her father might be, still came from the union between the two of us. Perhaps it was a union of more than two, but over time that union would round down—to Okāsan and me. Before Mirai was born, both of us suffered greatly. But one day, in the first month of Mirai's life, as Okāsan nursed her on the small tatami in our home, she turned to me and said, 'I want a peaceful home for our child, and for all of us. I want us to be a family that tries always to walk the right path. I think we should try to live so as not to create bad karma for ourselves or our daughter.' Her words astounded me. I never thought she had Buddhist leanings. And from then on we agreed to raise a family in such an atmosphere. I'm afraid we lost track of this promise to ourselves, but that doesn't mean we've done a bad job raising our daughters. Perhaps we became so focused on them that we let our marriage suffer. I suppose there's no avoiding it. For what is life if not suffering?"

Emmitt didn't know what to think. He appreciated his father-in-law's candor but regretted that it took what they'd gone through to draw it out of him.

"The place where Okāsan's former lover died—is that what really drew you here?"

"It's everything. But yes, before I get too old I want to visit the *ojizō-sama* statue erected where he was found and thank him for the life he gave me. And for the life he gave my family. If not for him, who knows how our lives would have turned out?

Maybe you'd like to pay your respects, too. It's possible that you wouldn't be in our lives either, or us in yours, if not for him."

"You don't know where the statue is, do you?"

"No. And after all these years it may not be standing anymore. But at the top of Hakusan is a shrine, a very important one. It's enough for us to pay our respects there."

"But we're still far from the lodge, and the summit is past that. And then there's the matter of getting back down the mountain. You hardly seem in good enough condition to make it much further."

"You underestimate me."

Up ahead of them, the strange light reached the crest of the trail and stopped moving.

19

THE LIGHT THEY WERE following disappeared before they reached the top of the ridge. Looking now across a long field of low, wind-blown scrub, they spotted a group of dimly lit buildings that became distinguishable from one another as Emmitt and his father-in-law approached them.

"We made it," Emmitt said, relieved. He felt weak from hunger, and thought his father-in-law must, too, though he'd made no complaints. Emmitt stopped again to rub his legs, which he hardly recognized as his own. For the last half hour he couldn't bend his knee without pain. His father-in-law also limped heavily.

"Not all the way." His father-in-law pointed to another summit still before them.

Although Emmitt realized that what awaited them in the distance was the lodge, it seemed incongruous here near the top of the mountain they'd struggled to climb. As they continued walking, he was grateful to have reached level ground.

When they got to the lodge, only one light was on inside the entire complex. At the steps leading into what appeared to be the main building, they saw through its front window a worker behind a check-in desk, reading a magazine.

As they pulled the door open and went inside, the young man behind the desk looked at them in surprise.

They tried to negotiate for a room but he wouldn't let them have one. He seemed uncertain with himself, and in particular with the lodge's rules. In the end he offered them a corner of the lobby and said they could spend the night on the sofa there at no cost. Too tired to argue, they agreed. The man ducked behind his desk and pulled out what blankets he had for them to use. Emmitt asked if the lodge had any food they could buy, but the young man shook his head.

Emmitt saw a clock on the wall behind him. It was only nine-thirty, yet it felt like the middle of the night. His father-in-law was walking to the couch to go to sleep, but Emmitt had another question for the man.

"We weren't the only hikers caught on the mountain after dark. There seemed to be an old woman ahead of us. We followed her from a distance all the way here. She must have checked in shortly before we arrived."

The man glanced toward the entrance and shook his head. "You're the only latecomers today."

"In that case, I expect she'll show up soon. If it wasn't for her, I'm not sure we'd have found the strength to make it here."

The young man looked at Emmitt strangely but didn't say anything.

Emmitt asked to use the lodge's phone to notify his wife that they had made it safely there. After some hesitation, the man nodded to the phone at the end of his desk.

Mirai picked up after the first ring.

"It's me," Emmitt said. "I'm with Otōsan at the lodge on Hakusan. We're hungry but fine."

Mirai let out a shriek, and he heard her turn away from the receiver to shout the news to her mother. "I was on the verge of calling the police. Where did you find Otōsan?"

"He was halfway up the mountain, resting on the path."

"Where is he? Can we talk to him?"

Emmitt called him to the phone but he wouldn't budge from where he lay. When Emmitt stood up his father-in-law waved for him to sit back down. Emmitt told Mirai he was already sleeping, but he assured her again that he was all right.

"If we're lucky we'll make it back to the car by late morning," he told her, "which means we'll arrive in Shiramine before lunchtime."

"Is there anything we can do? Should we meet you at Bettō Deai?"

"No. And you don't need to worry about anything, either."

"Are you sure you're both okay?"

"We're hungry, but fine. It's a relief to be where we are."

"Be careful coming back down, Emmitt."

Emmitt thanked the man at the desk and limped to the couch. He set the thinner of his two blankets on the floor, lay down on it, and pulled the heavier one over him. There was no pillow, but he was too tired to complain.

From the floor he could see the sky through the front window. There was no sign of anyone else coming to spend the night. He thought the old woman they had seen on the trail might work at the lodge, or had entered one of the sleeping quarters without being seen. He would look for her tomorrow morning when they made their final push to the summit.

For a long time Emmitt watched his father-in-law sleep. He couldn't stop thinking about the man who could just as easily be Mirai's father as the man lying bundled up on the couch above him. Did Mirai have some inkling of this, and if so, was that her reason for not showing more interest in her mother's past? Maybe he would never know.

He felt an intense admiration for how his father-in-law had handled his marriage in its early days and Mirai's paternity. If Mirai's reason for wanting to move to Tokyo had been an affair, Emmitt didn't think he could be as forgiving. His father-in-law's goodness exceeded that which Emmitt perceived in himself—or in anyone he knew. It was a revelation.

The more he replayed in his mind what his father-in-law had

told him, the more Emmitt was willing to question his own role in his marriage. Had he been as selfish as Mirai had accused him? Was selfishness what prevented him from considering Tokyo as a home for them? But if he had been thinking more of his own happiness than Mirai's, he knew that Mirai, too, was not the model her father had been. Her father had been uncommonly good.

His father-in-law turned onto his side, breathing deeply in his sleep. He had saved his family by giving up what Emmitt himself never could have.

Emmitt's mind went back to the artist Clifton Karhu and what Kimura had said about his life. Emmitt had never known or met Karhu, and could only guess at what made him give up the religious life that had brought him to Japan and turn to *shinhanga* prints. Clearly he had sacrificed much to lift his family out of poverty, but was it selfishness or selflessness that had resulted in their poverty in the first place? And which was it that helped save them? Perhaps it didn't matter. What mattered was that he found a way out for them as well as for himself. And it was by discovering a purpose for himself that he did so. Emmitt didn't need to have known the man to understand this.

He closed his eyes.

꙳

ONLY WHEN HIS FATHER-IN-LAW shook him by the shoulder did he realize he'd fallen asleep.

"What is it?" Outside, it was still pitch dark.

"It's 4:30 a.m.," his father-in-law said. "Come here and look."

Barely awake, Emmitt peered out the near window. On the black face of the final summit a chain of tiny lights snaked upward, slithering from side to side. He immediately thought of the old woman they had seen yesterday, flicking her lighter on and off, leading them up the mountain. With his mind still clouded from sleep, he didn't understand what he was seeing.

"What is that?" he said.

"Other climbers. They're ascending to watch the sun rise. The young man at the front desk agreed to lend us these."

Emmitt took the headlamp his father-in-law held out and checked to make sure it worked.

A minute later Emmitt followed his father-in-law outside, where they saw more people walking from their sleeping quarters to the summit trail. All wore headlamps or were putting them on.

A strong wind blew off the mountain, so cold that Emmitt thought they were about to climb blindly onto a glacier. He and his father-in-law were the only ones not dressed as if it were mid-winter.

Behind the lodge was a tall *torii* that led to a simple shrine.

"Is that where you want to make a prayer to your old friend?" Emmitt said, shivering.

His father-in-law shook his head. "There's another at the top. That's the one I want to reach."

Through the darkness Emmitt spotted a ghostly mist creep across the upper half of the summit. The path, a steep walkway made of flat stones, began behind the shrine, and Emmitt and his father-in-law moved toward it while rubbing their arms to warm themselves.

As soon as they started climbing Emmitt wanted to turn back. In addition to the freezing wind, his legs were sorer than they had been upon arriving at the lodge. Each step made him wince. He could see by his father-in-law's expression, and the slowness with which he, too, climbed, that they were struggling equally.

The higher they climbed the colder and windier it got. The

light from the headlamps above them had already disappeared in the mists or over the crest. In the darkness, only the steps they continued to climb were visible; they angled their foreheads down to illuminate them.

The smooth stone beneath their feet soon became rugged, and they had to be careful not to turn an ankle on the irregular surfaces of rock and gravel. The climb was as steep here as on any part of the path before, and their pace seemed impossibly slow and ineffectual.

As they neared the summit they could see, dancing in the darkness again, the lights from other hikers' headlamps. A wall of rock and a shrine it protected were also faintly illuminated. After a few difficult turns near the top they reached it.

Emmitt's father-in-law stopped moving and leaned against the rock wall. He was shaking, but it didn't seem because of discomfort.

"We made it," Emmitt said. "Are you all right?"

Rather than answer, if in fact he'd heard Emmitt over the wind and the people around them celebrating, he dragged himself toward the shrine.

A dozen hikers grouped around it, praying and taking photos. They didn't remain long, however, and his father-in-law soon positioned himself before it, beneath its double-eave and the sacred rope-and-paper *shimenawa* indicating the dwelling of Shinto gods. From his jacket he removed something scroll-like, which turned out to be a length of sketch-paper he had rolled up and brought with him. Climbing the mountain had flattened it against his body and he twisted it back and forth to give it shape. He opened it and set it down on a wooden offering board, then bowed before the shrine, clapped his hands, and bowed again. Emmitt watched his lips move in prayer.

When he stepped away, Emmitt came up to the shrine. He

made his own prayer for his family, then paused thinking of the sculptor who'd died somewhere on this mountain. The only prayer he could think to make for him was for peace.

He opened his eyes. As he walked behind the shrine he saw a tall elevation marker. Large rocks surrounded it, and his father-in-law sat on one looking down upon a layer of clouds that seemed to stretch to infinity. Above them, from the eastern sky, a faint light spread.

His father-in-law was holding the lighter he had found on the trail yesterday. Starting toward him, Emmitt saw him touch a flame to the drawing he'd brought up the mountain. Emmitt reached him as the flame consumed an upper corner of the paper only for the wind to snuff it out.

He stood behind him and, as the wind buffeted the sketch, peered at the picture he'd drawn. It appeared to be yet another statue, one Emmitt hadn't seen before, rendered in masterful detail except for where the statue's face should have been. His father-in-law had left it blank. Even without a face, there was something familiar about the figure. Yet without one, how was he to recognize it?

His father-in-law turned from the gusting wind and touched a new flame to the sketch. It caught, and the paper turned to ash. The wind launched it in every direction, and it soon disappeared into the clouds and mists.

Over a peak, the sun's rays colored the eastern horizon pinkish white. They softened as the clouds parted long enough for the sun to crest into view. Emmitt and his father-in-law watched the sun lift over a ridge directly opposite them. Its rays extended almost wing-like to the sides before lightening the entire sky. The other climbers on the mountaintop cheered, some bowing to the sun, others pouring sake over the stone marker behind them.

With the sun's appearance, the higher mists began to burn away, leaving only those still deep in the valley.

"Otōsan." When his father-in-law didn't turn to him or reply Emmitt came up beside him. "Let's go back. You climbed Hakusan exactly like you wanted to, and we were lucky to watch the sun rise. Okāsan and Mirai are both waiting for us."

"Give me a moment."

He had turned away from the bright sun and was staring at a western mountain still in shadow. On its dark slopes, still in the hands of nightfall, Emmitt spotted a flickering light moving slowly beneath its summit. Was it merely another hiker with a headlamp who had scaled a different peak? Emmitt looked back and saw his father-in-law raise his hand and flick his lighter several times. He wondered if his father-in-law thought that the light below, too, belonged to a *yamanba* passing through the range. But surely that was impossible.

Despite the cold and wind, they sat together on a rock above the clouds. The sun rose higher, gradually warming their backs and illuminating their surroundings. When they descended to the lodge to make their way back to Bettō Deai, the single light on the slope below them had long disappeared.

20

EMMITT SAT BESIDE HIS mother-in-law on the wooden steps of Renshōji temple. Opposite them was a weeping cherry tree that she claimed was one of the most magnificent in Higashichaya when in bloom. To its right was the wooden gate they had passed through after climbing a flight of concrete stairs. To its left was a small garden and cemetery whose boundaries overlapped.

A moment before, Mirai had left them to wander the grounds with a paper lantern she had bought on their walk here. She wanted to draw something on its removable paper to include in an ikebana exhibit next week at Kenrokuen Garden.

Emmitt's mother-in-law turned to Emmitt and smiled.

"We talked before about *Rukōshinsō*, the last story Kyōka wrote, but never got to visit where it was set. It's difficult to imagine what Renshōji looked like when Kyōka was alive, but that was eighty years ago and Kanazawa has changed since then."

Emmitt remembered how the bad weather and his work had prevented them from coming here last February. "I'm glad we finally made it." It felt surreal to be physically present in a setting Kyōka had brought to life so long ago. Being here gave him goosebumps. And yet she was right to suggest that the temple didn't match how he had imagined it. Certain things, however, seemed as if they had been passed down unaltered from Kyōka's time.

The most obvious of these were the dragonflies. Hordes of them flew overhead and zigzagged every which way. They perched in equal numbers atop the surrounding walls, around the ablutions basin alongside the garden, and on scattered tombstones,

not to mention up and down a telephone wire between the temple roof and main gate. Their presence made him feel like they
had walked directly into Kyōka's final story.

To Emmitt's mother-in-law, death and the specter of death
cast long shadows over *Rukōshinsō*. Not only did Kyōka die of
lung cancer shortly after completing it, but in the story he por-
trays an old man nearing the end of his life, too, his mind on
those who have already passed on. The old man visits this temple with the daughter of a woman he once loved. That woman
is dead and buried in the cemetery here, along with a woman
who drowned herself in the castle moat at a time when he, too,
planned to take his own life. It was her suicide that turned him
away from death, keeping him alive all these years. The story is
autobiographical. Kyōka had experienced a similar brush with
suicide, and *Rukōshinsō* was a way to honor the drowned woman,
even at the moment he himself was about to die. The story is a
testament both to the life he lived and to the writing he produced
and would soon leave behind.

Despite the motif of death running through *Rukōshinsō*, the
story wasn't depressing. In fact, Emmitt felt it expressed a pro-
found affirmation of life. That Kyōka set it in Kanazawa also
made it more interesting to him.

"Mishima Yukio once wrote that when he was fourteen
and living in Tokyo, his grandmother made him go to a bookstore to buy *Rukōshinsō*," his mother-in-law said. "Mishima later
described the story as having all the attributes of what Zeami
called the perfect ideal. It's funny, but Mishima's grandmother
was from Kanazawa. Though Mishima was only a boy when
Kyōka died, she had imagined her grandson becoming friends
with him one day. She had that sort of respect for Kyōka, as if her
grandson could aspire to emulate no better writer."

They continued talking about *Rukōshinsō* while Mirai strolled the grounds, stopping periodically to examine the dragonflies. Emmitt watched her settle on one to sketch: a bright red speci- men on a pale arm of the weeping cherry hanging over the gar- den. Even when Mirai approached to within a foot of the insect, it remained on the branch, as still as a bud waiting to bloom.

Mirai spoke to it coaxingly as she brought from her purse a colored pencil, bright red like the dragonfly, to draw with on the lantern-paper.

"Don't move now, don't fly away. Stay long enough for me to capture you as you are. Oh!"

As soon as she touched her pencil to the paper, another dragonfly descended from the tree's canopy and mounted the one Mirai planned to draw. For a moment they stayed like that, perfectly still on the branch.

"Did that really have to happen just now?" she said, laughing. "Well, I suppose I could change my vision for the picture. But an erotic *shunga* piece wouldn't go well with ikebana, I'm afraid."

Her mother clicked her tongue and said, "You shouldn't talk that way, Mirai."

"I'm only acknowledging the garden's life force. It's very much alive. Their mating reassures me that this place will always be filled with dragonflies. There's nothing vulgar about that, Okāsan. After all, that girl in Kyōka's story embroidered pictures of mating dragonflies."

Her mother looked pleased that she knew the story. And it was true what Mirai had said. In *Rukōshinsō*, the more successful the girl's embroidery had been, the more criticism her coworkers had leveled at her, and the more embarrassed she had become for having embroidered what she did.

"Wasn't that why she killed herself?" Emmitt said.

"She was caught unable to please everyone. Some people called her a disgrace and said her work was shameful, yet her pic- tures were very popular."

"It's hard to imagine that being enough to kill yourself over now," Mirai said.

Her mother turned to Emmitt. "I'm glad you appreciate the Kyōka stories I introduced to you. Naturally, his work will live on only for as long as people read him. I hope you'll find a way to bring his work to other readers."

He had heard her say similar things before, but when she said this now it had a different impact on him. "If I can, I'll certainly try to."

Emmitt had passed his translation certification test five days after climbing Hakusan. His results were better than he'd expected, and within a week of receiving them he'd begun working for a company specializing in medical translations. If he translated Kyōka in the future, he would likely have to do so on the side. Despite working again, he still had time to explore Kanazawa more deeply. Translating Kyōka would not be impossible. He had already picked three stories he wanted to work on.

After quitting his teaching job at the university, he had planned to take a year off to find a better way to live. He considered himself fortunate to have discovered a new path for himself as quickly as he had. And though it was too soon yet to declare that he'd achieved his aim, he had at least made a change in his life, and to him this was progress. At the same time, he felt that he and Mirai had found a middle road to travel together. That they had learned how to support each other's dreams, even as they promised to evolve, boded well for their future. Perhaps it was because they had learned this that the middle road had appeared before them. For a long time they had been turned away from it, unaware that its existence was so near. He hadn't "moved backward," as his father-in-law had worried he might, but he had found where he stood in relation to the past, and—in no small part due to the Kyōka reading he'd done—he was more firmly ensconced now between the old and new.

"I'm sure I've told you this already," his mother-in-law said, "but at Keiō University, on a visit to Kyōka's archives, I saw the original manuscript of *Rukōshinsō*. I'll never forget the sense it gave of Kyōka struggling to complete it before he died. Even then, he had something greater than himself to strive for. One day I'd like to show it to you."

"I'd like that, too."

She looked around them and said, "Kyōka's struggle to complete his final story feels especially meaningful, doesn't it? If he'd never finished it, we wouldn't be here now, and our lives might somehow be different—less than what they are today."

Emmitt smiled, agreeing that they were lucky Kyōka had given the world *Rukōshinsō* as his final work. It felt almost as if he'd written it for them.

"I'm going to explore the far end of the cemetery," Mirai called out.

Emmitt and his mother-in-law watched her walk over the gravel-lined path in that direction.

"It's too bad Otōsan and Asuka couldn't come with us," Emmitt said. Asuka, for the second weekend in a row, had come up from Tokyo and was staying at home. She was making a point to spend as much time as possible with her family before moving to Taipei in three more weeks.

"Neither of them would have liked it here. Besides, it's good for them to have this time together. He rarely gets to see her, and since leaving Kanazawa she's tended to communicate more with me than with him."

Emmitt's father-in-law had taken over Asuka's room to use as a space to draw and paint in. Asuka, rather than feeling put out, was happy to give her room to him and sleep on the sofa downstairs. Just that morning Emmitt had helped him rearrange her furniture so he would have a larger working area. Unlike before, there were no signs of the statues he had visited, photographed, and drawn. In a corner was an empty canvas on an easel. Beneath it, leaning against a wall, were pictures of trees awash in pink and white.

Emmitt hesitated before saying, "It must be satisfying to see him paint new things. What has it been the last few days, anyway? Cherry blossoms? Considering it's October, he's either half a year early or half a year late."

His mother-in-law looked away. After a long moment she said, "He told me what you talked about on Hakusan. About what happened in the past, before and after we married."

Emmitt nodded.

"Were you shocked?"

"At first I was."

"And now?"

"The shock's worn off. But it's true that I never would have guessed what Otōsan told me."

She looked toward the cemetery. "Have you told Mirai?"

He turned to her in surprise. "Of course not."

She sighed deeply, her breath catching in her chest. "One day I'd like to tell her. Not on a mountaintop, the way Otōsan told you, but maybe at home some evening. When it's just the two of us together." She met Emmitt's gaze. "I hope you start a family soon. Is it really so important to wait until you have your own house?"

"It's not as important as it was. And we do have a house now."

"That's true, you do."

Half a dozen dragonflies began to chase one another overhead. They circled around quickly before dispersing in different directions.

"Where is the sculptor buried?" The words left Emmitt's mouth before he realized how inappropriate they might sound.

She looked at him wide-eyed. "He's buried in Nodayama Bochi, a big cemetery near Daijōji." Regaining her composure she added, "You can see Murō Saisei's grave from where it is."

Emmitt knew the place. "It's one of the most beautiful cemeteries I've ever seen," he said.

"They should have buried him higher up. The sun barely reaches him through the trees."

The way she talked about it, it seemed she either still visited or she once visited so often that she could remember it as clear as day.

"But of course it doesn't matter now. What matters when you're dead, really? Cemeteries are for the living—which is strange, isn't it? Few people like to visit them. When Mirai was a child and we took her to our ancestors' graves, she would scream and kick until we came home."

"Has Mirai been to the cemetery at Daijōji?"

Again his mother-in-law turned to him. "She might have gone once," she said quietly. "I'm sure she doesn't remember."

"With her school?"

"It could have been."

She stood and went to the ablutions basin to rinse her hands. Afterward she patted her face as if to wake herself up.

"That girl is buried here, you know," she said from across the path.

"What girl?"

"The one who killed herself. And saved Kyōka's life. In the story he named her Hatsuji."

"I wonder where her grave is."

"I only know where Kyōka's relations are—his mother's sister and her own children." She pointed to a well-maintained area of the cemetery. "I believe the girl's grave was moved at one point, from the hill behind the temple. Just like in the story."

Emmitt wondered what was keeping Mirai. If she were with

them, they would be talking about something more lighthearted. He was tired of talking about the dead.

"I think I'll have a look around," he said.

"Please, take your time."

He walked off in the direction Mirai had gone.

She had passed through the cemetery and was standing near the bottom of a sloping path, drawing on her lantern-paper. Not wanting to disturb her, he turned where the path led up a hill.

Pushing through a cluster of branches, which crossed each other as if to keep people out, he reached an overgrown area. A number of graves stood here—a large one before several smaller ones—surrounded by nettle trees and *hisakaki* shrubs. The forest and rotting undergrowth became denser higher up; fallen branches and the trunks of two young trees blocked his way again. Past them were more scattered gravestones—covered in moss, leaning at precarious angles, and appearing as if they'd been forgotten. In ten or twenty years, he thought, the forest would swallow them up. Who were these people buried here? Could this really be where the woman who jumped into the moat and drowned herself in front of Izumi Kyōka now lay? Or was that merely fiction?

A half-dozen dragonflies started darting around him, their wings buzzing like motors. When they landed on him he shook them off. He didn't like them touching him here.

Mirai called to him on his way back to the temple.

"I spotted two dragonflies balanced together on a long blade of grass," she told him. "I managed to sketch them, one for each side of the lantern, before they flew off." Having refastened the paper to the lantern, she showed him her drawings. He shook his head, amazed. "When we get home," she continued, "I'll need to embellish them. Maybe I'll ask Otōsan and Asuka to help me. What were you doing up that hill?"

"I wanted to see where the path led."

Looking behind him, she apparently saw nothing to comment on. She suggested they see the temple's giant Buddha statue before going back home. She held out her hand and he took it.

He felt a resistance in her hand as he turned to the temple. Despite a hardening in her expression, her eyes were clear and soft.

"You understand, don't you, that I'm happy you've found a new path to follow? I finally see that you need to be free to find a way to reach your goals."

"But what made you see that?"

"I don't know. When you and Otōsan returned from Hakusan, I noticed a change in you. And I think it's finally made its way to me. Maybe it's just wisdom, slowly building up in me. Or an acceptance of truth. For a long time I didn't understand what you wanted from life. But now I do."

He pulled her close to him, and together they started back toward the temple.

Her mother was keen to visit the statue. The three of them approached the temple door and Mirai called inside.

A middle-aged woman appeared and pointed where to go. They took off their shoes and shuffled down the long hallway, past the prayer hall and a set of steps.

The tall Buddha here—Kanazawa's third "Great Buddha" statue—was carved from camphor wood. Its eyes were closed, and its hands, face, and upper body gleamed with gold leaf under the rooftop. Mirai's mother lit a stick of incense lying on a hand-carved table and placed it in an ash-filled urn. Each of them made a prayer and bowed.

When Emmitt opened his eyes he saw Mirai's mother peering at an old poster on the wall.

"Have either of you heard about this?" she said.

Mirai approached it and shook her head. Emmitt only saw that it was a walk across seven bridges on the Asano River.

"Mishima Yukio wrote a story based on this, though he set it on the Sumida River, in Tokyo, not here. The walk this poster describes is the *nanahatsu hashimeguri*. People say that if you cross the seven bridges in a certain order at midnight under the mid-autumn moon, dressed entirely in white, never once turning around, and never uttering a word, your greatest wish will come true."

Emmitt read the names of the seven bridges. "Otōsan did that walk, didn't he?"

"Yes, and I bet he broke all the rules." Mirai laughed. "He was coming back from Mt. Utatsu, where he'd been looking for a statue. He'd been upset to learn the city had recently torn it down."

"I remember . . ." Mirai's mother said thoughtfully.

"He walked across the seven bridges, but only for exercise. He said it was good to change his routes sometimes. It was right before he climbed Hakusan."

Mirai's mother stepped away and they followed her back through the hallway.

When they were outside again, Emmitt and Mirai started toward the main gate. The branches of the weeping cherry were so long that Emmitt had to pull them back to walk past.

"Where are you going?" Mirai's mother called out. "I wanted to show you something. We can use the exit by the cemetery to leave."

They walked behind her to the far end of the temple. The cemetery here was small, with at most seventy gravestones.

"This grave brings you closest of all to Kyōka. You can see the name 'Meboso Teru' here. In fact, the gravestones in this particular area all say 'Meboso.'"

"Who was she?" Mirai said.

"His mother's sister. In *Rukōshinsō* she was the model for the dead mother of the woman the protagonist accompanied here."

On top of her gravestone were three red dragonflies. Looking around, Emmitt saw that more sat motionless atop each grave in the Meboso family plot.

"Well, there's no point lingering," his mother-in-law said. "Let's go home. Otōsan and Asuka will be getting hungry, I'm sure."

They passed through the cemetery exit. The sloping path, where Mirai had drawn the dragonflies, led to a maze of narrow streets that would take them back to Higashichaya.

Mirai stumbled slightly, and the lantern she'd been carrying fell from her hand. Emmitt bent down to retrieve it, but the slope's angle caused the lantern to roll beyond his grasp. As it did so it hit a rock, rose into the air and, as if sucked into a current above them, sailed toward the houses below.

The three of them watched the lantern, enthralled. The images Mirai had drawn, even more lifelike and real from a distance, seemed to take wing among a cloud of dragonflies the lantern's movement had startled into flight.

❅ ❅ ❅

Reading Izumi Kyōka

THE JAPANESE AUTHOR IZUMI KYŌKA (1873–1939) and his works figure prominently in this novel and were an important influence on its creation (and on my own life in Kanazawa). Born Izumi Kyōtarō in Kanazawa, Kyōka moved to Tokyo at the age of seventeen to become a writer. Despite poor health and various eccentricities, he wrote numerous short stories, novels, and plays, which were often criticized for not following the naturalist literary trends of his day. Since the 1970s they have enjoyed resurgent popularity. The city of Kanazawa has commemorated Kyōka's life and work with statues (of him *and* his characters) and monuments, as well as by attaching his name to streets, food, sake, and an important literary prize.

The characters and plot of *Kanazawa* present deliberate instances of intertextuality. Certain scenes I've written interact with certain scenes in Kyōka's stories (and with his own life). If you have read Kyōka you may recognize these instances, or at least trace some aspects of their lineage, in my novel. I could never hope to achieve what Kyōka did in his stories, stylistically or literarily. I've merely tried to weave interesting pieces together to add a layer to the ways my novel can be read, understood, and enjoyed.

You can still read *Kanazawa* without first reading Kyōka. And you can also experience the same sense of recognition in reverse—by reading my novel first and then seeking out Kyōka's works.

For example, Charles Shiro Inouye's three publications on Kyōka are masterful. Two are collections of translated stories and one a critical biography. The former are *In Light of Shadows*

(University of Hawaii Press, 2004) and *Japanese Gothic Tales* (University of Hawaii Press, 1996), the latter *The Similitude of Blossoms* (Harvard University Press, 1998).

Donald Keene's chapter on Izumi Kyōka in *Dawn to the West: Japanese Literature of the Modern Era* (Columbia University Press, 1998) has long served as an excellent addition to what is available in English on Kyōka and his writing.

Cody Poulton's *Spirits of Another Sort* is another excellent source of translation (mostly of plays, of which Kyōka wrote more than five dozen), and of critical and biographical material.

The more recent *A Bird of a Different Feather*, translated by Peter Bernard, beautifully illustrated by Nakagawa Gaku, and appended with several short but interesting essays by Japanese Kyōka scholars, is also of interest.

There are other short publications that deal with the creative products of what Akutagawa Ryūnosuke referred to as "Kyōka's World," but the works mentioned here are the ones I've read and come back to often with the greatest pleasure and interest.

As Emmitt's mother-in-law suggests in *Kanazawa*, if foreign readership of Kyōka's work spreads, perhaps it will "help preserve something that's in danger of disappearing." I share her belief, and also hope that it might lead to Kyōka's work taking a more prominent place in Japan's highly regarded literary canon.

Acknowledgments

I'D LIKE TO TAKE a moment to thank the many people who offered valuable help and support as I wrote *Kanazawa*.

To Wayne Malcolm, Michael Chassen, Mark Harris, Abigail Munday, and Rick Broadaway for checking *Kanazawa*'s accuracy and authenticity and offering feedback. And for talking to me about it over sake, *yakitori*, and *banh mi* sandwiches, depending on my needs at the time.

To Takuo Hasegawa for submitting to interviews for the novel (as well as to my cooking—sorry about the goya), though regrettably I was unable to use what you shared. Except your restaurant, Huni, which appears in my novel in the guise of a gallery.

To Sol Gallago and Yuko Otoku for introducing me to Shira-mine (and letting me shovel snow from your driveway there—it was a good workout).

To Garry Powell, *obrigado* for our years of friendship and the support you've long given me—in writing and also in life. And *obrigado* again for hosting us most recently in Portugal. I will never stop being envious that you can have nearly free wine with every meal and *pastéis de nata* whenever you please.

To Jeffrey Gibbs, *çok teşekkürler* for being a true and faithful friend—usually over email, but sometimes (when luck is on my side) also in person. I look forward to having Japanese food and raki with you in Istanbul soon. *Mochiron, Jeff-san no ogori de.*

To Edward Lipsett for your time and encouragement, which set me on a path I ultimately and gratefully landed on.

To Rosemary Ahern, for reading and commenting exten-sively on multiple drafts of *Kanazawa*, which greatly improved under your steady and experienced eye.

To Writers in Kyoto for publishing a modified excerpt from *Kanazawa* in *Echoes: Writers in Kyoto Anthology, 2017.* (*Arigatō!*)

To Charles Shiro Inouye and Cody Poulton, whose incredible work on Izumi Kyōka changed my life in the best of ways, and without which this novel would never have been written.

To Shinji Kenichi, whose literary passion, encouragement, and friendship has meant so much to me (maybe one day I'll write a novel titled *Hiroba Café*).

To Lê Tuấn Đạt, who taught me what it means to be a poet (though I'm not one myself, sadly) and who has been a faithful friend through thick and thin.

And, of course, to Stone Bridge Press's publisher, Peter Goodman, to whom I owe a huge debt of gratitude. *Kanazawa* wouldn't have made it into the world without your support and your willingness to take a chance on it.

DJ

DAVID JOINER MADE HIS first trip to Japan in 1991—a five-month study program in Hokkaido—and three years later moved for the first of seven times to Vietnam. In Japan, where he has also moved numerous times, he has called Sapporo, Akita, Fukui, Tokyo, and most recently the western Japanese city of Kanazawa home.

David Joiner's writing has appeared in literary journals and elsewhere, including *Echoes: Writers in Kyoto 2017*, the *Brooklyn Rail*, *Phoebe Journal*, the *Ontario Review*, and the *Madison Review*. His first novel, *Lotusland*, set in contemporary Vietnam, was published in 2015 by Guernica Editions.